Praise for th

"Elizabeth Goddard has done it again. She's a brilliant romantic suspense writer with fast-paced stories that keep you hooked from start to finish."

Lynette Eason, bestselling, award-winning author of the Lake City Heroes series, on *Storm Warning*

"Elizabeth Goddard's *Storm Warning* is perfectly named. This book takes readers by storm as her characters face danger not only from outside forces but also from the deadly secrets that rage inside their souls. Secrets that could cost them . . . everything. Highly recommended."

Nancy Mehl, author of the Ryland and St. Clair series, on *Storm Warning*

"A fast-paced journey through beautiful yet isolated parts of the Last Frontier."

Booklist starred review of *Hidden in the Night*

"The author does a fabulous job of keeping the suspense level high, the danger coming, and readers like me on the edge of our seats!"

Reading Is My Superpower on *Shadows at Dusk*

"Close relationships, believable characters, danger, murders— *Shadows at Dusk* has it all."

Life Is Story on *Shadows at Dusk*

"Goddard weaves a gripping mystery."

Publishers Weekly on *Cold Light of Day*

"Elizabeth Goddard has once again proved she is the queen of romantic suspense thrillers."

Urban Lit Magazine on *Cold Light of Day*

PERILOUS
TIDES

Books by Elizabeth Goddard

UNCOMMON JUSTICE SERIES

Never Let Go
Always Look Twice
Don't Keep Silent

ROCKY MOUNTAIN COURAGE SERIES

Present Danger
Deadly Target
Critical Alliance

MISSING IN ALASKA SERIES

Cold Light of Day
Shadows at Dusk
Hidden in the Night

HIDDEN BAY SERIES

Storm Warning
Perilous Tides

PERILOUS TIDES

ELIZABETH GODDARD

Revell

a division of Baker Publishing Group
Grand Rapids, Michigan

Published by Revell
a division of Baker Publishing Group
Grand Rapids, Michigan
RevellBooks.com

Printed in the United States of America

Library of Congress Cataloging-in-Publication Data
Names: Goddard, Elizabeth, author.
Title: Perilous tides / Elizabeth Goddard.
Description: Grand Rapids, Michigan : Revell, a division of Baker Publishing
    Group, 2025. | Series: Hidden Bay ; 2
Identifiers: LCCN 2024051759 | ISBN 9780800746155 (paperback) | ISBN
    9780800747091 (casebound) | ISBN 9781493450596 (ebook)
Subjects: LCGFT: Christian fiction. | Thrillers (Fiction) | Novels.
Classification: LCC PS3607.O324 P47 2025 | DDC 813.6—dc23/eng/20241118
LC record available at https://lccn.loc.gov/2024051759

Scripture used in this book, whether quoted or paraphrased by the characters, is taken from one of the following:

The Holy Bible, English Standard Version® (ESV®). Copyright © 2001 by Crossway, a publishing ministry of Good News Publishers. Used by permission. All rights reserved. ESV Text Edition: 2016

The Holy Bible, New International Version®, NIV®. Copyright © 1973, 1978, 1984, 2011 by Biblica, Inc.® Used by permission of Zondervan. All rights reserved worldwide. www.zondervan.com. The "NIV" and "New International Version" are trademarks registered in the United States Patent and Trademark Office by Biblica, Inc.®

Cover design by Mumtaz Mustafa

Baker Publishing Group publications use paper produced from sustainable forestry practices and postconsumer waste whenever possible.

25 26 27 28 29 30 31   7 6 5 4 3 2 1

Dedicated to those who brave the
uncharted places of the heart.

Three may keep a secret if two of them are dead.

Benjamin Franklin

1

*Y*ou won't see danger coming . . . until it's too late."
Those words, shared by her mother moments before her death, had defined Jo Cattrel's life for the last three years, since she'd fled Michigan. And maybe the life of every dead or missing person whose case she'd ever worked as a forensic artist. As for suspects, she lived to take them down with nothing more than a pencil. But there was a downside to it. A morbidity.

So much time spent with the dead and the missing or drawing criminal faces meant that she couldn't trust people. It meant that she glanced over her shoulder more than the average person. Like right now. If anyone cared to notice, she might appear downright paranoid.

Was someone watching? Following?

She couldn't escape the fear that she'd made a mistake in leaving her hiding place in Hidden Bay along the Washington coast.

But Pop had left her a cryptic note.

Don't worry about me, Jo. I didn't mean to lead trouble to you. Please forgive me.

That message had compelled her across Puget Sound to the city, of all places, to search for her father. She'd only just found him three years ago. She wasn't about to lose him now.

And this note felt like . . . *goodbye.*

No way would she let him disappear on her. Was she a fool to chase after him? Yet another person to leave her? Didn't matter. She was here.

I'm doing this.

After living in the misty rainforest, she was overwhelmed by the city sights and sounds. Nothing like a lungful of concentrated exhaust. The towering skyscrapers impeded fresh air. Having parked two blocks away, she dragged in too many breaths of pollution as she ascended the slick uphill sidewalk on a cold, rainy day, hiking toward the tallest building in Seattle.

If Pop hadn't wanted her to follow, he should have responded to her many texts demanding an explanation. So she'd used a locator app they shared. Fortunately for her, he'd probably forgotten about it.

She couldn't picture Pop in the big city. Back in Forestview—part of the Hidden Bay region of the Washington coast—he owned and operated the R&D Auto Repair Shop, got his hands dirty, and was always in his coveralls, fiddling with tools and covered in grime. He called himself a grease monkey, so what was he doing in downtown Seattle at the Columbia Center?

Finally arriving at her destination, she peered up at the seventy-six-story building. Dizziness swept over her, so she stared at her feet instead. Got her bearings. Then pushed through the glass door.

The sleek lobby intimidated, but she pressed forward. She needed to act like she belonged. The locator app told her that Pop was here. Or at least he *had* been. But now when she looked at the app, she got nothing. Was he still here?

She started toward the bank and nodded with a friendly smile at the security guard, though she feared the "I don't belong here" look on her face would give her away. Jo's sling bag snagged on a brass stanchion, and she knocked the whole thing over. Of course, it banged on the floor and echoed. A few people glanced her way.

Her heart pounded as the security guard approached. He set the stanchion back in place.

"I'm so sorry. I'm just clumsy. I'm just . . ." She pointed. "I'm going now."

She hurried toward the directory. How in the world would she find Pop? He could be literally anywhere. Numerous businesses took up space. Tenants too. She could take the elevator and look around the Sky View Observatory. But she'd need to purchase a ticket first. Jo retrieved her cell and texted Pop again.

> I'm at the Columbia Center. Where are you?

Then she took a picture of the directory. Jo should really get out more often because right now, she couldn't feel more out of place.

I just want to go home.

But . . . Pop.

"Can I help you, ma'am?" The security guard stood next to her at the directory.

Yeah, she had a feeling she was giving off the wrong vibes.

"Actually, maybe. I'm looking for this man." She pulled up an image of her father on her cell and showed it to the guy. "He's my father. His name is Raymond Dodge. I was supposed to meet him here."

A little white lie. But the security guard didn't need to know everything.

"A lot of people come and go, but you're lucky. I remember seeing him. He left about an hour ago."

What? "Weird. Okay, I'll just wait at the Starbucks. I can text him that I'll be there." Now that she thought about it, the security guard might wonder why she hadn't texted Pop to begin with. Well, she had but never got a response. "Thanks."

Acid rose in her throat. Jo rushed through the exit without looking back. But there was nothing more she could do.

I never should have come.

She stepped out into the rain and hurried down the hill. Glancing over her shoulder, she happened to catch someone leaving the building . . . and stopping to watch her. She turned to get a better look. The watcher ducked out of sight. Frowning, Jo blew out a shaky breath. She was just seeing things.

Jo rushed forward, speed-walking her way around the pedestrian traffic until she got to the corner.

Another glance back confirmed that no one followed her. Still, the sounds, the rush of people, would give her an anxiety attack. She didn't wait for the light to signal but dashed across the street, receiving honks and a few choice words. At the parking garage, she raced to her vehicle in the corner. Another glance over her shoulder—because there could never be too many—told her others entered the garage, heading to their vehicles, oblivious to her.

Sayonara, Seattle.

Jo scrambled into her red Land Rover Defender, which Pop had customized. Starting it, she appreciated the deep rumble. Nobody was going to mess with her while she was in this beast. She paid at the gate and sped out of the parking lot.

Jo was done with the city. And . . . done with her father? The thought sent a pang through her heart. She wasn't done with him. This couldn't be the end.

Downtown traffic was maddening, and Jo didn't relax until she was on the ferry, crossing Puget Sound to Bremerton, where she could drive the rest of the way to Hidden Bay. Sitting in cold silence, Jo remained in her beast where it was safe, fighting the nausea erupting from the rocking motion of the ferry. The water was surprisingly rough today.

Jo glanced up from her cell and couldn't believe her eyes.

Waves crashed onto the deck with the cars, moving them around a little too much for comfort. She couldn't imagine this was a normal happening. Maybe she should get out. Another wave, and then the Toyota Camry in front of her nearly knocked into the Lexus next to it. Getting out now might be dangerous.

I should have stayed in Hidden Bay. She'd been hiding away for the last three years, and now venturing out into the world was giving her a panic attack.

The waves calmed. If she was getting out of her vehicle, now was her chance. She'd head up to the top deck. Grab some vending machine food. Jo weaved between the parked cars, noticing that she'd been the only one to remain inside her vehicle.

"What are you doing?" A muffled, fear-filled voice drew her attention.

The question hadn't been for her. She glanced around the shadowed car deck filled with vehicles. Hearing nothing more, she headed toward the steps, where she could make her way up. Pressing forward between the cars, she couldn't ignore the grunts that came with a struggle, and in the reflection of a truck window, she watched as someone slid down the side of a car. Someone else holding a knife appeared in the reflection and looked down at the body, then slinked away. The killer wore a heavy overcoat with the hood pulled forward.

Jo should scream.

But she couldn't breathe.

He hadn't looked in her direction, but he was aware she was there and watching—she knew that to her bones. Looking at her would send him to prison—whoever he was—because then she would see his face. She hoped security cameras caught him.

Jo hurried toward the stairs. She had to get out of here. Get away. He was still here somewhere, hiding behind or in a vehicle, she didn't know. Another wave crashed, sending water onto the loading deck. If she could just escape before he saw her. The intrusive waves rushed around her ankles, soaking her shoes in ice-cold water. The cars were moving with the waves again, and she could end up crushed.

She eyed the stairwell. Where were the two ferry crew members she'd seen earlier? Maybe someone would come down to check on the vehicles and see what was happening. She had no choice, really. Jo rushed between the cars and sloshed through the water, slipping a few times as another wave crashed.

A chill crawled over her. The tiny hairs on the back of her neck lifted. Her breaths quickened.

She sensed someone near and—

A hand covered her mouth as a strong arm seized her. She fought and kicked, but he treated her as if she was as weightless as a small plastic toy. He dragged her between the vehicles, then, at the last car, opened the door. Horror filled her when she saw a body in the back seat. The man he'd killed. A scream erupted in her throat, but he punched her in the face, stunning her. Pain shot through her head as it lolled. She struggled to find her way out of the growing darkness and failed.

Blinking, she suddenly realized she was in the driver's seat of a sedan. He'd knocked her out, but she was awake now. She scrambled to get out, but the car was already in motion, rolling over the edge. He must have removed the net barriers and forced the vehicle over.

Heart hammering, Jo screamed as the sedan plunged into the water. The man stared down at her from the deck, his face shrouded in darkness.

Except his eyes.

She'd never forget them.

And that's why he was killing her now, destroying the only witness.

I'm going to die.

The car slammed into the water, then bobbed and rocked on the rough, stormy waters. Icy cold seawater filled the cab as it sank faster than she would have thought. But she could escape. She could do this. She tried to open the door, but it wouldn't budge against the pressure of the water, so she tried the window button.

Hope filled her. She could swim through the opening.

Except the window stopped. What? Why had it stopped? No way could she make it through that small gap. "No, no, no! God, help me!" Jo cried out.

She just needed to break the glass.

The force of the water pushed her up to the roof, and it was then she realized her foot was tied to the accelerator. Even if she could get the window open, she was trapped. She yanked on her ankle, tried to undo the zip tie, but she couldn't free herself.

A knife, she needed a knife.

The vehicle was completely submerged now, and cold seawater poured in. Her entire body shook as she held up her face to breathe from the remaining air pocket. Her last lifeline.

She fought the window and the door. Taking what could be her last gulp of air, she opened the glove compartment to search for a gun or a hammer—anything to help her break the glass—or a knife to cut herself free. Papers floated out of the compartment.

A lump of terror squeezed her throat.

Panic engulfed her as fast as the rising water.

God, I'm going to die. All this hiding from one killer, and another one got me anyway.

Mom had been right.

Jo hadn't seen danger coming . . .

2

Standing on the deck of a small recreational cruiser he'd secured when he flashed a big wad of cash to the hesitant owner, Cole Mercer couldn't believe his eyes. A silver Lexus sedan had rolled off the Washington State ferry with someone still inside.

Someone do something! But people on the second level of the ferry simply watched the tragedy unfold. Nobody jumped in.

"Get me up there. Take us closer!" He shouted to the pilot steering the boat.

"But—"

"Now!"

Looked like Cole would have to be the one. He'd had enough traumatic experience when it came to the deep blue that he recoiled at the thought of jumping in. But he would do what he had to do.

The boat sped forward, closing in on the ferry, which kept moving. "Stop here!"

Bubbles erupted on the surface of the rough waters. The

vehicle had floated for about thirty seconds before sinking completely.

God, save whoever's inside. Keep them alive. Help me get them out! Cole shrugged out of his coat and took off his boots. Drawing in a big breath, he dove into the frigid, murky water. The shock of cold almost robbed him of breath. He caught the grille of the sinking sedan in his peripheral vision and, kicking hard, corrected course. His mind raced through the steps required to free whoever remained trapped inside. He feared he would be too late as he made it to the slowly sinking vehicle. At the driver's side, he found the window halfway down—not enough for someone to slip out. He tried the door, but it refused to open. He'd need to break the window. The front of the cab was completely submerged. Was there even a pocket of air left?

He tried to signal to the clearly panicked woman inside.

Big brown eyes stared back. His heart lurched.

Jo? And he might have released too much air. Even so, his pounding heart was using up too much oxygen. He removed his gun from the holster at his waist and waved her away. He hoped the water wouldn't slow the bullet enough to make it ineffective in breaking the glass.

She shook her head, eyes wide with fear. Was she stuck? Couldn't move?

Cole angled away from her and fired at the window. It shattered. The bits of glass floating away posed a danger of their own. But her path was free.

Except, she remained in the vehicle. She pointed to the floorboard. He suspected her foot had somehow gotten stuck, so he maneuvered until he could find the problem. And there it was. Her foot was zip-tied to the pedal. Fury rolled through him as he tugged out his pocketknife.

Cole dove into the space that grew darker by the second as the vehicle continued sinking. He couldn't see a thing, but he felt the tie, secured it away from her ankle as best he could, and cut, then he pulled the plastic away. Her body instantly floated free and upward in the space. Heart pounding, running out of air, he grabbed her hand. Noting someone else was in the back seat that he hadn't seen before, he shoved her forward and up toward the surface, but she tugged him toward her. Shook her head. The other passenger was gone.

And he and Jo would be too if they didn't get to the surface. The cold worked against his body, making his limbs numb as he kicked and swam toward the light. Breaching the surface, hauling Jo up alongside him, he drew in a long breath.

Jo sucked in air too. Treading water, she glanced around them, then zeroed in on him, giving him a brief questioning look that he could read only too well. Why his sudden appearance?

After all, he hadn't seen her in months. But he would answer her questions later. Right now, they were in survival mode.

Together they bobbed on the surface, the rough chop during this spring storm that tried to drown them. He'd get them through this. He fought the aggressive waves that pummeled him, draining his strength. Jo's too. Puget Sound waters were rough today, and the temperature was always too cold.

Now for the second rescue.

Kicking to stay afloat, he turned in every direction, searching for the ferry. There. Finally stopping, the vessel floated nearby. An orange life ring had been tossed out, and Cole and Jo swam for it. They finally made it and held on while they waited for the rescue boat.

Finally, rescuers pulled Cole and Jo from the water and transported them back to the ferry.

Aboard the MV *Chimacum*, they sat inside the upper deck, blankets wrapped around them both. Cole held Jo in his arms. He tried to ignore the fear-spiked adrenaline still pumping through his veins and instead simply be grateful for this moment.

She was here.

He was here.

I almost lost you . . .

He wanted to kiss her blue lips and put some color back into them as well as her pale face. But that would be totally selfish. He might have kissed her before, back when they spent time together, but he doubted she'd want that from him now. Even if she wanted him to show her just how much he missed her, they had an audience. A public display of affection wasn't happening. Standing around, far and wide, ferry patrons watched them, zooming in with their cell phone cameras, no doubt. Mumbling and questioning what had just happened.

A car had rolled off the ferry and into the water. That's what. While that wasn't *ever* supposed to happen, this wouldn't be the first time, though maybe not on this particular ferry. Cole didn't know.

He *did* know that this had been no accident.

Jo told the *Chimacum* captain that she'd witnessed a murder, and the killer was responsible for stashing her in the vehicle, along with the body of the murder victim, and sending the vehicle into the water—as if no one would notice? Dropping her overboard along with the body, attached to some kind of anchor, might have been a better way to hide his crimes, but he'd chosen to . . . what? Make a statement?

Two crew members had been found bound and gagged. At least they hadn't been murdered. But they hadn't seen the man's face. Neither had Jo. How was that possible?

Cole was just glad he'd made the decision to come after Jo and that he'd been there at the right moment to pull her from the cold depths of Puget Sound.

The ferry master had contacted the Seattle PD Harbor Patrol, who requested the *Chimacum* return to the ferry terminal in Seattle, to the utter displeasure of all the patrons who needed to get to Bremerton. But the authorities would need to question and investigate. Regardless of who had jurisdiction, law enforcement would get the man who'd done this. Except Cole had a feeling the killer would slip through the noose before it could close around his throat. Either he was a complete idiot, or he had planned it all out and wouldn't have murdered someone on a ferry with no plan for escape. Next to him, Jo shifted, drawing his focus back to her.

Questions, accusation, rose in her big golden-brown eyes. He suspected she wouldn't soon overcome the shock of witnessing a murder and then almost being killed herself in a dramatic and horrific way. After nearly drowning, she must have questions about why *he* was the one to rescue her.

He had questions too. Answers wouldn't come until the dive team recovered the murder victim's body. Still, he suspected the question burning through her right now had nothing to do with that.

Explaining his reasons for being here would be . . . complicated. As he looked at her, he had so much he wanted to say, to explain. His chest ached with the need to get back what he'd left behind in Hidden Bay.

Jo Cattrel.

But he hadn't walked away by choice. The threat of criminal charges and the manipulation of the truth had been held over him to coerce him into participating in a classified, covert mission.

So what was he supposed to tell her when he called her from DC?

It's me, not you?

The other, equally painful truth of it was that Jo had already been through so much, and he was a mess. He had no business falling for her. Making promises he feared he couldn't keep. But how did he tell her that? It sounded lame, even to his own thoughts. The two of them together were headed for massive heartbreak.

"What are you doing here?" she asked. "Why were you on the same ferry I was on?"

I wasn't. "I'll explain all that later. I'm just glad you're alive. Let's focus on that right now." And keeping her that way.

On the bench, Jo scooted away a few inches. Understandable. She'd struggled with trust issues, and he hadn't made it easy for her to trust him, even after saving her life today. The color returned to her cheeks and lips. Good, at least her outrage at his sudden unexplained appearance was causing the blood to flow.

"Were you *following* me?" Fire erupted in her eyes. Fire and fear. "Because I had the feeling I was being followed. I mean, I know I get that a lot. But you know why."

Seeing the pure confusion in her eyes cut through him. He wanted to reassure her, but he couldn't have this conversation in front of witnesses, some with their camera phones out. "Some privacy, please?" He glared at the onlookers.

"No, Jo." He lowered his voice so only she could hear. "It's not like that. I wasn't following you as in stalking you."

Then he turned her away from the cameras, and they both faced the windows looking out over the water. Her eyes grew even wider as though she finally got it. "Cameras. Oh no . . ."

Exactly. What if the videos went viral? What if the wrong person saw them? She'd been hiding at Cedar Trails Lodge in Hidden Bay for years now.

Shivering, she hung her head. "I shouldn't have come here."

And that was the whole reason *he* was here. He'd come to try to end her need to hide, if she would allow that. "Let's get you out of here and just get through what comes next as quickly as possible. I promise, I'll explain everything." *I just have to figure out how.*

"I haven't seen you in months, and you just show up . . ."

To pull her from a sinking car.

Again, he leaned in, whispering in her ear. "I can't stress how important it is to keep your head down and not say too much in front of the world."

Because right now, the world was watching as the images filled up social media and either died or grew viral or appeared on the evening news. With her wet hair, pale features, and dark circles under her eyes, she didn't look like herself right now. Good. That could work to her advantage. At some point, her name would be attached to the images. Maybe even her current address.

Cole hoped that Jo wouldn't push him away before he got the chance to explain. In the meantime, they watched through the window as the *Chimacum* slowed on approach to the ferry terminal. Law enforcement vehicles were already waiting. He wasn't sure what jurisdiction this murder on a ferry would fall under in the tangle of law enforcement entities—Coast Guard, Washington State Police, King County or Seattle PD, or Harbor Patrol—none of this was good for a woman who'd been hiding from danger.

His insides twisted up at the thought of Jo having to answer their questions. Exposing the truth of who she was and *where* she was hiding to even one more person was dangerous for her.

Cole tugged her closer to keep her warm and was relieved

when she didn't pull away. Honestly, he needed that extra heat too. "Don't worry. It's going to be all right."

But he feared the opposite was true. Regardless, he would do everything in his power to protect her.

Her lack of response troubled him. What was she thinking? What would *anyone* think after what she'd just been through?

The ferry docked, and authorities from the Washington State Police confined everyone to the vessel. Passengers were upset but understanding. A murderer needed to be caught. Evidence gathered. Passengers questioned. What a nightmare to be kept on a ferry because of someone else's crimes when you had places to go and people to see.

Jo and, fortunately, Cole—because she'd insisted—were transported to the state police offices in Seattle. She'd also insisted that someone retrieve her cell phone from her vehicle. They'd been questioned separately, and Cole had explained to Detective Hargrove his reasons for being in the boat chasing after the ferry. Hiding anything would only create suspicion and ignite questions later, and he hoped to secure an ally—someone he could work with in protecting Jo. She might not realize it yet, but hiding in Hidden Bay, working at the Cedar Trails Lodge, was no longer good enough.

Three hours later, an officer took Cole and Jo back to Cole's rented vehicle—a black Yukon—parked at the ferry station. Her vehicle had been offloaded from the ferry and remained at the Bremerton ferry station. Offloading it here would have been too complicated. She'd need to pick it up at Bremerton. That had been the destination to begin with.

"I know you don't want to talk about this anymore," he said. "But I don't know what happened." She hadn't shared the details on the ferry because too many people were watching, then she'd been separated from Cole to give her statement to the detective. "And I need the details."

He expected her to ask why, but she started right in. "I saw him standing over the guy, the body was . . . um . . . it slid down the car . . ." Her voice grew thick with emotion as she shared the entire sordid story, even the part he knew. It was surreal hearing his rescue from her point of view.

"I didn't get a look at his face," she said, "but I drew the eyes for them."

She showed him a copy of the image. "I get it now, from the other side."

"The other side?"

"When victims of a crime are asked to describe their attacker, sometimes they can't remember much, but they always remember the eyes." She turned away and swiped at her cheek.

Oh, Jo. His heart ached for her. He looked at the sketch. Dark eyes that were filled with hatred. Just so much detail. How could she have seen so much and yet missed the rest of his face? The sketch of eyes peering out from beneath a rain jacket hood. He suspected that, in that moment of desperation, believing she was going to die, that image had etched into her mind forever.

He could barely swallow as he took in the sketch. Cole had seen a lot in his life, so his reaction to this surprised him, but then again, this had happened to Jo. The images bombarded him again. The sinking car, then Jo's face and hands pressed against the window as the cab filled with water.

She blinked, clearing the unshed tears. "If you hadn't been there, I probably would have died. You saved my life, Cole. Thank you."

His heart beat a little faster at her gratitude. "I guess that makes us even. You saved my life on the beach that day."

She hung her head a moment, then suddenly lifted her face. "I still don't know what you're doing here. I thought you were back to gallivanting around the world on special missions."

Partially true. At least her assumptions would make it easier. Cole drew in a long breath. How did he untangle this complicated story? He pressed his lips into a thin line and, to his shame, looked away.

"Are you going to tell me? Because if not, then I'm getting out and going home."

Same take-charge Jo he'd met on that beach last winter. He thought back to that moment, when she'd heaved his battered, shot-through body from the rocks and assisted him out of danger. *She* was *his* hero. And he hated to add another layer of anguish to her day.

Cole faced her. "I was hired to look into your mother's murder."

3

She sucked in a breath, filling her lungs with outrage. "Now I know you're lying."

Jo watched his reaction closely.

His mouth opened as he gave a small shake of his head. Incredulous? "It's the truth. Why would I lie?"

"No one believes she was murdered except me. Not the police. Not anyone." She glared at him, her anger over what happened to Mom burning in her gut.

No one had truly listened, even after she'd become a target. No one believed her mother's death was connected to the threats on Jo's life. Or at the very least, none of it could be proven.

"Listen to me, Jo. I believe you. And now the police are leaning that way, calling her death suspicious."

Jo narrowed her eyes. Whoever had hired him knew something, or else why hire him? The police maintained it was an accident. "Who hired you?"

"Her name is Naomi Bancroft. I was already looking into things when Mrs. Bancroft contacted CGIS and requested an investigation into Mira Cattrel's murder."

"CGIS?"

"Centurion Global Intelligence and Security."

"And you work for them, then?"

"It's basically a directory for veterans with specific skill sets. They connect clients with investigators, security and protective services, threat assessments. That sort of thing. I know the guy who runs it, and he knew I'd want to work on this case."

Jo nodded, satisfied with his answer. "Why does this woman care? What's the connection?"

"Apparently one of your mother's last forensic art assignments identified a man who murdered someone at an ATM. The police have recently identified Mason Hyde as the killer, and he's wanted for questioning in your mother's death."

"What?" Jo gasped. "I don't believe this. Finally, they're looking into it." Her heart pounded erratically, and her hands shook. "No one notified me. Oh yeah. They couldn't reach me if they wanted to." Because she'd intentionally disappeared. "But that doesn't explain the connection."

"Mason Hyde is Naomi Bancroft's brother." Cole took her hand and squeezed.

"And now you're working for the killer's sister?" She jerked her hand away.

"Will you hear me out? Naomi believes he's been set up. That he didn't kill anyone."

"And you were all too eager to jump on it? Cole, how could you?"

Cole rubbed his temples and shook his head. "I should have led with the fact that I was already looking into your mother's death on the side. Working through CGIS for a client, I could dig into things officially and get to the truth, Jo." His gaze pleaded with her. "For you."

Jo looked away. She didn't know what to think. *I should*

just get out and get away while I can, before I get hurt again. Then again, she wanted to know *everything* about her mother's murder investigation. She would definitely stay.

"I'm listening."

"I had to start with the police reports, and then I needed to talk to you."

The way he looked at her right now, she could almost imagine that he *wanted* to talk to her and his reasons for being with her now went beyond this investigation. But that was Jo's imagination. Her pitiful desire to have Cole come back for her with an explanation that she could accept and live with so they could be together again. Pathetic. So much more was going on now. Pop had left, and now Mom's murder might actually get solved. Still . . .

One question burned in her chest. "Why were you looking into the investigation to begin with, Cole?"

She shouldn't care, she really shouldn't. But she had to know why he was really here.

He lifted a shoulder, and his brows furrowed as if he struggled to answer her question. After a few breaths, he finally replied, "I wanted you to be free, Jo. Free to live your life the way you want, not holed up in . . . yeah, a beautiful place, but you have so much to offer the world."

She let his words sink in.

The world. And Cole? A few months ago, he hadn't wanted what she offered.

He roughed his hand over his mouth and chin. "You shouldn't have to hide or fear for your life."

She nodded and glanced around. They'd just been sitting here in his Yukon in the parking lot, talking things through. Catching up. The rain had stopped. Cars parked and cars left. People trudged along sidewalks on a rainy day. The world kept turning, oblivious to Jo's personal battle.

Glancing at Cole, she angled her head. "That still doesn't

explain how and why you were there to pull me from the car." *At the exact moment I needed you.*

"I went to Cedar Trails first to see you. Remi told me where you were headed."

"That traitor." Jo half smiled. Of course, Remi Grant would want Cole to find Jo. Remi was her boss at the lodge and her dearest friend of late. Remi hadn't wanted Jo to chase her father down. "Why not call me or text me?"

"Would you have responded?"

"I don't know."

"Exactly. Remi told me what you were driving and that you'd texted you thought your dad was in the Columbia Center. I couldn't miss the big, loud Land Rover racing around a corner to the ferry, and then I spotted you in the driver's seat. Stupid traffic kept me from making it myself. So I paid a boater to follow the ferry. I was going to catch up on the other side. I thought to head you off."

"Head me off. Why? You could have just waited for me at Cedar Trails."

"I was trying to catch up. Thought I could help with your father. Look, I don't know what's going on there, that's beside the point. I tried to follow, and I missed the ferry. That's when I witnessed the vehicle going into the water."

"Nothing else? You didn't see the suspect?"

"No. I saw the vehicle *in* the water, I should say. I wasn't looking at the ferry. I was looking at the car."

Jo sat up. Leaned closer. "And you didn't know it was me in the car?"

"I didn't."

Wow. She couldn't believe this. "You just dove in . . ." Cole hated the water. He might have been traumatized one too many times. Maybe even had PTSD, but that didn't stop this man. He'd faced his fear to save a stranger.

"Someone was in the vehicle, that was all that mattered."

He averted his pained gaze. "I was shocked to see you." His voice hitched.

This strong, quiet professional was showing some kind of emotion for her? Jo wanted to lean into him and forget that she hadn't heard a word from him in months. Forget that he had acted like he didn't care at all. What she saw now seemed to prove otherwise. But she'd been burned too many times, and even today her own father had let her down. She wasn't trusting anyone again. Not for a long time, if ever.

"If there's anything I can do to help you with your father, just let me know."

Her life was one big, twisted roller coaster. She wanted to know about her mother. She wanted to know about her father. "I don't know where he is. He's just . . . gone. I tracked him to the Columbia Center, where his cell said he was, and the security guard told me he'd left. Now the little red dot is gone."

"Remi said he left a note," Cole said.

"Yep. Said that he was sorry he led danger to me."

"Did you tell the police about that? Maybe the murder on the ferry—"

"I wasn't the target. I was just the witness." Jo glanced out the window again and shook her head. "This is what I get for leaving my hideaway."

"While I don't know what kind of danger he could have brought your way, and that raises a lot of concerns, is there anything more we can do while we're here to look for him? Because, if we find him, we can get answers."

"It's a dead end. I'm going to go now. I'm taking the next ferry."

"Across the sound?"

"Yep."

"You were just attacked. Took a dunk in the water and almost . . ."

"You don't need to remind me."

"I'll go too. Maybe you can tell me the facts surrounding your mother's death back in Michigan along the way."

"I'll consider it. I'm just exhausted. I need to think." *And I need space.*

An escape from Cole would be nice, but how do you ask the guy who just saved your life to get lost?

She wasn't sure about anything anymore, except it seemed like someone always wanted to kill her. If she thought about it too long, furious tears would surge, and she couldn't let Cole see her like that. He'd only known her when she was strong. Never vulnerable.

"I have an idea." Eyes bright, he stared at her. "I'll see if I can get security footage. We could find out where your father was going. I don't like the idea that you followed him, potentially putting yourself in harm's way—whatever the danger is—but I'm here, and I can protect you now. What do you think?"

She angled her head. "I mean, he's a mechanic. What kind of danger could he have gotten himself into?"

"He could owe money to the mob. I don't know."

"Pop? No way." She quirked her face. "What's your *gut* feeling about this?"

"I'd like to know what he's involved in so I can assess any threat against you."

"Maybe there's something we can do to help him," she said.

He rubbed his jaw as his face scrunched up. "Maybe. So have you tried to contact him?"

"Are you kidding? I've texted multiple times, and I've called, and I get no response."

"I've met your dad a few times, of course, but I wouldn't say I know him that well. Other than he is an auto mechanic, what can you tell me about him?"

"You mean you haven't already run background checks and looked into everything about my life, which includes my parents?" She studied him, trying to get a read on him.

"I read the police report about what happened in Michigan. I came to talk to you. That's it. Now we're here in Seattle. What would you like to do?"

"I guess, yeah, let's look at the security footage." She knew some of how law enforcement worked but not about the kind of private agency for which Cole worked.

She got out her cell again and looked at the locator app. Nothing.

"Okay, then. We'll head to the Columbia Center parking." He steered from the parking lot.

"Back to my question about your father," he said. "What can you tell me about him other than he's a mechanic?"

"Pop is my biological father. I only just met him three years ago. I grew up with a different father. His name was Dale, but he left when I was a kid. I never heard from him again because he died from a heart attack." A vise clamped down on her throat, strangling her. "I don't know where that came from." Cole hadn't asked about Dale.

Cole touched her arm. "It's okay, Jo. That would be hard on any kid. Believe me, I've got my own family horror stories."

She knew there was tension between him and Hawk growing up. Still, they were as close as any siblings she'd known. But Cole had never talked about his family with her before. He claimed that after everything that happened, he wanted to focus on the good things, the present and the future. She'd done the same, leaving the past in the past.

She wiped away the tear that leaked and glanced at him. "Will you tell me sometime?"

As if that opportunity would come because they were

friends and would have plenty of time to talk about it. That wasn't happening.

"Sometime." He shifted uncomfortably. "What happened? Why'd Dale leave?"

"I was ten when I overheard Mom and Dad—Dale—fighting, and then he left for good. Walked out on us both. I never knew why. All I knew was that I really hated my mother. I thought she had sent him away. It took me a long time to get over it." A friend had invited Jo to church, and she learned that she was supposed to forgive. That didn't mean she would forget that her dad left her. But she'd forgiven him, and she'd forgiven her mother and had even followed in her footsteps to work as a forensic artist.

"That's hard to get over."

"Three years ago, Mom finally told me *why* he left. It just took her sixteen years to get around to it. I was twenty-six. For the first ten years of my life, she'd let Dale believe that he was my biological father, and he left when he found out the truth. She hadn't cheated on him, so she says, but she was already pregnant when they met. They had a whirlwind romance and married in just two months."

Jo dragged in a long breath, then continued. "And that's when she dropped another bomb. She told me that if anything happened to her, I needed to leave and to hide. That she'd left instructions for me in our bank safety-deposit box. Her hands were shaking, so I could tell that she was upset. Scared, even. Can you imagine how that freaked me out? Mom had been angry and hurt by his actions too, that much was clear. She'd kept that from me, to keep from hurting me. But something had triggered her—I realized after the fact, of course—to finally tell me the truth. She tells me the truth about my father and warns me something bad might happen all in the same breath."

"And your biological father?"

"She left me hanging. I don't know if she just didn't know who he was. Or she wasn't willing to tell me. But she died before we could talk it out."

"What happened after she told you the truth?"

"I was so stunned—so furious with her—that I stormed out. I took a long walk in the park near my apartment. Worked through things. Prayed. Finally, I blew off enough steam that I went to her house to talk to her, but she wasn't there. I had a key. Still had a room there. I made cookies while I waited. Thought we would talk. Everything would be fine again. I loved Mom. I fell asleep on the couch waiting. She never made it home. I learned about the accident hours later."

Her heart had been utterly shattered.

It wouldn't be the first time, and as she looked at Cole's profile . . . she knew it would definitely not be the last.

4

'm so sorry." He hadn't meant to bring back the painful memories, especially not here. There was more to the story, but they could talk about her mother after they learned more about what her father was doing here today and why he'd left the cryptic message.

Since they were here in Seattle, they might as well finish this business and find out what she came to find out. The traffic slowed them down, and he got stuck at yet another light. They'd gotten off track, so he shifted the conversation.

"So, back to your father and the present. You came after him, leaving Hidden Bay when he warned you away. Why?"

"He didn't warn me away."

"It kind of sounds like he's in some trouble," Cole said, "and didn't want you involved. He was afraid he might have led danger your way."

Jo's features were drawn. "You don't have to be here with me, you know, challenging my decisions. I need to find Pop safe and sound. Let him explain to me in person. That's why. Are you satisfied now?"

He suspected that her reaction—needing to have her

father explain everything to her face—had everything to do with her stepfather, Dale, leaving her when she was ten. What more could there be to *his* story? Cole couldn't see anyone leaving his child, even after learning he wasn't the biological father. But people reacted differently.

He looked out the raindrop-studded window. For Jo's sake, he hoped she would find her father and all would be well. But this kind of start to a day never ended well.

"If it was *your* father—someone you cared about—what would *you* do?" she asked. "Call the police?"

"I don't know. Did you tell the WSP detective about what brought you to Seattle?"

"Not in so many words," she said.

"And why not?"

"What would I say?"

"I hear you." He hated saying his next words. "You know for sure this guy is your real father?" The question sounded ridiculous. There was a resemblance, but that didn't always mean a blood relation. Yeah. Dumb question.

Jo's face scrunched into a deep frown. "I'm not an idiot."

He'd said the wrong thing. "Of course you're not. I didn't mean to imply you were. But people want something bad enough, sometimes they see something that isn't real. Isn't there." He was digging a deeper hole. He should shut up already.

"Just please explain to me how you met your biological father." Her mother dies, and then this man claiming he's her father shows up. Cole believed that he probably was. But how does that happen?

"You don't understand," she said.

"That's right." Cole braked to keep from rear-ending someone. "I don't. Please, help me to understand."

Then he circled the block so he could find a parking spot right on the street, and that was going to be tough, but it would give them more time for this conversation. She sighed. Closed her eyes. Was he pressing her too much? Still, he needed the truth so he could better understand what he was dealing with.

"Okay. First things first. That night, after Mom told me the truth about my father, when I was waiting for her at the house, I thumbed through her Bible and found a picture of her with a man. An old picture. I don't know. I wondered if he was the one. So when I finally left Michigan, I drove through the Midwest. I was a couple of days into my trip when I stopped in Kansas at a hole-in-the-wall place for breakfast. That's when I spotted a man sitting in a booth on the other side of the small café. He was watching me. And I realized, he was an older version of that same man in the picture with Mom. He didn't look so different—you know how some people do when they age—that I couldn't recognize him. He was in good physical condition but had some gray. And his brows and eyes were like mine. I don't know what it is about eyes, but I'm drawn to them—I guess like most people are—and I remember them. I start there, as an artist, if I can. And I just knew."

She looked at Cole with her own big browns, and he knew he'd been a complete fool to even ask her how she'd known. "That he was your father."

"Yes." Tears welled in her eyes.

He'd never seen this version of Jo, and right now, he wasn't sure he'd even known her at all. "Tell me, Jo, what'd you do next?"

"I approached the booth." She sucked in a breath. "I can just remember that conversation, see it in my mind as if it happened yesterday. I asked if I could sit down. He replied that he thought I'd never ask. So I sat and we stared at each other. It was just so surreal. I said, 'Are you who I think you are?' I mean, how bold was that?"

"And what'd he say?" Cole asked.

"He responded that he thought he might be." Jo angled her head and frowned. "That confused me."

"You figure if he was your father, he would know."

"Right. So I said, 'What do you mean you *think*?' And he said, 'You have my mother's eyes.' I said, 'I have *your* eyes.'" Jo smirked and shrugged. "He has a *distinct* look."

Cole smiled. "Like you, Jo." She really stood out with those almond-shaped, golden-brown eyes. "*You* have a distinct look. As for your father, I always saw the resemblance." But still, he needed to ask about this guy who appeared out of the blue into her life not long ago.

"Anyway, I was still confused and asked him why he never showed up in my life. Why I didn't know him. Why now? Was he following me or what? You know what he said to me?"

"No idea."

"He said that he didn't know about me until a few days before!" Incredulity twisted up her features. A tear leaked from the corner of her eye.

Cole thought for sure she was holding many more of them back. Rather than say anything—because there were no adequate words, really—he kept quiet. Listened.

"I tell you, I don't understand any of this. But I asked how he found me. He said he wasn't even looking. He said that he'd loosely followed Mom's career over the years and was sorry to hear about the accident. He came to the funeral and then figured it would be weird and awkward and so decided to leave before he joined those at the gravesite, and that's when he saw me. And he *knew* that I was his daughter. So, yeah, he followed me until he could figure out how to approach me. Said he suspected it would all work out, and it did. I approached *him*."

Tears leaked out both eyes then. "I had so many questions.

I was so mad at my mother. Again. I had so much to ask him. But instead of any of that, I blurted out that I needed to hide."

Interesting. For all Jo knew at the time, her newly found biological father was the person she needed to hide from. How could she know? Unless she hadn't shared everything yet, and her mother had told her more. "What did he say then?"

"He told me that he knew a place. Didn't even ask me questions. He brought me to Hidden Bay, where he'd lived and worked for thirty years."

Well, that explained a few things. Cole wanted to continue this conversation, but it was after 4:00 p.m., and he didn't want to lose the chance to get at the security feed. Columbia Center was just around the corner, and he finally found and parked in a spot right in front.

"How'd you get this spot? I had to park in the garage two blocks away and walk uphill in the rain."

"You didn't happen to notice I drove around the block a few times?"

Cole pictured her making that hike and could just see her, slipping or maybe tripping a couple of times. She had to be the clumsiest person he'd ever met, and weirdly, it was one of the things he absolutely adored about her. Adored? Yeah . . . at some point, he needed to talk to her about . . .

Us.

We need to talk about us. If there is an us or can be an us. Now who was the clumsy one? When it came to talking to Jo about *them*, he was the worst with words.

Jo cleared her throat. "Listen, I think . . . um . . . yeah, you're here about my mother, officially, and now you're sort of helping me with my father, unofficially. But I want to get one thing straight so that this isn't awkward—at least for me, because it doesn't seem like it's awkward for you at all. But whatever we did before—dated, whatever—we can work together now without any of that affecting our relationship. So we can keep this completely professional. Deal?"

Aw. Jo . . .

She thrust her hand out for him to shake, which felt completely off to him, like she was trying too hard. And she was pushing for the exact opposite. Cole forced a smile, more heartbroken than he had a right to be, and then he shook her hand.

"So what next? Should I wait here? I was already inside, and I don't want the security guard to be suspicious when I show up again with you."

"It'll be fine." He wouldn't think of leaving her here since they were tracking a man who was involved in something hazardous, and she'd just witnessed a murder. "I know what I'm doing."

They got out of the vehicle, and the rain had stopped. He might have taken that as a good sign, if Jo hadn't laid out rules he didn't much feel like abiding by.

He held the door while she entered the Columbia Center building. Then he went straight for the directory, and she followed him. "Is that the same guard that was here earlier?" he asked.

"No. He's different."

Okay. Cole hoped he could work his magic. No one was required to help him or offer him security feed, and sometimes they demanded a court order, but he had a knack for getting what he wanted, and he had a feeling about this guard. "Why don't you sit in one of those chairs over near the bank and wait?"

"Okay. Sure." He watched Jo find a seat as he scanned the place without giving away that he was checking all egresses—complex in a structure like this—and making note of every person. Then he headed for the security guard, who had definitely noticed and appeared to size him up. Cole needed to make sure the security guard understood that he wasn't a threat.

So he introduced himself and flashed his private investigator credentials. "I'm hoping you can help me."

"Nick Freeman. You're former military?" Nick asked.

Nick was obviously trained to read people. Vets or current servicemen often had a certain posture and demeanor about them.

"Army. You?" Cole preferred not to offer more information than necessary.

"Army. Thirty-Eight Bravo, Civil Affairs. Then I was a local cop for twenty-five years. The security guard gig keeps me home at night. My wife is happy. We're raising grandkids, so everyone's happy."

"I hear you. I list my services with CGIS, which is owned and operated by vets. They connect clients with vets who offer protective services, investigations, you name it."

Nick leveled his gaze on Cole. "What can I help you with?"

"Maybe you can put me in touch with the head of security. I'd like to review footage from this morning. Sometime between eight o'clock and noon. What do you need from me to make that happen?" Properties had their own security policies, but sometimes a person could get around the hard rules. Rules might be rules, but people were people.

"I'll see what I can do." Nick got on his radio and asked for another guard to cover for him.

Cole figured that he'd made a friend. That Nick would help him.

"Have a seat, and I'll come get you. I'll take you over myself."

Cole nodded, appreciation in his eyes. He rarely ran into

issues. As long as a person knew how to play the game and asked nicely, they got what they needed without having to push the edge of the legal envelope. He took a seat next to Jo and told her about his conversation.

Another guard approached Nick, and they talked, and then Nick gestured at Cole, waving for him to follow.

"Stay here."

"But why?" she whispered.

"I'll tell you everything, don't worry." Bringing her along could complicate matters. Thankfully, she backed down.

Jo flipped open a magazine, and Cole left her for a few minutes. He walked with Nick down the hall, and then Nick unlocked a door, and they entered into a security room, monitors revealing the various cameras around the building—the tallest building in Seattle, previously the tallest on the West Coast. Nick introduced Cole to two other guards.

Nick found the footage of the day, and they scanned the images for the timestamp. "There. I think that's him."

Though the man looked *nothing* like the Raymond Dodge he'd met, in terms of his demeanor and how he dressed—the grease monkey, as Jo had called him—it was him, all right. Raymond ambled down the hall on the forty-sixth floor and joined a couple of men, walking with purpose. Cole was familiar with that tactic and could tell Dodge did it to blend in. Then Dodge entered an office.

"What's that?" Cole asked.

"Advanced Technologies." That could be anything.

"What do they do?"

"No clue."

He could figure that out later.

"Is that it?" Nick asked. "Are we good?"

"Let's wait a couple of minutes. I want to see what he does next."

45

Nick seemed more fidgety, as if he was ready to shut down this operation. "I'll make you a copy and send it to you. Give me your contact information."

Cole handed over his card while he continued to observe, but Dodge never left the office, at least while Cole was there to watch. Nick gestured to the door. Cole got it. Nick's supervisor might not approve of this activity. Cole thrust his hand forward, and Nick shook it.

"We'll be in touch," Nick said.

Cole exited the office, then found Jo.

She stood when she saw him approach, dropping the magazine on the table. "Well?"

"Let's take a walk." He led her to the elevators, which they rode to the forty-sixth floor. They weren't alone, so Cole said nothing.

Exiting the elevators, along with another person who took a right, Cole turned left and walked the hall and found two businesses. He suspected that Advanced Technologies took up half the floor.

He said nothing, just walked with her toward the main entrance. Next to the company name was an emblem that had three dots inside a flashy circle. "That's where he went. Does that ring a bell?"

"Not at all. What even is it?"

"I don't know."

She almost stopped in her tracks, but he nudged her forward.

"Are we . . . are we going inside? What would we do or say?"

A couple of burly men exited through the double doors. They had the look of personal security guards and seemed somewhat out of place here. To avoid looking suspicious, he smiled and laughed and grabbed her hand, turning her with him, and they walked toward the other company on the floor—IncuTech. He pulled on the door and entered to get away from those men.

Inside, he snatched a brochure—IncuTech was a "sprout lab," designing containers and storage for sprouts.

"Can I help you?" A woman looked up from a tall reception counter.

"No, I think we're good." He pulled Jo with him out into the hall, took the elevator ride down forty-six floors, then exited the building.

His heart rate didn't slow until they reached his vehicle. Normally, he would have gone inside to find out what he needed to know—in this case, from Advanced Technologies—but Jo was with him. Coming here might have been too much of a risk, after all.

He opened the door for her, and as she slid in, he whispered, "I'm supposed to get a copy of the security footage so we can review things later."

Once he sat in his vehicle next to her, he took a deep breath. "I barely recognized him."

"What do you mean?" She gave him a concerned look. "Are you sure it was him?"

"Oh, it was him, but he looked like a different person."

5

*H*e looked like a different person."

Those words played over and over in her mind. Cole said nothing more, for which she was grateful, as he concentrated on driving in the pouring rain, through heavy traffic and oblivious pedestrians. They approached the ferry station. Jo's breathing hitched. Could she do this? Could she get onto another ferry so soon after everything that happened this morning?

The Yukon inched forward behind a crimson Volvo mid-size SUV.

"Are you sure about this?" he asked. He must have noticed her tensing up.

"Sure about what?" Might as well play dumb when she didn't want to admit what a coward she was.

"We could always just take the Tacoma Narrows Bridge."

"At this time of day, the traffic would be awful. We're here."

"If you're sure."

"I'm sure, okay?" She snapped at him. "I'm sorry. Thanks

for checking. To be honest, I'm not sure, but I don't want to fight the traffic."

In fact, while they rode the ferry, maybe she could answer his questions, and then, on the other side of the sound, they could part ways. That would be for the best. He'd hurt her, and even though they agreed to work together as professionals, it was harder to maintain that emotional distance than she thought.

I really am a coward.

Her elbow on the armrest, she rubbed her temple. "You had questions about my mother. Why don't we talk about that?"

"It can wait. I know you're stressed. I'm not in a hurry."

Maybe I am. "Talking about what happened before would distract me from getting back on the ferry." She noticed they'd switched out the *Chimacum* for another one. Maybe that's because a murder had been committed and portions of the ferry were deemed a crime scene.

Cole inched forward behind the line of cars and steered onto the ferry. Jo couldn't believe how much her pulse raced. Was it just this morning that she'd witnessed a murder? Nearly drowned? A shiver or two or three crawled over her. She tugged her jacket tighter.

God, I just want to be home in my bed. I just want to be back in the rainforest and pretend I never came here. That Pop was still working nearby. "Ask me questions, Cole, please." She'd already told him a lot, but there was more.

"All right. So, you mentioned your mother never returned home. You said she warned you that if something happened, you needed to hide. But you didn't at first. You waited."

"No. I didn't. I stayed. I grieved. I worked. Mom had told me to hide if something happened to her. But I didn't listen. I didn't open the security box. Not at first. I was too shocked.

I tried to get the police to understand that she had warned me of something."

"Makes you wonder what triggered her to suddenly warn you. Had she received some kind of warning herself?"

"Not that she told me, but that makes sense that she could have. And if she had told me what it was, then I could have shown *that* to the police. Obviously, something set her off."

"Did you show them the safety-deposit box?"

"I was scared that whatever was inside might have been more indicting than helpful." Wow. Saying that out loud made it sound bad.

"Yeah, I can see that. Good call."

Oh, good. Cole understanding her logic reassured her. "Plus, they could possibly prevent me from using the tools she left. I made a mistake. Okay? Besides, I wasn't going to leave, I wasn't going to run before her funeral. I wanted to know what she was afraid of. I wanted her murder solved! A few days before she was laid to rest, someone followed me. He grabbed me, pulled me into an alley, and I kicked him where it hurts most. I was able to get away. When I got to my apartment, I found it had been trashed. Now I wish I would have turned to look at him. You know I would have remembered his face. Drawn it, and he would be behind bars. But in that moment, all I could think was to run."

"That thinking saved your life, Jo. And the police?"

She shrugged. "I mean, what are they going to do? They investigated. Even went as far as dusting for prints, which they don't for every situation. But I worked with them, free-lancing like Mom, and so they did it to give me the benefit of the doubt."

"Please tell me you didn't stay in your apartment until the funeral."

"I didn't. I stayed with my friend Becky Stobbe, who had

moved back in with her parents. I was there until the funeral."

"And the safety-deposit box?"

"Before the funeral, I opened it. I should have listened to my mom. Inside I found cash—lots of it—along with a note explaining that I should take the enclosed passport with a new ID and travel with it so I couldn't be followed. Use the fob to the vehicle at a storage unit. Disappear for good." She turned to him, her eyes wide. "Can you imagine my complete shock?"

"I think I can, actually. And you *did* disappear."

Almost. But she still used her real name and not the new ID.

"Yes. I was completely out of my element, but she had prepared for this day for a reason big enough to get her killed, and I was next. After the funeral, I grabbed luggage I'd packed, got the car out of the storage unit, and traveled across the country. Unfortunately, she didn't tell me where to go. Just to disappear. That's how I ended up in Kansas. Before I left, I told the police everything, including my mother's warning, but they still didn't rule her death as a homicide or even suspicious. They didn't find whoever trashed my apartment. They still maintain that her car accident was nothing more than an accident. Her car was found overturned in a flooded ditch. There wasn't anything suspicious connected to her death."

"Until now," Cole said. "Now there's movement. The police are looking into her death again."

"I want to talk to the Michigan detective. Who is he? I hope he's someone new on the case."

"Rick Wilson is a detective in the cold case unit. Does he sound familiar?"

"I don't know him, but I mean, seriously, a cold case already?"

"In Michigan, a case is cold after a year. The fact they considered it a case even though it was ruled an accident tells you something. But it's been three years."

Had it been that long? Why hadn't she done something—tried to find Mom's killer—before now? As for the new detective, she wasn't sure if that was a good thing or a bad thing, but fresh eyes and new interest had to be good, right?

"I think talking to him is a great idea," Cole said. "Remember, I'm looking into this too, and working with the police is the best way to go. I'll try to set something up."

Jo leaned her head against the headrest. A murder on the ferry. Her mother? Her father? What next?

She skimmed her smartphone. Maybe she shouldn't, but she wanted to see if her story had gone viral. She spotted multiple news stories about the murder on the ferry, and her gut clenched. Nausea erupted. But she needed to see. She needed to know.

"Oh . . . no . . ."

"What?" he asked.

"Too many viral images of me." She looked up and held his gaze. "What was I thinking, coming out of hiding?"

"Let me see." He leaned in as she held the phone for him to view the screen.

He watched a few moments, then sighed. "You look different here, Jo. Maybe you won't be recognized."

Then again, maybe this was all good. Stirring up trouble could be the best way to get answers. Hadn't she hidden long enough?

"They'll still publish my name. Someone is going to find me. Whoever chased me out of Michigan, whoever killed my mother, now knows I'm in Washington. They could already be here."

"They only know you were here. They don't know you

live here. People travel across Puget Sound for multiple reasons. Tourists. Business travelers."

"That doesn't make me feel any better."

"We'll figure it out. I'll find a place for you to stay."

"You don't have to give me protection. I know you have other obligations. Other commitments."

"That all involve you." He held her hand and looked at her, deep and long.

This wasn't the professionalism she'd asked of him, but Jo was powerless against the gentle caress of his thumb and the longing in his eyes. The way he squeezed her hand made her want to move closer and melt into him.

Get a grip.

"Nothing . . . nothing is more important than your safety," he said. "Solving the mystery of your mother's murder isn't more important. Figuring out what's going on with your dad isn't more important. My job isn't more important. *You* are what's important to . . ."

He let his words trail off. What had he been going to say? *To me . . .*

He'd almost said it. She *knew* it. She couldn't breathe. *Oh, Cole . . .*

Jo pulled her hand away. Now she could breathe. "Solving her mystery can help me to be safe."

Hurt flickered briefly in his gaze, but then he smiled, and that reassured her. "I'm glad you see it that way."

Jo turned her attention to the cars ahead of them, willing the ferry to go faster so she could put distance between them. A lot of space. Getting out of this vehicle would go a long way.

"You do understand that your safety is my priority, Jo, don't you?"

"Yes."

"So please let me help you. I'm good at this."

Though she kept her focus ahead, she smiled at that. "I have no doubt."

"I can give you a list of protective detail references if needed."

So he was keeping it professional and not so personal. He was sending her mixed signals. "No need. I'll accept whatever you can offer, Cole." But he hadn't mentioned cost. She'd figure that out later when she got some space from him.

Cole got out his cell when a text came through and stared at it, leaving her alone with her thoughts.

Last year, after the mayhem settled down and Cole was supposedly cleared of all suspicion, he remained in Hidden Bay and stayed with his brother. Hawk owned a helicopter and had established a helicopter tour business out of Cedar Trails Lodge, and as a result, he and Remi had been growing closer and spending a lot of time together. And Jo had a thing for Cole. Fortunately for her, he finally asked her on a date. And the next thing she knew, she was in a relationship too. Or so she thought. She never imagined she would fall for such a rugged former soldier. He had layers upon layers of intrigue she wanted to peel away to get to know him.

And when he looked at her, he made her feel like nothing else in this world existed for him. Then it all fell apart. Hawk proposed to Remi, and everyone was happy, except for Jo and Cole. Because then, he suddenly got called away to yet another briefing in DC—so maybe he hadn't been cleared of all suspicion—and he never came back. Never even called. She knew he was still alive because Hawk mentioned him.

Cole's sudden departure after she'd let herself trust him so completely, maybe even love him, had hollowed her out. And now here he was again, out of the blue.

I don't know what I think about this. I just don't know.

Flashes of their shared kisses gripped her, and she had to shake them off. Was he thinking about those kisses too? Or had he completely wiped them out of his mind? After all, he'd stayed away for so long. She didn't understand it. She had to stop thinking about this or the hurt would well up again. Somehow she had to keep this professional and platonic.

Why was it so hard?

Cole put his cell away.

"Good. That's great," he said. "There are multiple investigations surrounding you now, at least two officially, and the other one is your own search for your father."

"Who was that from? What did the text say?"

"Allison. She's my tech and intel assistant at CGIS. Divers are in the water now to retrieve the body."

She shuddered. "Do they know who he was? I mean, without diving?"

"There are other ways to identify him, I'm sure, but we won't know who he is until the public knows, probably. Family has to be notified."

"I didn't get a look at him," she said. "I saw the top of his head when he slid down the vehicle." Her throat tightened, and she strained to get the words out as the horrific images bombarded her. "And . . . when I came to, I was inside the car going into the water. I just saw a body in the back seat, and his face was angled away. It was dark and I was in a panic, and I just didn't even try to see him. That . . . that makes me seem cold and harsh."

"It makes you seem normal and human. You were fighting to survive. He was already gone."

He got his cell out again. "I'm calling Washington State Detective Hargrove."

"So, you really think he's just going to tell you everything?"

"I saved the girl, after all, and he knows my military history. I work with law enforcement all the time. It's important to keep the lines of communication open."

"I saved the girl . . ."

She loved those words and smiled inside. She'd missed Cole so much. But really, she had to stay focused on the reason he was here and the matters at hand.

"This sounds uncaring, but given all that's going on—my mother's murderer potentially finding his way here, my father leaving—why is it important that we know the identity of the victim on the ferry?"

The call went to voicemail, and Cole left a message, then ended the call. "We'll know soon enough. After they notify the next of kin, it'll be on the news. As for why it's important, I think it's vital to know every detail around what happened today."

Hmm. She'd already been through so much that she didn't need another incident that would try to define her life. "The sooner I can get this behind me, the better. I should have just gone up onto the deck with everyone else. Sticking to the crowds is best. It just seems weird to me—I spent my days in a job that would help police solve crimes, identify the dead, put criminals away, and I can't seem to escape that in my own life. My mother didn't escape. She's dead."

Before he could respond, Cole's cell chimed. He glanced at the number and answered on speaker. "Cole Mercer here. Good to hear from you, Detective Hargrove. I have Jo Cattrel with me on speaker."

She was surprised he called Cole back, honestly. He had to be so busy.

"Good. You'd said as much in your voicemail. That's why I'm calling. This is a courtesy call to let you know that we haven't apprehended the killer. He escaped before we could detain the passengers, or he has us fooled, but we've logged everyone, and we'll be reviewing the manifest and the interviews."

"No one matches the eyes I drew?"

"Nope. That's why I think he somehow escaped. Got off the ferry before Cole even pulled you from the water. He could have had help. But you need to know because you're a witness, and he's already tried to kill you once."

She glanced at Cole. "I've hired protection, Detective. Cole Mercer is a professional."

Cole glanced her way, his eyes narrowing then brightening.

She hadn't exactly officially told him he was hired before this moment.

"I've vetted him and agree he's top-notch," Hargrove said. "I feel better knowing you've hired him. Let's keep in touch, Mercer."

"Any news on the victim's identity?" Cole asked.

"Gotta go. I'll be in touch." The call suddenly ended.

She needed some air. Jo got out of the truck and started toward the stairs. This was déjà vu, and her knees shook, but she had to see this through. Cole joined her, following her, weaving through the vehicles with others toward the steps. She released a pent-up breath. Somehow, she'd have to hide from him just how much his presence affected her, but it also reassured her. Because, hey, big, strong former Green Beret. Who wouldn't feel more confident facing danger?

"How did he get off that ferry?" Cole asked. "How did he evade law enforcement?"

"The billion-dollar question. Let someone else answer it. That guy doesn't concern me right now. Pop concerns me right now."

"You witnessed a murder. You're the only witness. And you saw the killer. You *should* be concerned."

"Bad enough someone was already after me." Okay, now

she had to sit down. Jo found a bench and slumped onto it. And Cole sat with her.

He took her hand.

She focused on the strength there. The calluses too. What did he do to get calluses?

"I know it's a lot to take in."

"I thought that eventually I would go back to Michigan. After a while. After things died down and, I don't know . . . try to figure out my mother's warnings. What happened to her. But I built a new life. Pop, Remi, and the Cedar Trails Lodge staff are my family. The people in town, I know and love. Pop . . . he really is the best dad. Dale, I loved him like a father, and . . . I still do, even though he left and died before he could maybe come back, but Pop cherishes me. You know? A person can tell the difference. I didn't want to lose that, so I let go of solving the mystery behind my mother's death. Left behind any danger to me. Sometimes I think that I might have imagined it after all."

"You didn't imagine it. I read the reports."

Instead of responding, Jo listened to the roar of the ocean, the crashing of waves. The ferries usually took the smoothest paths, but that didn't seem possible today. At least this new ferry wasn't being battered like the one this morning. She might have stayed in her Rover and none of this would have happened. After she was back at Cedar Trails and the small town of Forestview, she might not ever ride another ferry. Still, she'd only gone to Seattle because of her father.

God, please let Pop be okay.

She tried him on the cell again. Nothing. Cole's concerned expression almost brought on the tears.

"It's not like him," she said. "Totally not like him."

"You can kick me later for asking the hard questions."

Really? "What now?"

"What do you really know about him? His past?"

And now *Cole* was doing the kicking. Kicking her when she was down. It wasn't enough he had to know *how* she knew that Raymond Dodge was her father.

"He's owned the R&D Auto Repair Shop for thirty years. Everyone in town loves him."

"Anything before that? Did he grow up here or move from somewhere else?"

"He was from Texas. It's where he met Mom. Loved Tex-Mex and made the best chili. Said after they went their separate ways, he moved up to the Pacific Northwest to get away from the memories and the three months of Texas blazing sun along with three-digit temps. Beyond that? Who knows anything about anyone going that far back?"

Still, his question left her unsettled.

6

The question had to be asked. Given his experience and his present line of work, his mind automatically jumped to some of the worst-case scenarios. Was Dodge a former murderer in hiding? He didn't seem the type, but Cole had witnessed stranger occurrences. Often the worst sorts of criminals lived in plain sight, involving themselves in a community that had no idea about their past. But it wasn't fair for Cole to attach those thoughts to Jo's father, a man in whom she'd placed her trust. Not until he knew more.

In coming to Washington state to find her, Cole had prepared to ask her the difficult questions about what happened in Michigan regarding her mother's death. Was it murder? He would uncover the truth. He'd come here with the thought that at least she had her father for support. He never could have imagined that her father had put her in danger. He admired Jo for her strength and how well she held up under pressure. If only Cole could have come to see her without bringing investigative questions with him.

The ferry neared the Bremerton Ferry Terminal dock. Along with the other passengers, Cole and Jo returned to their vehicle on the ferry. After docking, Cole steered the Yukon, following the line of cars disembarking. Detective Hargrove had informed Jo she could pick up the keys to her vehicle from the vehicle maintenance supervisor at the terminal.

What a complicated day.

Keys in hand, he parked next to her vehicle in the Kitsap Transit parking lot. "I'll follow you back to Forestview. If there's any trouble while—"

"Trouble?" She cut him off. Looking exhausted, she angled toward him and arched a brow. "What kind of trouble are you expecting?"

Was she serious? "I'm not expecting trouble so much as planning for all contingencies. If anyone were to follow us, let me handle it. I'll text you or call you. I'm just asking you to follow my lead if anything happens."

"I'm not worried about anyone bothering me while I'm driving that monster. Maybe I should give it a name. What do you think?"

She could make him crack a smile at the weirdest times. He loved her sense of humor. "I'll have to think on it. When did you get that anyway? You were driving an old Ford pickup last time I saw you." Why'd he bring up the reminder of his disappearance? Yeah, he dug himself into that hole.

"Pop got it on a steal. He was always into customizing and modifying vehicles. Insisted I should drive it, and he wanted me to have it." Without another word, she got out of his Yukon and climbed into her custom Land Rover on twenty-two-inch wheels, so not really a monster truck with gigantic wheels. But it looked good and mean.

And that gave him a thought.

Had Dodge suspected a day would come when he'd have to leave Jo? And on that day, he wanted her to have a good, solid, intimidating vehicle? Nah. Cole was overthinking. If

Cole were trying to protect someone, he would have gone about it in another way. A Hummer, maybe.

The Land Rover rumbled to life, sounding intimidating. What was under the hood? Would Jo even know?

Cole followed her out of the parking lot. You couldn't drive *across* the Olympic Peninsula because there were no roads through the mountains. You had to drive along what looked like, on the map, a coast-hugging lasso around the mountains. Jo chose the northern route through Port Angeles, taking Highway 101 around the peninsula to the west side of the state. He followed right behind her. It could take two to three hours to get there, so he streamed Christian artist TobyMac's upbeat music from his cell to keep him awake and alert. At some point, he'd lose cell reception and then he would wish he'd downloaded the songs.

But this time alone in his vehicle would give him a chance to reflect on the events of the day. He wasn't sure how far Jo wanted him to go when it came to her father. Should he have Allison run the background checks and dig into his past? That would definitely be part of the threat analysis to protect Jo, but this was a touchy matter for her, so he'd tread very carefully.

Via his Bluetooth head unit, he called Allison before he lost reception. She was a tech genius and a great resource for any detective agency, especially one utilizing military vets.

She answered quickly. "You're out there making a name for yourself."

"What, no 'Hello, how are you doing, Cole?'"

"Do you know you're all over social media?" she asked.

"Not *me*. Jo's the one."

"No, *you*. The media has identified *you* as a hotshot private detective."

He cringed inside. "I don't want to hear it. Nothing I can do about that."

"It's great for business," she said. "You're a hero. CGIS has actually been getting calls from people who need protection detail."

"Okay. Moving right along. I need you to look into a few things for me. First, Jo's father—Raymond Dodge."

"Her father? What does that have to do with the incident on the ferry?"

"It doesn't."

"I need some context here, Cole," Allison said.

"She was trying to find her father when she was on the ferry." Or rather, she'd given up on finding him. "Look into him, and also look into Advanced Technologies. They have offices in the Columbia Center, downtown Seattle. Dodge was there today. I want to know everything you can find out on both."

"And this has to do with her mother's investigation, then?"

"Nope. But that's the other thing I need. Monitor the ferry incident, and I need to know what you can find out about the victim."

"If it's separate, why are you spending time and energy on the ferry incident?"

"I'm not. You are."

"Funny. I'm happy to look into it, but knowing what you're thinking can help me expand the search."

"I don't know what I'm thinking other than I need to understand the details behind all the moving parts," he said.

"So you give *me* the hard part."

"That's why you get paid the big bucks." Cole chuckled inside.

"Do I?" Allison asked, but her tone was teasing.

She'd had his back before, and he trusted her. "Yes. You do get paid well."

Probably more than Cole, but he wasn't doing this for the money. If it was about money, he would be doing something else entirely.

"Is the ferry incident somehow related to Jo's father?" Allison asked.

"Could be. She was looking for him, had fled and felt like someone followed her."

"Please forgive me for overstepping, but I seem to remember you mentioning that Jo was a bit paranoid. Always thinking someone was following her."

"And she has a right to be. She was hiding for a reason. That's why I started investigating to begin with."

"Okay, thanks. I just wanted to make sure I'm tracking with you. So you believe that someone could have followed her onto the ferry."

"Possibly. I don't know. I'll remain in touch with the local police here too. Washington State Police Detective Hargrove is on the ferry case."

"Which investigation do you want me to give priority to?"

"That's a hard call."

"I'm just kidding. I'm a great multitasker. I'll get back to you shortly." Allison ended the call. He'd been so fortunate to recruit her.

While he'd been talking to Allison, he continued watching for a possible tail. Jo was driving a little slower than the speed limit, which made sense with the rain and wind. She occasionally passed slower cars, and that surprised him, but he easily kept up with her. Michigan detective Rick Wilson called, and he answered again via the Bluetooth head unit.

"Cole Mercer."

"Detective Wilson."

"Detective, what can I do for you?"

"You mentioned tracking Jo Cattrel down since you're looking into her mother's death. Did you find Cattrel?"

At least one person hadn't seen the news about the ferry incident. Jo's vehicle swerved, making his heart jump. A deer leapt out of the way. He slowed but then caught up to her. He didn't feel at liberty to talk about Jo, who had remained hidden away in her secluded corner of the country until this week.

"Why do you ask? What's happened?"

"I don't have her contact information. I can't get ahold of her to let her know that we have a person of interest in her mother's suspicious death. If you've found her, I assume you told her."

Detective Wilson hadn't shared with Cole about Mason Hyde when he'd spoken to him before, but the case had not been reactivated yet. Naomi Bancroft had shared about her brother when she'd hired Cole.

His gut clenched. "Can I ask you something? What took you so long to finally identify Mason? What's tying him to Mira's case?"

Cole had read through the reports of the cold case. Just one investigator worked the cold cases. Wilson had been deep in another investigation, and Cole hadn't gotten the chance to ask the question he'd wanted to ask before heading to Washington to find Jo.

"It started with an anonymous tip—someone recognized the image of our freelance forensic artist, Mira Cattrel. The caller said that Hyde had murdered her. I'll say, Mason Hyde's sister wasted no time hiring you."

"Can you blame her?"

"No. We can't locate Hyde, and his sister isn't talking. Won't tell us where he is."

"You might get more answers from the tipster. Whoever

made the call could know a lot more. Sounds like they know everything, or they're possibly framing someone."

"That's what Bancroft thinks, I'm sure. The hotline isn't set up to track callers who want to stay anonymous. So that's why I'm calling you. I'm worried he might come after Jo."

"Why would he come after Jo?"

"Come on. You read the reports. She's in hiding because she believes whoever killed her mother is after her."

Cole wasn't sure that Wilson believed that, though.

"Where are you?" the detective asked. "We should meet to talk about this in person."

Fishing for information? Sounded like the detective planned to grill him. "I can't meet you right now. I'm in the middle of another case." True. He was *protecting* Jo. And stalling. "I'm happy to answer your questions. I appreciate your assistance as well."

"I need to speak to Jo Cattrel. If you find her. I'd like to tell her the news myself. She could be in real danger, if she wasn't before."

A fact that Jo already knew. "And you have more questions for her."

"I'm reviewing the police reports now and, yes, will probably have questions. But I have to find her first. I hope you can help with that."

He didn't want to stand in the way of an investigation or hold up progress, but he avoided answering the detective directly. Jo might not want to be found. She already knew she was in danger. Then again, he'd told her today that working with the police was the best way to go.

"We're on the same team, Wilson. I'll see what I can do and try to set up a call." With the words, he pretty much admitted he'd found Jo.

"Fair enough. Alternatively, we could use a videoconferencing app," Wilson said.

"Good idea. I'll be in touch." Cole ended the call. Jo was already in danger when she'd landed in Hidden Bay, and now her father could have dragged her into something else. But what? He hoped Allison found intel that could help, and soon. At least he had someone of her caliber on his team.

While conversing, he'd kept his eye on a vehicle approaching fast from behind. Passing the other traffic. Finally, it accelerated toward him, then the black Toyota Sequoia, which looked like it had been off-roading recently, sped around him, rudely cut in front of him, and nearly forced him off the road. He laid on the horn. Maybe the driver had meant to do just that. Most times, Cole remained levelheaded and refused to succumb to road rage, even in the nastiest of situations.

But this wasn't one of those times.

Especially when the Sequoia accelerated and rammed into Jo's Land Rover.

7

Her body jerked forward then fell back. She'd seen the SUV cut Cole off and she'd floored it, fearing the worst, but she hadn't acted fast enough. Heart pounding, she glanced in the rearview mirror. The muddy black SUV accelerated, catching up with her. Again.

Oh yeah? She could accelerate too. Pop had put a big engine in this. She couldn't recall what it was beyond a V-8. What made the pursuing driver think he—or she?—could take Jo out in her souped-up Land Rover? Then again, the Sequoia could also have a big, bad engine.

A thought suddenly hit her. An epiphany, really. The reason her father jacked up her truck with big tires and a powerful motor could have been for this very kind of harassment. She floored it, driving too fast for comfort along the slick road that hugged the Strait of Juan de Fuca. One wrong move and she could end up in the strait. Pop had known all along, or at the very least suspected, she might face this kind of threat one day. Because of him? Or because of what happened to Mom?

Where are you, Cole?

Wasn't he supposed to be protecting her? Her safety fell on both their shoulders. The Sequoia caught up and rammed her from behind again.

"Come on!" she growled through gritted teeth.

The vehicle then swerved into the eastbound lane heading west, then edged forward until it was right next to her, keeping pace. Was someone going to shoot her now?

Should I duck? But then she wouldn't be able to see the road. She accelerated, but the aggressive vehicle kept pace, even as she approached a curve in the road. Jo had no stunt-driving experience.

Her chest grew tight.

Her breaths shallow.

Her knuckles white as she gripped the steering wheel.

They weren't going to shoot. Given the ridge to her right, pushing her off the road made more sense. Terror streaked through her. Terror and determination.

"Oh no you don't." She floored the accelerator.

Racing along this slick highway had to be a bad idea. But the Sequoia increased speed too, keeping up. Almost.

Jo didn't like taking the switchbacks at a high rate of speed, and she slowed just a little so she wouldn't lose control and slide right off the road. That could very well be what they wanted—for Jo's inadequate response to get her killed.

She was on the ride of her life.

Her cell went crazy. It had to be Cole. Like she could answer at this moment, when she was in the battle of the big SUVs. She had to focus completely on the road and react to whatever else the Sequoia might do.

She wasn't going to play into their hands and lose control of the vehicle, or her thoughts. Jo breathed in and out slowly, hoping that would reduce the shaking in her hands, feed her brain oxygen so she could think. She had no plans to outpace the Sequoia now, even though they were still in position to force her off the road in the event that she didn't lose control and go on her own.

Oncoming traffic forced the other vehicle to slow down and move into the westbound lane behind her again. Though she was still in imminent danger, that took a little pressure off so she could think.

"Hey, Siri. Call 911!" She couldn't just assume that Cole had made the call. Help couldn't arrive fast enough, so for now she was on her own unless Cole figured out a way to stop this. He'd said he would handle any threats, but she would work this as if she were on her own.

Siri made the call. Jo focused on the road while she waited for someone to answer, then her call dropped. Of course! She should have answered Cole's call via Siri, but she had been focused one hundred percent on not going off the cliff and into the water.

"You have a text message from Cole Mercer. Do you want to hear it?" Siri asked.

"Yes!" Jo hadn't meant to shout at the digital assistant.

Siri read the message. "Slow down. Don't do anything out of the ordinary. I've got this."

Whatever you say.

Jo instructed Siri to call 911 again. Dispatch answered immediately, and Jo explained the situation and her location.

"Someone has already called in this incident, and units are on the way," the man said.

"What should I do? Keep driving? They're going to force me off the road and off the ridge."

"Remain calm. If you're able to get somewhere safe, do that. Keep your doors locked."

Best advice she'd ever heard, but not anything useful. "Somewhere safe? Are you serious?"

"Ma'am, please remain calm."

"I'm going to end the call now so I can focus on staying safe."

She cut the dispatcher off to tell Siri to end the call. Jo pulled in a few breaths. Up ahead was a severe drop into the strait. She had no intention of landing in the water again after her experience earlier in the day. Against her better judgment, but trusting Cole to take it from here, she turned off onto the pullout right before the most dangerous section of the road, fully expecting the harassing vehicle to follow her. But she would let Cole take care of them.

The SUV sped past her on the road, surprising her. Relief blew through her as she watched the vehicle heading west.

Cole's vehicle slid across the gravel, coming to a stop, and he jumped out and ran to her. Lights flashing and sirens screaming, a county sheriff's vehicle sped past them, giving chase to the Sequoia. Another county vehicle pulled in behind Cole's Yukon.

His expression taut, Cole yanked the door open to reach for her and Jo slid right into his arms. He squeezed her tight until she thought she would suffocate. Shaking, she clung to him too. She might never let him go.

That was close, much too close. Just like earlier today. Just like back in Michigan. God, what is going on?

And now, clinging to him, she realized that she was much too close in another way. Cole . . .

I missed you.

Jo had to pull herself together. She tried to step away, but she was trapped by the Land Rover at her back.

Cole wouldn't let go, but he held her at arm's length, his intense gaze searching, taking her in. "Are you all right?"

No! I'm not all right. But yes, she was alive. She wasn't injured. Still, the words wouldn't come, so all she could do was nod. Gravel crunched, and she peered around Cole at the approaching deputy. Cole's lips pursed into a serious line, and his eyes turned dark with anger—at whatever this was. She got that. Fury surged through her as well, now that she could shake off the pure terror.

Stepping back, he addressed the deputy and introduced them both, then explained what happened. Jo confirmed his story. The deputy asked for their identification and registration, the usual. Jo grabbed hers from her wallet while Cole grabbed his.

The deputy studied her ID, then looked between her and Cole. If he recognized them as being part of the incident involving a murder earlier today on the ferry, he said nothing.

"Please wait here." He moved to his vehicle.

"Is he running our license plates and registration? We're not the bad guys here. What's going on?"

Cole shrugged. "He's doing his job."

She didn't like standing out in the cold as the wind rushed off the strait, but thankfully the rain had shifted to mist and wasn't soaking them at the moment. She pulled her jacket tighter, wishing she could just wait in her vehicle. Wishing that Cole would say something about what just happened. She assumed that he didn't have answers about any of it, including the ferry today. But he was here with her. That was something for which she should be grateful.

Thank you, God.

She thought back to that moment when Cole had yanked the door open and might have pulled her out, except she'd moved instantly into his arms. Or maybe he had pulled her out. She wasn't exactly sure, but now that she thought about it, she'd never seen Cole that shaken.

The deputy returned. "You're free to go. Be aware, our office might contact you if we have more questions."

"I'll walk you to your car," Cole said to the deputy but nodded to Jo, gesturing she could get back in her vehicle.

And she did just that but positioned her rearview mirror so she could watch them.

She imagined that Cole was talking to the deputy about keeping Jo safe and letting him know he wanted an update on anything they learned. They stood out in the weather, talking far longer than she would have thought necessary. But Cole—he had a way about him. He was good at this job. He was great at every job. But maybe he wasn't so good with relationships.

Jo had once had a job she'd been good at, until her life had been threatened. She'd left everything behind, and for what? Someone had found her anyway. This was all on her—she'd been the one to go to the city to look for her father. Still, this venture out of Hidden Bay brought clarity and made her realize that she had been living in a dream world, where the outside world didn't matter, and pretending that evil wouldn't eventually come for her. Leaving Hidden Bay, even for one day, had put her back in danger.

She didn't regret that decision. It was time to end this—one way or another.

Cole finished the conversation with the deputy, who then got in his vehicle. Had the other deputy who'd given chase caught up to her pursuer? The parked county vehicle suddenly raced away, sirens flashing. Cole approached her vehicle and knocked on the window.

She lowered it. "Yes?"

"I don't like this, Jo. If the deputies don't catch whoever pulled this stunt today, that means the guy is still out there and could come back. There's only one road you can travel."

He hadn't meant those words to be philosophical, but part of her would mull that over later.

"What can we do about it?" she asked.

"Let me drive you home," he said. "I can arrange for someone to get your vehicle and bring it."

"You can ride with me if you want. My vehicle is big and has a lot of power under the hood. You can send someone for yours."

His pursed lips and narrowed gaze told her he didn't like her idea. "We'll take your vehicle, then, but I'm driving."

"What? You don't trust me?"

"I trust you, but do *you* trust you? If they come after you again, do you want to be at the wheel?"

"You might be a former Green Beret, but do you have some kind of special training in road-rage warfare?" Maybe she should have laid off grilling him because now she was only making him mad.

He crossed his arms and angled his head to stare at her. Then the rain started. "It's getting late. Are you really going to grill me about my experience now?"

Mom had always said she had to pick her battles—a metaphor for only fighting when the cost was worth it. This wasn't a battle worth fighting. Her hands were still shaking after trying to stay on the road. Admitting she'd rather not be behind the wheel didn't make her weak, it made her reasonable.

"Let's head to the nearest town. You can leave yours in a grocer parking lot," she said. "Safer that way. Let's get out of here."

She'd had two too many threats to her life today. She might not survive another one.

8

Jo had to admit, she was relieved Cole insisted on driving. He stared at the dash, got himself familiar with the Land Rover, and then peeled out, spitting gravel at the small grocery store off Highway 101 where he left his Yukon parked for his brother, Hawk, to retrieve later. Cole had already texted him about their situation.

The shaking in her hands had settled to a slight tremble, but more than that, she was much too distracted. Her mind raced to catch up with too many events occurring in one day. The rain and wind had picked up, and frankly, she preferred to be alone with her thoughts, or rather preferred that someone else be at the wheel right now. She was not in a good place after witnessing a murder, being left to drown in a sinking car, and—oh yeah—being rescued by none other than her ex–almost boyfriend, Cole Mercer. She was grateful beyond words he'd shown up, but her emotions were tumbling down a staircase of confusion into a dark dungeon of anguish, at least where he was concerned.

She wanted him here.

She wanted him gone.

She wasn't too proud to admit that she needed his protection. She needed his assistance and connections for two separate investigations, though he was working for someone else on her mother's investigation and unofficially helping her learn more about her father. Where had he gone? What was the danger?

How had this all happened in one day? When she woke up this morning, the stormy day seemed like any other in her life. A person just never knew what the future held. Only God knew, and he had her in the palm of his hand right now. She had to believe that and lean into it if she was going to survive this mind-warping experience.

Cole's cell buzzed, and he turned it on speaker as he drove so she could hear the Clallam County deputy.

"We have deputies all over the county looking for the aggressive driver and have notified the troopers for a statewide search." Cole glanced her way.

She shared his concern that someone after her was still out there.

"The Sequoia license plate revealed the vehicle had been stolen."

Figured.

"Thank you for your information," Cole said. "Stay safe out there."

"You keep her safe," the deputy said.

See? Cole really knew how to make friends with law enforcement.

The call ended. He accelerated as they steered around Lake Crescent.

He floored it, and the vehicle took off. "What's under the hood? Feels like a turbo."

"For all my mechanical prowess, I really couldn't tell you." Now she wished she had taken more interest in the work Pop had done. She thought it was just a hobby. She hadn't for one minute considered it had been part of a proactive protection plan. Maybe it was just a hobby, and Jo, per usual, was overthinking and living in fear.

"I had a thought when that Sequoia rammed into me, I didn't feel it all that much. It could have been worse. It would take a lot more than that to move this vehicle around or off the road. So I half wondered if Pop knew something was coming and just added this extra layer of protection. But that sounds ridiculous now that I say it out loud."

"No, it doesn't. I had the same thought. Still, we could both be way off."

"He could have done it just for fun."

"Did he customize other vehicles?"

She scratched her head. "That wasn't really his business. Not what he was known for, but occasionally, sure, he would add some headers, upgrade the wheels and tires, and yeah, turbochargers."

"Sounds like you should know what's under your hood, Jo."

She lifted a shoulder. "I know a few words that I sling around, nothing more."

"You're saying he never asked you to hand him a wrench? I happen to know that you're pretty good with a wrench."

Okay, now he was making her blush. "Not on cars. I can fix . . . showerheads. I wish I had paid more attention to him. To the details of his life. Maybe he was trying to tell me something. Or left a clue. Something."

As soon as she could, she would stop by the shop. Sit in his chair in his dusty, messy office. He had to have told his two employees that he'd gone. In fact, now that she thought about it, what would happen to R&D? Was Pop coming back? Was he selling it? What had he told Sarah and Jessie?

Cole pressed the accelerator with a brief punch, and the

engine gave a deep, guttural rumble. "It handles really well on the slick roads."

"You sound like you're interested in buying this from me. It's not for sale."

He chuckled, flicking his gaze to the mirrors.

Small talk. Jo didn't need it and would rather get lost in her own thoughts. A knot lodged in her throat, and tears threatened. She stared out the window at the lush evergreens, and beyond them, heavy gray clouds hovered over the Pacific Ocean.

———

Jo woke with a start. They were here at Spruce Hollow—the name she'd given to her tiny house in the rainforest. How could she have fallen asleep? She glanced at the house, then back at him. "Um . . . Don't I need to drop you off?" *Because you're absolutely not staying here to protect me.*

A vehicle pulled in behind them. Hawk. That made sense.

"I've got a ride. I wanted to clear your house first. Unless, of course, you're willing to stay at the lodge tonight, just until we figure things out."

A small laugh burst out. "Seriously, I'm good. This place isn't even in my name. You know about it because I brought you here. As for clearing it, you can see everything from the front door."

"Okay. Then I'll take a quick look." Cole hopped out and then followed her up to the door, which she unlocked. "Hawk is checking the perimeter."

"Really?" She opened the door wide to let Cole inside.

"Really." He stepped past her and gave her a "get real" look.

"I'm taking this seriously, Cole," she said. "Don't act like I'm not."

He cleared her house so fast it was almost laughable,

then stood in the doorway. She looked at him, and that unwanted memory of them standing here kissing good night rolled through her. Awkward. He could probably hear her pounding heart. Heat flooded her cheeks, and Cole stared at her face. The way he looked at her, she knew he was thinking the same thing. Longing erupted in his gaze, then he shuttered it away.

And that hurt. But it shouldn't have. She should have been the one to hide her emotions.

Hawk clomped up the steps, breaking the moment. Relief flooded her.

She closed her eyes, grateful for the rescue from her own embarrassment, then quickly opened them. "I'm good, boys. You can leave now."

Cole didn't appear convinced, his face serious, as if he was about to jump out of a helicopter on a covert operation in a forbidden jungle. He stalked to Hawk's vehicle. Honestly, she was surprised she'd gotten rid of him that easily.

And there it was again. That thought to get rid of him, when deep inside, she wanted the exact opposite.

If he looked back at her, maybe he could read *that* on her face.

You don't have to leave, Cole.

Cole opened the truck door and turned to her. "We need to talk soon, Jo. I'll be in touch but call me if you need me."

"I will." She shut the door.

Alone at last. She'd wanted the space from him and to be alone with her thoughts, away from anyone and everyone, but now that she was here—no Cole, no passengers or city dwellers, no exhaust, and nothing but fresh rainforest air— regret coursed through her. She missed Cole and wished he could be with her here in her small corner of the property behind Mrs. Crawford's house. Spruce Hollow.

She sighed a weirdly happy sigh, given her day. But every

time she looked at the place, a sense of peace engulfed her. She'd put her heart into decorating, letting the vines grow over the outside walls, except for the windows, so it would meld into the rainforest. Her small—very tiny—place in this world, hidden away in this corner of the Olympic Peninsula.

Inside the home, she sat in the plush chair and looked out the window at her view of the lush moss-covered branches and trunks of the evergreens and ground cover.

God is good.

She believed that once. She had to keep believing that now. But sometimes it was hard.

Like when your dad left—oh, and by the way, he wasn't your real dad. And when your mom was murdered and nobody believed you, and your real dad left too, and the man you thought you could love turned up after hearing nothing from him for months and months.

God is good. I know you are, God. It's not you, but it's people who have left me in pieces, who aren't so good.

She pushed the morbid thoughts away and focused on the beauty of God's creation through her big window. Answers would come. She just had to wait for them.

Her mother's framed picture hung on the wall near the window. Mom needed justice. Pop could take care of himself. The thought didn't soothe the pain in her heart. As for the incident on the ferry, she had told the police all she knew. But who was the victim? A father, a husband, and a son?

There was too much death in this world.

The next day, Jo blew out a breath and pretended like yesterday had been a day like every other day. After she showered and dressed in jeans and a T-shirt, she did a few chores—part of her mission to put normalcy back into her life, if only for one day. Remi knew she was back and told her to take the day off.

By late afternoon, Jo had run out of things to do and debated settling in with a bowl of popcorn and a good movie. Whatever. Jo couldn't just sit anymore, and she'd put Cole off all day. He'd texted her one too many times to check on her, to which she'd replied,

I'm fine. Need space.

Though she hadn't said the words "from you" because she wasn't entirely sure it was him as much as it was the situation. She looked through her sketches and added the eyes from the ferry killer to the other unnamed people she'd sketched. She was a people watcher and often found herself sketching faces of random strangers. Other sketches were of nature, like the bridge in the rainforest over the Pulsap River. Pop had taken her there a lot. It had been a special place for him, but he'd warned her not to ever go there on her own. The old logging bridge had been decommissioned and was off-limits. Maybe she couldn't go to the bridge, but she knew exactly where she would go.

That was it. She would go to Pop's. He'd lived in a small apartment above the shop. God willing, she might find a clue about where he'd gone and why. Jo grabbed a coat, her bag, and keys and locked up the tiny house. She hopped into her Rover, started it up, and placed her hands on the wheel. Cole's hands had been here yesterday. In fact, she could still smell his cologne. Musky. Masculine. How weird was it for her to think about that?

She steered out of her hidden space and onto the road into Forestview. Along the main strip, she found Pop's R&D Auto Repair Shop. He did much more than just mechanical work. He did body work too. Sarah and Jessie—if they had even remained to work—would have already locked up for the evening. Or did she have it all wrong? Had they been let go and the shop completely shut down with her father's departure?

At the back of the structure, she hiked up the steps to his apartment above the shop, then unlocked the door using the key he'd given her. Flipping on the lights, she entered the one-bedroom space to find the old furniture remained, less than half of his clothes were still in the closet, the kitchen and the fridge were emptied of food—so at least he'd cleaned that out—and with that, her shoulders sagged. He wasn't planning on coming back any time soon, if ever.

She moved to the window and ran her finger down the sleek, professional-grade Meade telescope. Pop was serious about his hobbies. Maybe that's why he'd never bought a nice house. He hadn't even married—as far as Jo knew, anyway. He preferred to focus on what was important to him, like looking at the night sky. Exploring the Creator's universe, he'd called it. He'd take the telescope to the coast when the skies were clear and spend hours looking at the stars. Olympic National Park wasn't officially a "dark sky" park, but it might as well have been.

She could hear Pop's voice in her head now when they viewed the Milky Way at Ruby Beach. *"One day soon, we'll go back to the moon, Jo. I can feel it in my bones. I might even still be around by the time we make it to Mars. Only the good Lord knows the future."*

A pang shot through her heart at the memory. Pop was a nerd who obsessed over things, but she could tell that, beneath the surface, he was a tortured soul. She shoved the melancholy away. While she hated to leave his expensive telescope here, it was too much to take apart and load in her vehicle right now. She'd have to come back for it. That he'd left one of his prized possessions behind showed his state of mind.

She locked up the apartment and bounded down the steps. With the shop key on her key ring, she opened up the back door to his office and flipped on the overhead fluorescents, which flickered. Only half the lights worked.

Jo plopped into Pop's rolling chair and stared at his desk, which was uncharacteristically neat. That was because he'd cleaned it off. Usually it was stacked with paperwork—parts orders, manufacturer specs, and customer needs—all handwritten. He'd left his old desktop behind, probably because it was too ancient to be useful. She searched through the drawers and found nothing of value, just random papers and junk. She wasn't even sure what she was looking for. Just figured she'd know it when she saw it.

Over on the corkboard, the pinned images drew her attention. A few cars he'd customized as well as a Polaroid photo of Jo smiling next to her Rover. She got up and snatched the picture off the board. There had been two such photos pinned. Maybe he'd taken one for himself and left one for her.

This wasn't getting her anywhere. He hadn't left any clues. He was too smart for that. His office might have been messy, but he'd always been meticulous when it came to his hobbies. She plopped back in the chair, and her eyes landed on the shelf on the opposite wall. She rolled across the room to study his model-car collection. One by one, she picked them up. Corvette. Aston Martin Valkyrie. Lamborghini Diablo. Shelby. Had he painted them himself? The die-cast models had already been here gathering dust when she got here. The only thing he'd said about them was that the smallest details could have the biggest impact.

He apparently liked fast vehicles. She blew the dust off now, and it made her sneeze. She moved down the row that included military stuff. Cannons and tanks, and then single-engine airplanes, a space shuttle, and a rocket. She picked up one of the planes and flew it around like she was a little kid. But she hadn't known him as a kid, and now she came to the awful realization that maybe she hadn't known him at all, even after three years.

The thought sickened her, but more because she was worried, hurt, and angry all at the same time. Yeah, she was in that proverbial mental dungeon right now.

Time to get out. She could work at the lodge tonight.

Because . . . shoot . . . her mind would not shut down. Too many questions about murder and mayhem rolled around in a brain already filled with paranoia. She'd only slept last night due to utter exhaustion. Tonight would be different.

Jo drove the short distance from Forestview to the Cedar Trails Lodge, which was perched on a cliff that overlooked the Pacific Ocean. Every season brought its own kind of coastal beauty to Cedar Trails Lodge.

Parking, she risked a glance in the mirror. *Am I really such a mess?* She scraped her long dark hair into a ponytail and got out of her Rover to go in search of Remi. Jo wanted to let her know that she was back and needed to work. Anyone in their right mind would curl up in a ball and shiver until all the confusing thoughts passed. Or at the very least, collapse into bed and sleep it off. But Jo had too much nervous energy to burn off. She could always find something to fix at the lodge. The physical labor and problem-solving required her complete focus, so she had to shut everything else out.

She really wanted to pretend all was well.

Pop was at his shop working late, and Jo was just the local lodge fixer of everything. Working as a maintenance engineer was so different from her job as a forensic artist. But she hadn't taken another job in the same field because Mom had said to run and hide.

Now she was here.

Hiding.

Apparently, even her father wasn't someone she could trust. She should have known he was too good to be true. As it turned out, no one was to be trusted, especially men. Every man in her life had left her.

Inside the lodge, she spotted Remi over by the big panoramic windows, which offered amazing views of the ocean and the waves battering the rocks and sea stacks. Remi finally glanced her way and excused herself from a conversation, then she headed toward Jo. Maybe she hadn't thought this through, because she really didn't feel like answering questions. But Remi was a person Jo could trust. With a severely concerned look in her eyes, Remi grabbed Jo's arm and ushered her down the short hallway and into her office. Then shut the door.

Remi turned to face Jo. "Did you find him?"

And Jo just lost it. Remi had been right to drag her into this office. She fell against her friend and sobbed. Remi held her. After entirely too long, Jo stepped back and swiped at her eyes.

"I'm sorry, Remi. I'm so sorry. That was unprofessional."

"Come on. We're family here." Remi snatched tissues from a side table and handed them to Jo, who wiped her face clean.

Remi crossed her arms. "I thought you would have poured all that out on Cole's shoulder."

"How do you know that I didn't?"

Remi gestured to the sofa. "You want to talk about it?"

"No, actually. I just wanted you to know that I'm done with my day off, and now I need some work. Got any major leaks that sprang up while I was gone?"

"If you want to wait around a half hour or so, I'm sure something will come up. Tell me what I can do to help?"

Okay, well, maybe she did need to talk about it. At least she could tell Remi what happened. "There's more, Remi. Much more." Jo explained about witnessing the murder. Almost getting killed.

"Okay, that's it. You are officially on paid leave. You need time to recuperate."

"I don't need time off. What I need is to work."

"Look, I get that. I really do."

"Are you saying you're not going to let me work?" Jo lifted her trembling chin. And she lifted her hands and wished she hadn't.

They were shaking. "I need to use these. I can think better, I can clear my mind."

A knock came at the door. Great. She moved to the exit that led outside. "I'm leaving. I'll find something to do."

The door opened, and both Hawk and Cole stepped inside. Cole's eyes zeroed in on her, concern twisting his features, and maybe a hint of relief in his eyes that he'd found her.

And just like that, her heart skittered around inside her rib cage. She really couldn't get this guy out of her system. But she had to try.

9

'm glad I caught you." Cole steeled himself against the hurt. He'd texted her multiple times to ask about coming out to check on her, but she'd wanted her space.

He'd wanted to talk about her father. Her mother. The ferry killer. And well, maybe he'd wanted to finally talk to her about . . . them. Maybe he wanted to explain where he'd been in the many months since he'd seen her last.

But she was pushing him away now. As soon as she'd seen him, she'd taken another step out the door. Jo peered out into the late evening. Yeah, he hadn't seen her in twenty-four hours, and it might have driven him out of his mind.

Hawk had come into the office with him and closed the door to the lodge so they had privacy.

"Jo?" Remi approached the door where Jo teetered between staying and going.

Remi pulled Jo inside and shut the door. "Let's talk it through. Make a plan. I just want you to be okay."

What had Jo told Remi? After yesterday, would she ever be okay again?

Funny about running and hiding, Jo had done it once

before. He suspected by that look on her face that she might consider doing it again, especially since her father had taken that same path. But Cole couldn't see Jo leaving behind her new friends, especially Remi.

And Cole? Who was he to talk? He'd done this to her a few months ago. He'd left and not come back. He couldn't talk her out of disappearing again if she slipped into the night without saying goodbye.

A pain jabbed at his heart. *Please don't go, Jo.*

If only he could say the words, but he had no right. Not until he told her everything about why he'd stayed away. He hoped Remi could persuade her to stay with her friends here. People who loved her and were prepared to protect her. How long could she survive on her own with what seemed like multiple nefarious entities coming at her from different directions?

She looked at him. Held his gaze. Maybe she read the complete dejection on his face because suddenly her shoulders dropped as if all the pent-up energy had drained out of her.

She drew in a breath. "Okay. Let's make a plan. Then I need to go home. I'm exhausted. I thought I needed to work because my mind just will not stop, but I can't do this anymore."

"You need to rest," Remi said. "I could come over and stay with you tonight. Or you could just stay here in the lodge."

"I want my own place, and I'm fine, Remi. I'll be fine. My tiny house misses me. Spruce Hollow needs me now."

Cole smiled at those words filled with so much love for the place she'd created at the edge of the rainforest. And that same emotion surged in his heart—for her. If only he could fix things between them. Fix it all.

"Jo, there's something you need to know," Cole said. "Why don't you have a seat?"

"Look, I've had a long, hard day, so just tell me already."

"Remember Detective Rick Wilson? I mentioned him earlier."

"Yes."

"He called yesterday when I was following you, and then again today. You said you wanted to—"

"You didn't."

"I didn't tell him that I found you, no. Not yet. But you said you wanted to set up a meeting. Have you changed your mind?"

She sighed. "No. I need to talk to him, but that doesn't mean I want him to know where I am. For all I know, some cop in Michigan doesn't want my mother's murder solved. I can't trust anyone." She took an involuntary step forward. "What else?"

"He said that you could be in danger."

"Ya think? That's why I left. What an idiot." She grimaced. "I'm sorry. That wasn't called for. But I left because I thought I was in danger. They weren't helping to keep me safe."

"I think he really just wants to talk to you and wanted me to give you up."

"Talk. Talk. That's all they do anymore. People, especially women, often die by the hand of a person under a restraining order. The police tell them there's nothing that can be done. Until, of course, after someone dies. Then a murder suspect is taken into custody. Or not. They have to be caught first. Evidence must be gathered."

"And it has to hold up in court. I hear you, Jo." She was venting like never before.

"I've worked in that world long enough that I know how hard it is to bring justice." Jo sank onto the sofa and hung her head. "So I fled instead of standing my ground and fighting for justice. Instead of fighting for freedom and for safety for myself and justice for my mother."

Cole didn't want to say anything in case she wasn't finished getting it all out. Hawk and Remi remained perfectly still and quiet, listening and watching.

Jo leaned back and closed her eyes as if the world was closing in on her and her mind was the only escape.

"So I'll set something up, then," Cole said.

Jo opened her eyes and sat forward. "Don't tell me he's coming here."

"He doesn't know where you are. We can do it over videoconferencing."

Remi took a step closer. "What do *you* want to do, Jo?"

"Set it up, Cole. Tomorrow, even." She stood and moved to the door. "But tonight, I'm going home."

Jo left them all standing there.

———

At Hawk's house in Forestview, the wind and rain lashed at the windows, mirroring Hawk's tone. Cole wasn't being fair. Hawk didn't sound nearly that harsh, but Cole didn't like that his older brother was jumping down his throat. But he'd always done that, and he might feel he had the right.

Cole paced, ignoring Hawk, who grilled him incessantly about the last many months he'd been away and about Jo, her situation and his response to it, his relationship with her or lack thereof, and life in general. The sound of his brother's voice was starting to knife through every nerve ending, especially since it had started earlier this morning when Hawk had taken Cole to retrieve his Yukon. Then the rest of the day, Hawk had been busy and left Cole to work on his multiple investigations that were going nowhere. Allison had caught Covid and was working slower than usual. She shouldn't have been working at all, but he knew she'd try.

"Are you even listening to me?" Hawk asked. Maybe he finally realized that Cole had pushed Hawk's grating words out of his mind.

No? They were back to their usual sibling rivalry, except now it was more brotherly banter, and he knew they would be fine on the other side of it. Hawk was just filling his role as an older brother and trying to look out for Cole.

When Cole's phone vibrated, he sent Hawk a smirk. "Saved by the cell."

He answered without even looking to see who it was. "Cole Mercer."

"It's me," Jo said.

His heart did that erratic beating thing it did when he heard her voice. He wished he was with her now, but she apparently still needed space. Still, she'd called.

"I've been thinking." Her voice was soft. Sweet. And thoughtful.

"Yeah?"

"You came here to talk to me about Mom's death. Everything else, with my dad at least, is just a distraction. He can take care of himself."

Cole frowned at that. She needed to take the possible threat from her father's world seriously, but on the other hand, it was good to focus on something, and he'd take that. He was glad she'd found clarity back at Spruce Hollow. He smiled to himself, again. He was doing that a lot lately—when it came to Jo. "Okay. What else?"

"Did you set up the call with the detective?"

"Yeah. We're shooting for tomorrow. He'll get back to me with the details. How are you doing, Jo? Everything okay?" *Anything suspicious going on?* He wanted to ask her about coming out to check her place again, but he doubted she would go for it. He'd checked the perimeter deep in the woods last night after she'd gone inside.

Why had she really called? Did she want to hear his voice too?

He stomped out the thoughts. His nerves were about shot at this point. Hawk pretended to chop a salad—since when did he eat greens?—but he probably didn't miss a thing in this one side of Cole's conversation. Cole didn't plan on giving him ammunition to shoot down his plans.

"Everything is fine," she said. "I wanted to make sure you understand that I want to focus on solving Mom's murder. I'm sorry that I kind of blew up at everyone. Give Hawk an apology for me. I already called Remi. But getting it all out like that helped me realize what's important. Mom. She needs justice. And I need peace. I need the freedom you were talking about."

"She does and you do."

She was quiet, but he sensed she had more to say. He wanted to crawl through the connection to be with her. He once again paced and stared at the floor, envisioning her. Why had he stayed away for so long? Idiot, idiot, idiot.

It's Jo. It has always been Jo, from the moment she saved me on that beach. Why do I have to mess everything up?

"Can I do anything for you, Jo?"

"You've done enough. I'll be fine. I've survived here this long . . ."

Without you. He finished her sentence for her. Surviving before, when no one knew where she lived, was different. Now she was on someone's radar. Or two someones, he just couldn't be sure. But he wouldn't argue with her. And he'd just have to check the forest around Spruce Hollow without her permission. He knew how to blend into the jungle, and the rainforest was his second home, if he thought about past missions.

"Get some rest," he said. "We'll talk in the morning. How about breakfast at the lodge?"

"No. Come to my place. Eight o'clock sharp. We'll have more privacy here than at the lodge. I don't need more people in my business."

In other words, Cole in her business was already one person too many. "See you in the morning."

He didn't like the idea of having to wait all night to see her. Now that he was here, he wanted to protect her, and he wanted answers. They didn't come fast enough. Cole ended the call and released a heavy sigh. Hawk looked at him across the island, waiting on details.

"I'm meeting her for breakfast at her place," he said. "I hope I'll have more information from Allison by then on all fronts, especially before talking to the detective working her mother's case."

Though Hawk's expression remained stern, his mouth curved a little, and he chopped another carrot. "That's a step in the right direction."

Since when did his brother give relationship advice? Or was it more Remi's influence on Hawk? Considering they were engaged, that made sense, but Cole needed to focus on keeping Jo safe, not wooing her.

"I'm not concerned about a romantic relationship right now when Jo's in danger." And he'd gotten into this to begin with to help her because, yeah, his care for her went deep. He wanted something "romantic" with her, but he just didn't know how to get there. Not until all this was behind them. And maybe even then he wouldn't know how.

And he needed the chance to explain why he left . . . and never contacted her again.

"What can I do to help?" Hawk asked.

"If something comes up, I'll let you know." He and Hawk were tight. They'd been through more than the average siblings. Cole didn't know why, but he just wanted to do this on his own. Growing up, he struggled to feel like he would ever measure up to Hawk and his accomplishments, especially because their father had seemed to prefer Hawk. Then Cole had carried those same insecurities into adulthood. Hawk had been Army, and Cole had followed him. Maybe he'd still been competitive, even in adulthood, which was ridiculous. Then Cole had gone dark for months. He'd had no choice, but he'd left Hawk wondering, fearing, and searching. For that, Cole was sorry.

Hawk moved around the counter and crossed the room, pulling Cole's thoughts back to the moment. His expression told Cole that Hawk might be reading his mind. That he understood Cole's stubborn, independent need to prove himself. Instead of saying as much, he simply squeezed Cole's shoulder.

"I'm here for you," Hawk said. "You know that. I've got your back too. We're brothers."

"I do. Thanks." Cole snatched up his keys and headed for the door.

"Dude, where are you going?"

"To check out the area around Jo's house. Make sure there aren't any anomalies. I would have suggested that she stay somewhere else, again, but I suspected that she wouldn't listen."

"Does she know?"

Cole sent Hawk an incredulous look. "No. I mean . . . I went last night. Did you not even know?"

Hawk shook his head. "You think she's been compromised?"

"Most definitely. I'm not sure who was driving the Sequoia that tried to run her off the road. On the other side of the country, whoever tried to harm her in Michigan has probably seen the images of her on the ferry. They could already be here. Reporters could be digging and searching, and they could put out information about where she lives.

Or that information could somehow have been leaked from the police report from the ferry incident." *I hope not.* "Call me paranoid."

"I call you cautious."

"And I prefer to be overly wary."

"Have you considered that the murder on the ferry is related to her father's sudden disappearance somehow? He mentioned he hadn't wanted to lead trouble to her. Trouble has found her. Could it be connected?"

"Right now, everything is on the table."

"You want to stake her place out tonight, protective duty? I'm all in," Hawk said.

"Oh yeah?" Cole put on his coat. "I thought you had a hot date with your future wife?"

"I do. But I can cut it short if you need me. Remi would understand. She wants Jo safe too."

"I hate to see you ruin all that hard work you're doing cutting vegetables for a salad. Besides, I need to be gone so you can have time with Remi. If I had known you had plans, I could have made plans to crash somewhere else."

"You're making sure Jo's safe, and that'll take you time. But you're welcome to stay for dinner before you go. I'm sure Remi would love for you to join us."

"Why, so she can grill me too?"

Hawk moved his head like he was hemming and hawing, dancing around what they both knew to be true. Finally, he said, "I'll tell her not to grill you."

"But Jo is her friend, and Remi thinks I hurt her." The thought that he'd inadvertently hurt Jo jabbed at his heart, and he winced.

"She doesn't *think* you hurt her. You *did* hurt her, Cole."

"Wasn't my intention." He couldn't catch a break. He couldn't take more of this, so yeah, he was out of here. "I'll let you know if I need any help tonight."

He stepped out the door and got into his Yukon and steered over to Jo's, driving slowly by the house in front until he'd passed it completely, then navigated through the neighborhood. Jo's tiny house was up against Olympic National Forest—the rainforest—which could be a deterrent and, then again, depending on who wanted to harm Jo, could be a perfect cover.

But those woods were as dense as he'd ever seen, and he wasn't driving his vehicle into that. He steered through town and then found the forest road he'd used last night that followed the Pulsap River. Turned down a side road and parked in the woods.

With a round in the chamber of his Glock 19 semiautomatic handgun that he gripped, as well as the handgun at his ankle, he hiked through the woods behind Jo's Spruce Hollow, making sure no one was already here. Then he would make sure that no one decided to come after her. A full moon shining behind the clouds illuminated the night. He trudged forward, pushing through the lush greenery, slogging his way over and around thigh-high sword ferns and every imaginable kind of foliage, along with plenty he couldn't begin to identify. He made his way around a significant swath of the forest near her home but saw nothing suspicious, and he hoped it would stay that way. But the quiet seemed too quiet.

A sixth sense told him that he should be worried. Very worried.

He trudged deeper. To get here from the north, a person would have to traverse a ridge or cross the unsafe logging bridge over the Pulsap River that Jo had shown him before he left.

Before he left . . .

He shook off the depressing thoughts.

To come from the east, they'd hike in from the road like

he'd done. The west was the ocean and the south was Forestview, so the north or the east he had to watch. He'd prefer to talk her into letting him just sit on her porch. He had plenty of experience in VIP protective duty, and sometimes it was just standing at the door. Instead, he was out in the elements, and sure, working on operations in special forces, he'd gotten his fill. Still, right now, the cold, wind, and rain were not his favorite part of this venture.

As he approached, close enough that he saw the back of the cute, tiny house that depicted a domestic and creative side of her not easily seen, he admitted she would think he was spying or stalking, neither of which was true.

He didn't like this part of the venture either.

No curtains or blinds covered the windows. Anyone could see inside. He looked away before he could see her. What was she thinking? A sniper could take her out. But that was his Army brain working. The rest of the world just didn't think in those terms. But Jo should start.

Cole turned to walk back to the Yukon, remaining vigilant and aware of his surroundings. He stopped and stood still while a five-point elk passed by as if not even noticing Cole or registering that he was a threat.

Through the trees, he could see his Yukon sitting far enough off the path. It melded into the forest, and a figure leaned against it. Tensing, Cole squeezed his handgun.

A raincoat hood covered the face and the arms were crossed, but Cole recognized the slant of shoulders.

I'm in trouble.

10

Leaning against Cole's Yukon, Jo kept her composure.

She figured she probably couldn't find him in the rainforest. After all, as a quiet professional, he'd been trained to blend into a crowd of people or a dense forest. Jo only had an artist's eye.

Not to mention, she wasn't stupid. She didn't want to accidentally get shot for stalking around in her own backyard. Still, she did not believe for one minute that Cole would have mistaken her for a bad guy. Just like right now, he knew exactly who was leaning against his vehicle, even though her face was hidden deep in the shadows of her raincoat hood.

Shoulders taut, he emerged from the dark woods and stalked toward her, looking every bit the hero that he was. Her heart beat erratically at the sight of him. She vacillated between fury at Cole for intruding into her life and appreciation for the former special forces hero who was here to help her. To protect her. She should be grateful. She *was* grateful, but still . . . it rankled that he took so many liberties.

A thrill rushed through her core.

I'm in dangerous territory.

His frown deepened as he approached, raindrops sliding down his handsome tanned face, tracking through his stubbled cheeks. His lips flattened. And honestly, she couldn't tell if he was happy to see her or angry that she was here.

"What are you doing?" His thick brow arched.

Yeah. Angry. But then she saw a spark behind his dark eyes. She pushed from his vehicle to stand. "Me? What are *you* doing here?"

"Someone tried to kill you. You need to take that seriously. I'm here to make sure no one is going to try to come for you at home."

I did this to myself. Three years of hiding, and all it had taken was going out of her little corner of the world in the Olympic Peninsula. But it was time to crawl out from under the rock and learn the truth. Cole's sudden appearance to look into her mother's death was all she needed to keep the momentum going.

Cole shifted his gaze, searching the woods around them. The sound of a passing car drew his attention, but no one drove up the rutted path. Wary and suspicious, protective, Cole couldn't be anything but himself. A hero. Maybe she shouldn't be giving him a hard time. "You could have talked to me about checking the rainforest around my house first."

"Would you have agreed?"

I don't know. A cold gust in the face felt almost like a rebuff. Just as well. "It's getting late. Let's go back to my house and talk about it."

Without waiting for his response, she trotted around the truck and climbed in on the passenger side. In the driver's seat, he started the vehicle. The heat blasted but didn't chase away the chill. Though it was typical Pacific Northwest cold and rainy, she relished the beautiful forest painted in thick, green moss.

With trees closing in around them, Cole couldn't turn around on such a narrow road, so he backed all the way to the highway, then steered onto the two-lane road returning to town.

"You hiked all the way out here?" he finally asked. "How did you even find me?"

"I decided I needed a breath of fresh air," she said. And the lush rainforest always settled her thoughts and heart.

"In this weather?"

"Yeah, well, I took a long walk in the woods because, like you, I started wondering if someone might decide to approach my house to watch me."

"Are you carrying?"

"Always."

"A gun? Not just the wrench?"

"You'd be surprised how often 'Little Jo' has saved me." Not counting a time or two she wished she'd had a deadly weapon that could be used from a distance. "But yes, I have a handgun too."

"Good."

"While I was out walking, I saw a vehicle and decided to check it out, then recognized it. I figured you'd be back soon. I was only waiting a few minutes. I'm not going to lie, it was getting cold, and I was about to head back to my tiny, safe house hidden in English ivy. Even though I enjoy walking, I'm glad for the ride."

"You sound relaxed, Jo, and while I'm glad the fresh air and nature did you good, I don't like that you were out walking alone." He entered the small town of Forestview and turned right at a stoplight. "Have you heard anything from your father?"

"Nope. I'm not sure I want to." She stared out the window.

"I don't believe you."

"All right. All right. Just considering the possibility that maybe I shouldn't count on hearing from him." Was it wrong she wanted to protect herself from being hurt again?

"But more than anything, you want to know that he's okay."

"I want to know what and who he's running from, and I want to—" Tears choked out her next words. She couldn't finish. "Like I said, he can take care of himself. I need justice for my mother, and I figure since you're looking into it, along with the Michigan cop, that it can finally happen."

Cole said nothing, and Jo appreciated the way he listened. He knew when to press her, and he understood when to give her time to think and process. He gave her space. Cole knew entirely too much about her. She'd let him get too close.

Maybe she had run him off. Because she'd needed space, and he'd left to give her all the space she needed. Then he just kept going. Yeah, that was all on her. She didn't know how to cross the emotional abyss between them. Or why he would suddenly show up and be all in to help her.

God, help me, I don't know why.

Images of their passionate kisses seized her heart and mind, and she forced them away.

Whatever happened between her and Cole just wasn't as important as the fact that Cole was now investigating her mother's murder.

"You've got a lot on your plate," he finally said.

"It's weird. Just three days ago, I was fixing a toilet. Nobody wants to fix a toilet. That's the job for grunts. The bottom-of-the-rung stuff. But you know what? I wasn't stressed. I had no anxiety. I was looking forward to making a taco casserole Pop wanted to try." She looked at Cole. "I'm not a Texan, but he introduced me to the food, and you really can't get true Tex-Mex food here in Washington. Oregon either. I tried."

"You can get it in Spokane," he said. "There's a couple of chains there."

"Well, I didn't know that." A small laugh escaped. Here they were talking about Tex-Mex food when her life was falling apart. But sometimes you had to cling to the small familiar things to keep your head on straight.

Cole slowed to the requisite fifteen miles per hour through the neighborhood. He turned up the driveway, passing Mrs. Crawford's house, then onto the easement to Spruce Hollow. "How did you work out this arrangement to live on the property behind her house anyway? You never said."

"How do you think? Mrs. Crawford is friends with Mrs. Monroe." Evelyn Monroe was an eccentric elderly woman with a heart of gold who lived in a mansion on a cliff overlooking the ocean, and she owned the Cedar Trails Lodge. She maintained secretive connections that allowed her to assist those who needed to disappear or hide from the danger pursuing them. Jo had been one of those people. Jo had told him all about it back in their short, very sweet romance.

Maybe she'd only imagined it. After all, they had both been recovering from a severe near-death trial.

Mrs. Crawford came out onto the porch. Jo waved to let the woman know everything was okay. Cole steered toward the house in the back.

"Doesn't it look like part of the forest?" Jo took pride in the vines, greenery, and moss.

"It does," he said. "Except you have all the lights on and anyone can see inside."

"I don't like the curtains drawn. The forest is like a work of art on my walls. That reminds me, I have some drawings I need to show you. They could mean something."

"Mean something how, and to which case?"

"I'll explain when I show you." She didn't remember seeing this person back in Michigan, but the face was in her mind, and now in pencil and charcoal, and even in the sand on the beach in the summer. She might try to sculpt it, even. If she showed it to the investigator in Michigan tomorrow, would it mean anything to him?

He continued steering slowly toward the house, then parked in front.

They got out and Jo led him to the door, unlocked it, and entered. "At least I know if someone is inside or not. There's nowhere to hide."

"But they could just attack you from the outside. You have no protection here."

"Do you always have to be so cynical?"

"You have to ask me that? You know some of what I've done in my life. Where I've been. I spent too many years serving on protective details and conducting threat assessments, before that was actually my job description."

She stepped up to the counter to make coffee. "You'd have me live in that World War II bunker on the coast, wouldn't you?"

"Never. I'd have you live free of danger." He stepped closer, and the brooding look he gave her sent chills over her. The good kind. And maybe some of the bad kind too.

"I want you to stop having to look over your shoulder," he said.

She couldn't swallow. Couldn't breathe.

"Me too." But she'd been looking over her shoulder long before she'd had anything serious to worry about. Part of her job, she guessed.

She pulled her gaze from the intense exchange and turned her attention to the window. Cole was right. And with that, he'd destroyed her peaceful haven. With all the lights on in the small house, all she could see was darkness staring back from the windows that served as frames to nature during the daylight hours. The downside to a home snuggled up against the forest—the darkness closed in faster.

And that had never bothered her . . .

Until now.

11

Cole's hackles raised. Threat Assessment 101 . . . this wasn't the right place for her. Cole had to get her out of here. But she needed to come on her own terms. Jo was no fool, and she would come to that conclusion soon enough. He would try not to push, even though Spruce Hollow was not safe in his risk analysis. The thin walls and big window provided no real protection in an attack and were completely unacceptable.

His chest tightened. Shoulders tensed. Emotion, fear, and panic didn't normally grip him and, for the most part, had been trained out of him. But this was Jo, and he found it increasingly difficult to keep his head about him.

"What happened to you staying at the lodge?" he asked. "You have space there, don't you?"

"When I'm working and it's busy, they want me on the grounds, yes. But I like my own private space, and you can see why, can't you?"

"I can, yes." He looked at Jo—her big brown eyes and long dark hair—a true beauty and she had no idea, which made her all the more appealing.

She moved to close the curtains, and he joined her, assisting in covering the panoramic view of the rainforest. He could barely make out the giant moss-covered vines hanging in a tangled display.

Rain suddenly lashed the window, and they both jumped back, startled. A laugh burst from Jo, then she scrunched her face up with an apologetic look and shrugged. He wanted to join in the laughter and have fun with her—like they used to.

But now wasn't the time. "That wasn't funny."

Even if it was only the rain catching them off guard. She approached with that lazy grin that he'd always liked, and maybe even loved.

Her warmth suffused him, and he wanted to take her in his arms like he'd done before, but he kept his hands to himself. The wind rustled the trees outside and creaked through the small space. She'd turned on the flames in the gas fireplace, ramping up the cozy feel.

"It was a dark and stormy night," she said with a dramatic tone. "You know, the first line of some novel that's now cliché. I mean, the line, not the novel."

She loved reading mysteries. Now she was in one. Cole couldn't allow himself to get sucked into the ambiance. Standing here with beautiful, captivating Jo—who was happy to fix toilets and called a wrench "Little Jo" and who was in a playful mood tonight—drove him crazy inside. This woman might be more than he could resist. But he could try.

He moved to the small writer's desk against the wall. "Tell me about these pictures you've sketched."

"Sure. Coffee's ready," she said. "Want some?"

"Not yet."

She joined him at the desk, and Cole snatched up the images. "The eyes from the ferry killer." He let that one slide onto the desk, then examined another sketch. "What about this face? Who is this?"

"A face I kept working on until I got it right, I think. I can't be sure."

"What's the context?"

"Michigan. After Mom died. I felt threatened."

"You were followed, attacked, and then someone trashed your home. You didn't just *feel* threatened. And you have a face. Did you show this to the police?"

"No. I didn't see the face of the guy who threatened me. If I could have seen his face, he'd be arrested, charged, and hopefully incarcerated. I can't know if my stalker-attacker was responsible for Mom's death, but it would fit that context. But *this* face, I don't know if it's that guy or not. He could be a stranger I saw on the street, so I'm not sure. Some faces interest me, and so to keep up my skills, to practice, I draw them, sometimes even from memory. I expect victims to remember, so I try to remember too."

"Then why did you say the drawing had to do with feeling threatened?"

"It was during that time that I drew the face. I can't tie it to anything."

Interesting how her mind worked. "That's impressive, really." He let the image drop. "And just so you know, Jo, yes you told me about what happened, but I already knew much of it."

She looked at him long and hard. "So you really have read the reports on not just Mom's case but *my* reports on someone stalking me?"

He might have memorized every word. He was that determined to save Jo from the danger that stalked her. "So why didn't you show this to the police anyway? The face could be related."

"Well, for one, I hadn't completed the drawing. I only

recently finished it. It's just something that has been com-ing to me piece by piece. I have to draw faces and images to get them out of my mind. I plan to show the face to the detective tomorrow. See if he recognizes him. He could put it in the computer software too, but to be recognized, the person has to be in the system somewhere, on social media maybe. It's not a perfect system."

"I could let Allison work on it."

"Allison? That's your tech and intelligence assistant?"

"Yes."

Jo angled her face and studied him. "You've known her a long time?"

He'd met Allison in the Army, and she'd been a lifeline. "She had my back last year."

Jo pursed her lips.

"It's not like that," he said. "I don't ever see her. We work together. She has a boyfriend."

Jo scrunched her face. "It's not any of my business, really."

But she'd asked. Cole had seen the spark of jealousy, and he wanted to dispel that. Didn't he? That she was jeal-ous told him she might still be into him. She'd been giving mixed signals, pushing him away, and tonight she was a little bit flirty.

She snatched up the image of the man again. "Go ahead and take a picture so you can send it to Allison. Maybe she can figure out who this is. Probably nobody since they sup-posedly have found their suspected killer."

He quickly took a picture of the sketch and forwarded it on to Allison.

"They have only identified a possible suspect based on a tip. They haven't located him yet." He took her hand and turned her to face him. "I wish I could tell you that you're safe now."

She didn't resist and stared up at him. He brushed the

hair off her shoulder, loving the feel of the soft tendrils. That was a mistake.

With a sharp intake of breath, she stepped back. Her gaze flicked from him to the next picture on her desk.

"Thanks, Cole. For everything. Really."

She'd already thanked him. No need to keep doing that. He was just glad he'd been there.

And he was glad she was trying to put his focus back on the pictures. He shuffled the images to look again at the eyes behind the hood on the ferry killer.

"Any chance you can create the rest?" In the short time he'd known her, he'd easily seen her extraordinary talent. Detective Wilson had mentioned she'd been like her mother in her gift—it was like a gift from God, he'd said. Not every artist could do what Mira had done, and Jo was equally as gifted. The department had been sorry to lose two forensic artists in a few short weeks. Artists who had helped them solve crimes.

"I'm not sure."

"If given the chance, Jo, would you go back to work as a forensic artist?" he asked.

"Maybe." She was the one to study the next sketch.

The dangerous off-limits bridge over the Pulsap River near the coast. She chewed on her lip.

"What is it?" he asked.

Before she could reply, his cell rang. He glanced at the screen. "It's Allison." Then answered. "Allison?"

"Glad I caught you," Allison said.

"How are you feeling?"

"I'm young and healthy, and this cold feels barely there. I'm on the mend. Don't worry about me. I called because I've got the information on Advanced Technologies."

"Good. Let me put you on speaker." He set the cell on the table. "Jo's here too. Go ahead."

"Oh, hello, Jo. Nice to meet you. I'll get right to it then. AT—Advanced Technologies—is involved in researching and developing products for the air, sea, and space sectors. They're headquartered in Seattle but have additional facilities in Nevada, California, and Texas. Oh, and they're looking for manufacturing and test engineers, software engineers, in case you were interested. I wonder if Mr. Dodge visited for an interview. He's a mechanic as far as you know, right? Maybe he's got some engineering experience in his background. Just a thought."

And a big stretch, unless there was more to Raymond Dodge. Cole had asked Allison to look into Jo's father in *addition* to Advanced Technologies. Maybe she had information on him but was holding back to learn what Jo might say.

Jo gave him a look. She'd asked him to focus on her mother's investigation. If he was going to protect her, he needed to look into her father too.

"Interesting." Cole held Jo's gaze, willing her to just hold on. "Does that mean anything to you, Jo?"

She shrugged, looking confused. "I have no idea. Maybe he has a friend there and was meeting him for lunch."

"Right after leaving you a note that sounded like he was gone for good," Cole said, "and warning you about danger."

Jo's mouth flatlined at the news. Obviously confusing to her as well.

Cole should wrap it up quickly. "Okay, thank you, Allison. Anything else?"

"Well, yes, there is. I'm not sure this isn't for your ears only."

"I'm sorry." Cole sent Jo an apologetic look.

"It's okay. I'll just get us that coffee I made." She moved to the kitchen three steps away.

He snatched up the cell and took it off speaker, then put some space between them, standing at the door. He peeked out into the stormy night. Though partially illuminated by the porch light, the trees were barely visible as they swayed in the wind.

"What is it?" he asked.

"It's about Jo's father." Allison hesitated and sighed. "You wanted me to run backgrounds on him, and I dug deep. I don't believe that Raymond Dodge is his real name. I've looked into his background. I've been working for you, doing this specifically, and sometimes for the intelligence communities at large. I know the signs. If the government or some agency had done this, he would have at least a fake background, which I could spot, but not even that exists. He wasn't planning on anyone digging. He probably made sure he never gave them a reason to look, even avoiding social media and hiding with his alias. So in that way, he was smart about it."

"Until Jo."

Cole couldn't say that Raymond Dodge possibly using an alias surprised him, but would it surprise Jo? "Do you know what his real name is?"

"No. If you have a photo you could share, that would help."

"You mean you were working without an image?"

"You were kind of preoccupied. Given that Jo has been in hiding, she too has avoided taking pictures or being in pictures, and so no chance of me finding his image on her social media because she doesn't have a social media account and never did, as far as I can find. If you send me an image, I'll run it through all the relevant software, though we still might come up empty-handed. So what's the plan? Are you going to tell her?"

He slumped against the wall. Jo so did not need to hear this—that is, if she didn't already know. "I'll handle it and let her know."

This could be a blow to her, depending on how much she knew. Her reaction would tell him a lot, and whether she withheld the truth from him, but he believed she would be surprised.

"And that's a wrap," Allison said. "I'll keep you updated as I learn information."

Cole ended the call and dropped his hand to his side as he gripped the cell and continued to stare out the window.

Jo came to stand by him and offered him a mug of black coffee. "What will you let me know?"

He turned, took the mug, and gave her a soft smile. "How do you know I'm talking about you?"

"I don't. But the way you're looking at me now . . . you have news I'm not going to like."

"Depends."

"On what?"

"How much you already know."

"You know everything I know, Cole. Please, just tell me what she said." Jo glowered.

"Raymond Dodge isn't your father's real name."

She stepped back as if punched. "Oh. Well." Her chest rose and fell with her heavy breaths. "What is it, then?"

"I don't know."

"Does Allison know?"

"She doesn't. She would tell me if she did, and I would tell you."

Her eyes narrowed. "Wait . . . you think that I somehow *knew* this?"

"I wouldn't blame you. After all, you were hiding here. He brought you here with him where *he* appeared to have been hiding." From danger. Someone had found him, and that's why he left. Cole would let Jo work that out on her own. "You shared that your mother had created a fake passport for you with a new ID. So it's not a stretch."

112

"Well, I didn't know!" Her cell dinged with a text, and she glanced at it with a gasp. "It's Pop!"

The words were in all caps, and he could easily read them upside down.

BOMB! GET OUT OF THE HOUSE NOW!

Cole grabbed Jo and yanked her with him out the front door. She snatched her sling bag from the coatrack. They leapt off the porch, rushed to his Yukon, and scrambled inside. He quickly started it, then shifted in reverse and floored it. The tires spun out, slowing their egress, but this would take them farther and faster. Finally, the wheels gained traction, and the vehicle raced in reverse along the path through Mrs. Crawford's property.

Time slowed for him. The tiny house exploded. The walls burst outward. The roof splintered, chunks of it flying into the air in multiple directions. Debris rained down, landing in the pristine forest. Jo screamed. He might have screamed too.

A chunk of wall nearly hit the Yukon, bouncing on the ground near where he'd braked. Maybe he should have continued putting distance between them and Spruce Hollow, but the bomb had gone off. Now he sat in shock.

Watching.

The Land Rover sat off to the side and had escaped damage—that he could see from here anyway. A fire erupted. Had the bomb been an incendiary device? Or had the destruction caused a gas leak and subsequent explosion and fire?

Jo had stopped screaming. He pulled his gaze from the complete decimation to look at her. Tears streamed down her stunned face. He had to get her out of here. He never should have agreed to let her stay at Spruce Hollow and should have fought harder. The tiny house had obviously been discovered by the wrong people.

The text from her father remained forefront in his mind. Bile rose in his throat at the thought that the man *had*, in fact, brought danger to Jo. He continued backing away from the house.

"Cole, what are you doing? Where are you going?"

"I'm getting you out of here."

Mrs. Crawford ran out of her home, and he stopped. Lowered the window. "Get in!"

She stood in shock. Cole hopped out and grabbed her hand, but she resisted. "I have to find my dog. Gizmo's gone! I let him out—"

"I'll find him." He ushered her into the back seat, and then he pulled away from the property and steered up the road before he stopped.

"What are you doing?" she protested. "I have to find Gizmo."

"I promise I'll find him," he said, "but your safety is a priority."

"I'm calling 911." Jo's voice sounded high-pitched.

Mrs. Crawford cried in the back seat. "What is going on? What is happening? Was it an earthquake?"

He could barely understand the words through her sobs, so he was unsure if he heard correctly or how to respond. Jo informed emergency services about the explosion and gave her address. She ended the call and slumped.

Cole parked on the shoulder.

"Jo." He got her attention. "You get in the driver's seat and head to Cedar Trails Lodge."

Pain etched her face. "Where are you going?"

"To find Gizmo."

She frowned but nodded and got out. He hopped out so she could climb into the driver's seat.

Cole peered at Mrs. Crawford in the back seat. "It's all right. We're safe now. We're going to find out what's going on. I'll get Gizmo."

"You're a stranger," Jo said. "What if he won't come to you?"

"He will." Cole wasn't sure, but he would try. "Go. You need to get somewhere safe. We'll let the authorities figure things out."

Like who planted the bomb and how her father knew to warn her about it mere moments before it went off.

"What's to figure out?" Jo eyed him but didn't say the word *bomb*.

"I'll let Hawk know," he said. "He and Remi are on a date tonight. She can meet you at the lodge."

Jo hesitated, pressing her hand over his. "No, I won't leave you."

"You need to take care of her." He gestured to the back seat. Jo wouldn't resist protecting her neighbor. "She's upset. Take her somewhere safe. Cedar Trails it is." For now.

She dug in her bag. "Here's the keys to my Land Rover. You can use it. Or call me, and I'll come back to get you and Gizmo."

"I'll be all right. Please, Jo, just go."

Fear twisted her features, but she nodded, understanding she couldn't stop him. He watched her drive away and then jogged to the back of Mrs. Crawford's house. He unholstered his handgun and called out for Gizmo. Mrs. Crawford said she'd let the animal out, and honestly, he feared the dog might have come across whoever had set the bomb off. The authorities could determine what kind of bomb, if it was on a timer or triggered by a simple cell phone.

If Raymond—or whatever his real name was—hadn't warned them, they would be dead. For a moment, he couldn't breathe. This had been a close call. They could have died instantly. Fury burned through his core.

What had Raymond gotten his daughter into by mere proximity? Cole hadn't come here to dig into Raymond Dodge's life, but he was almost inclined to push Mira Cattrel's investigation completely aside for now. Yes, she needed justice, but she was with Jesus in heaven and in a better place. Her justice could wait.

"Gizmo? Here, boy. Gizmo!" By calling out for the dog near the woods around Mrs. Crawford's house, he was calling attention to himself if the person responsible for the bomb had remained behind to watch his handiwork and see if Cole and Jo had died. If so, then Cole would be ready to take him down. He crept through the woods, hiding behind trees, using them as protection even as he called the dog, which seemed counterintuitive.

Letting his gaze search the dark woods, he remained completely aware of his surroundings. Cold rain dripped on him, and he figured that would put the fire out as well. Sirens erupted, and finally the volunteer fire truck rumbled up the path to the destroyed home, along with a deputy driving a county vehicle.

While he wanted to talk to them, he'd told Mrs. Crawford he'd find her dog, and he wouldn't go back on his word. Cole continued to search the woods, looking for two-legged creatures in addition to Gizmo. She hadn't mentioned what kind of dog he was looking for. Maybe he should have asked. Through the trees, he could see that another emergency vehicle had arrived. Then he spotted Gizmo—a medium-sized brown poodle—emerge from a hole in the crawl space under Mrs. Crawford's house. He raced across the yard to the familiar face, who bent over to pet the dog.

Cole tucked his gun away and jogged forward to meet

his brother, who stalked toward him holding Gizmo in his arms.

"We have a problem," Hawk said.

"You think?" Cole gestured to the destroyed house. "Would you believe that we'd be in that pile of rubble right now if Jo's dad hadn't warned us in a text about the bomb? You'd be digging me out right now or searching for pieces of me." *And Jo.*

God in heaven, thank you . . . thank you. Cole was still unsteady on his feet, and when the adrenaline crashed, so would he.

Hawk's face twisted up. "Stop. Don't say any more. You're alive. Let's focus on that."

"Did you hear me? Jo's dad warned us."

Hawk's brows lifted. "That's telling."

"Who is this guy?" Cole asked. "You've spent more time with him than I have."

"Not really. People work. They live their lives. I didn't see him that much."

"Are you telling me that you saw Gizmo enough, he knows and trusts you on the scariest day of his life? You saw him more than Jo's dad?"

Hawk shrugged. "I met Gizmo twice. Once was all it took for him to trust me. I never had a long conversation with Ray."

"You never needed your vehicle repaired?"

"Once. Remi's twice. The other mechanic took care of it."

Cole watched as the volunteer fire department put out what was left of the fire, and two deputies stood back, talked, and looked at the devastation.

"And you never suspected anything was off with him?"

"Dude, there's a lot off about people around here, but no, he's just the local mechanic and auto-body guy. He knows how to fix cars inside and out, from what I'm told. Been here for almost thirty years, if not more."

"Well, apparently, he's much more than the local mechanic," Cole said.

"That aside, we have another problem."

"Well, what is it?"

"A reporter showed up at Cedar Trails looking for Jo. Her safe haven is blown."

And I just sent her there.

12

reathe. Just breathe. Jo tried to focus on the road. Think about Mrs. Crawford in the back seat. Anything to avoid the awful images seared in her mind of her beautiful haven blown to bits.

Her father's text. What did it mean? What did it all mean? Anguish squeezed her insides. Why hadn't her father told her his real name? Maybe he was the danger Mom wanted her to run from all along—because how would she know? Mom hadn't even told her about him.

Nausea erupted, but she held it together because she was delivering a scared woman to Cedar Trails. If Jo had been driving alone, she might have just pulled over and lost it on the side of the road. Or she would have stayed with Cole.

"Jo, honey, I'm sorry about your house," Mrs. Crawford said. "It can be rebuilt, but you're alive, and I'm praying for you."

The woman sounded like she'd composed herself and found the strength needed to make it through this, and she'd found it in her faith.

If only Jo could be so strong. "Thank you."

Jo finally steered the Yukon up the long drive to Cedar Trails. On this dark and stormy night. She chuckled through her tears and swiped at her nose. She'd been flirting with Cole. Actually flirting with him when the outside world came crashing down on them. Jo shoved thoughts of Cole away.

Remi was already running from the lodge and toward Jo when she swerved into a parking spot. Jo hopped out and assisted Mrs. Crawford. The woman hugged her long and hard. Remi joined in, the three of them ignoring the cold and rain.

"Let's get inside and out of this weather," Mrs. Crawford said. "Remi, dear, Jo's going to need your attention."

The woman's words surprised her. She'd gone through it too, except, well, her house was still intact.

"I'm fine," Jo lied.

She wanted to be anywhere but here at the moment. This place only reminded her of Pop, who had brought her to Hidden Bay to begin with. She started toward the lodge, but Remi held her back. Mrs. Crawford kept moving, unaware that Jo remained by the Yukon.

"Jo, there's a reporter here, hanging around. I tried to get rid of him, but he's going to stay until he finds you and talks to you. I just wanted to warn you to be on your guard. Maybe you can just wait in my office."

"What? I'm not going to hide. But I'm not going to stay."

"We could go back to Hawk's place."

"As if I won't be found? No, I'll just go somewhere. I'll let you know where."

"I'll go with you," Remi said.

Jo grabbed Remi's hands. "You're needed here. Mrs. Crawford is the one who needs attention. I'm going back to Spruce Hollow to check on Cole. I'll be okay."

Remi frowned and then glanced at Cedar Trails—the

hundred-year-old lodge perched on the cliff overlooking the ocean. Jo took advantage of her distraction and climbed into the Yukon. She was already backing out when Remi turned back.

"I'll text you!" Jo shouted over the wind, then closed the window and sped away into the night.

Filled with outrage now, she gunned the Yukon, putting as much distance as possible between her and Cedar Trails Lodge, a quiet and private rustic resort. Her privacy had been invaded.

A reporter . . . *a reporter!* . . . had shown up trying to get the inside scoop into Jo's life. How had that happened so fast? And why? Then again, someone might think a ferry losing a car with a woman and a murder victim inside made for a sensational headline.

She wanted no part of it. Needing a few moments of peace, she pulled over to the side of the road to calm her racing pulse. And send Pop a text. She hadn't heard a word from him since his cryptic last message—and then bam, he texted her about a bomb?

I'm alive. Thanks. What is going on?

She stared at the bright screen on her cell. She shouldn't expect her father to respond. Miracle of miracles, a response appeared. Her pulse jumped. Seriously?

Meet me. Tell no one. Keep it our secret.
You'll see my truck. The old Chevy
Silverado.

Then he sent an address. She knew the truck. He'd purchased it two months ago from a salvage yard and had it running in no time. She took the time to connect her cell on the head unit and put in the address. It was a small airport just over an hour away, out in the middle of nowhere.

She got back onto the road out of Cedar Trails Lodge and Resort and got on 101. Would this be the last time she would see him? Was this for one last goodbye? Whatever his reason for wanting to meet her now—after a bomb—she would not miss this chance to ask him the hard questions. If she got the opportunity, she needed answers from her father.

Face-to-face.

Heart pounding, she took the curve in the road too fast and swerved into the opposite lane. A car coming toward her honked, and she jerked the wheel back.

Her heart jackhammered.

"You'd better have a good explanation for this, Pop." Should she even be meeting him? Maybe she should call the county sheriff, law enforcement, police, FBI, but Pop wouldn't be there long enough for anyone in law enforcement to show up.

And Jo *needed* this moment with him. She needed to understand. She hadn't gotten the chance with Dale or . . . or with Mom. A big, wide crack remained in her heart at the way her last moments with Mom had unfolded.

If only she'd known they were her last. But no one ever knew the last time they'd see a loved one.

Now that she thought about it, she hadn't gotten a last goodbye with Cole before he'd left because she hadn't even considered she wouldn't hear from him again for months. Though he was temporarily back in her life. Emphasis on temporary. She wasn't entirely sure of the real reason. Yes, he was working on a case involving her mother, and yes, he claimed he wanted her to be free. But why did he care so much if he was able to walk away from their budding romance so easily?

Those thoughts were only a distraction. She didn't have

the answers, but one thing she did know was that the Green Beret turned private investigator–bodyguard would not be happy that she'd traveled to meet her father without running it by him or bringing him along. She suspected he assumed she was with Remi at the lodge, and she'd driven in peace for almost an hour before her phone started going crazy with text messages that she ignored.

Jo didn't care. She was doing this. Maybe connecting her cell to the head unit had been a mistake. Because the guilt was getting to her. But Pop said not to tell anyone. Instead of asking Siri to read Cole's messages, she let him know that she was all right. She needed space. Cole understood that about her. But he responded immediately. She wasn't getting rid of him so easily, especially since she had stolen his ride.

Siri read the text from Cole.

Why are you going to the airport?

Of course he would know exactly where the vehicle was heading. The rental vehicle had GPS tracking, and he'd tapped into that information. Technology had its pros and cons.

She steered into the small county airport as her cell rang, and this time, she answered.

"What are you doing?" he asked. "Why did you just take off in my vehicle? Why didn't you answer my texts?"

The fury in his voice was edged with deep concern. As if he cared about her more than anything or anyone. Or maybe she was imagining it.

"I can't talk long. I'll explain after—"

"After? After what? Just where do you think you're going?"

"You actually think I'm getting on a plane and I'm going to fly somewhere? I'm going to hide again?" And if she was, then she wouldn't bother telling him.

"Am I wrong? Because right now, that's what it looks like."

"No. Nothing like that, although now that you mention it, that seems like a really great idea."

Then she spotted Pop's truck at the end of the parking lot. "Gotta go."

Jo parked Cole's vehicle and turned everything off. *Everything.* Including her cell. Not to stop tracking—because it would still give off that signal—but to stop Cole's interruptive calls and texts.

She sat in the Yukon and took a deep breath. Her hands shook, and she needed to remain calm for seeing Pop—possibly for the last time.

She'd done it now. Her little excursion on the ferry had cost her anonymity. Cost her secret place, and now look at her—she was braving the world at large, coming to a small-town airport. At night, of course.

The parking lot could have been better lit, if someone had asked her. Like those big bright lights at Home Depot or some big-box store. Lights to chase away the monsters or just common thieves. Now she just had to find out where on that list her own father fell.

Chills crawled over her. Sure, it was cold tonight, but more than that, this place was creepy. Pop had to be leaving on an airplane, and he was waiting to give her one last cryptic message, but she prayed for all the answers. She hopped out of the Yukon and headed for the small terminal but hesitated. Cameras were inside—weren't they?—and Pop wouldn't be in there. He'd told her he would meet her at the airport. But where?

A figure stepped from the corner of the building, barely out of the shadows. Barely noticeable.

"Jo."

She recognized her father's whisper.

Her heart jumped. She tried to act normal and sauntered over to the corner and disappeared into the shadows with him. Was she trusting him entirely too much? Maybe. But this was Pop. She knew that he loved her, even though he was causing her pain.

She shoved every ounce of hurt away, deep inside. She had to become granite so he wouldn't hurt her again. Was it even possible? Maybe not, but she could block any sympathy for his sob story or whatever explanation he might give. In the end, she wanted the whole truth.

"What is going on?" And with those words she crumpled, sobbed against his shoulder.

Oh, Jo, you're so weak. Get your act together.

He held her, as comforting a moment as ever a father could offer. A bittersweet moment. Then he stepped back to peer at her. A sliver of light from the security lamp sliced across a portion of his face, giving her a look at the deep regret in his eyes.

Jo didn't bother wiping the tears from her cheeks. "Tell me everything, and don't hold back."

"I'm so sorry, Jo. I never meant to hurt you. I should never have come into your life."

"How dare you? How dare you insert yourself into my life until I don't know what I'd do without you, and now you're deserting me?"

The regret in his eyes turned to anguish.

"All I had to do was stay away once I saw you and knew you were mine. I didn't, and now I've ruined everything. I hate this more than you'll ever know. Please . . . go. Find a new safe place. I have to put a lot of distance between us. Please know that I'll always love you."

"That's it? No explanation?" About the bomb? About any of it?

Tears filled his eyes as he shook his head. "I'm sorry."

"Can't you even tell me your real name?"

Now he was the one who was granite.

Her heart might burst. "Oh, Pop. Just tell me . . . are you a criminal? Are you running from the law?"

"You aren't meant to know me, Jo."

He turned and walked toward a back gate, where she realized someone was standing in the shadows. The gate creaked as the stranger opened it for him. Was Pop getting through without going through the normal security channels? She didn't know. But if so, then she was complicit with his crimes if she stood here and said nothing. Then again, he could be getting on a private jet for all she knew, and she glanced out into the airfield, where a couple of prop planes sat.

Pop walked with the stranger to the small plane, then got in alone. The man who'd opened the gate kept his distance. Pop . . . was the pilot? She hadn't even known that about him. She assumed the stranger had completed the preflight checklist for Pop. The single-engine plane fired up, then it taxied and accelerated before disappearing into the night. This man here tonight, he wasn't the one she'd known for three years. The greasy mechanic who owned his own shop. Fixed everyone's vehicles. Whose fingernails were dirty. And he smelled of oil and grease. This man . . . *this* man, here tonight, she didn't know him at all.

She listened to the sound of the prop until she could no longer hear it. Then the sound of other vehicles and air traffic, a helicopter here and there, filled the night.

The wind had died down. The rain too.

Maybe she should follow Pop's lead. Get on a plane and fly somewhere. Someplace she'd never been and start over. Alaska. No, Hawaii. Or maybe the desert this time. No more rainy season.

Footsteps approached, rushing up at her, and she reached for her weapon and pivoted.

"Jo!"

The words came out breathless as Cole grabbed her. "Are you okay? Are you hurt?"

"Cole? How did you—"

He hugged her to him and squeezed tight. "Don't ever do that again."

Said in desperation and filled with passion, the words cut her to the core. If he'd said them any other way, she would have stood her ground. But Cole had somehow, overnight, turned into her anchor, and she needed to hang on with all she had or else she would be lost, so lost.

He'd followed her. She should be furious. Instead, she pressed into him, knowing she shouldn't trust anyone else. Those she loved, those she cared about, left. Her stepfather, her mom, and now Pop.

Maybe if she was a stronger person, she could withstand the force that was Cole. But she needed this man for this moment in time.

13

Cole needed to calm his pulsing nerves. Holding her in his arms only ramped up the ache in his body and heart. But at least he'd gotten here and found her safe, though maybe not sound. He wanted to keep her safe and hold her tight, but his better judgment told him he needed to hold on loosely to this one.

I don't want to let you go.

He slowly dropped his hands and stepped back.

"What happened? Why are you here?" Though, if he had to guess, it had to do with her father.

She swiped her nose. "First, how did you get here so fast?"

"Hawk brought me in his bird."

"Seriously, Cole, what if I *wanted* to disappear? You won't let me even if I wanted to."

Disappear. If she left and he couldn't find her, what then? He'd kept his distance for far too long, and in the back of his mind, he had counted on finding her again—when he decided he wanted to find her. What a jerk. He was no good at this relationship business, though maybe that had all started with his family life, and his brother. But he should only blame himself.

"Jo, please, we can talk about this in the Yukon. You know, *my* rental vehicle that you took off with." He injected a teasing tone.

Hanging her head, she jammed her hands in her pockets and trudged forward, looking more than dejected.

"It's your father, isn't it?" he asked. "You met him here."

"I don't like that you seem to know everything. It's almost like you're a spy or something." She glared at him, accusation in her eyes.

"I deserve that, but honestly, it was just a good guess. What else could it be? *Who* else?"

Did he need to remind her that her life had been threatened not once but three times already? It took everything in him to hold back what he really wanted to say, but he had no right to berate her. That would only put more distance between them, a distance he was trying to close. He opened the door to his vehicle for her, and she climbed into the passenger seat with the demeanor of someone who might be giving up.

Before he got in, he sent Hawk a text and let him know he could go.

Thank you, God, for my brother's help.

Or else Cole would be pulling his hair out to get to the airport in time to stop Jo. He'd thought she was leaving or that she was walking into a very dangerous situation. Head down, she sat in the passenger seat. Before he opened the door, he drew in a deep breath as he sent up a silent prayer.

Help me with this one, Lord.

Cole got in. He wasn't entirely sure he could drive while they talked, but he started the vehicle and noted the gas tank was almost empty. She'd gone on this crazy adventure with a near-empty tank. *His* near-empty tank.

"So, you talked to your dad. What did you learn?"

"He didn't tell me anything. Just said I was never supposed to know him." The words came out choked with tears.

He wanted to hold her again, but that was turning into a habit, and at this rate, she could spend more time in his arms than out of them. He had no adequate words to comfort her. Then she told him all the details, which didn't add much to the story.

"I don't know what to make of it," she said. "He said I was never supposed to know him. What does that even mean?"

Good question. "Look, I'm sorry you're having to go through this. I'll do whatever I can to help you, Jo, you know that."

But you have to let me in. You can't just run off like this.

"Good, because I want to officially hire you to find out who my father really is."

"Are you sure you want to know the answer to that question?"

"I do." Her voice broke. "I have to know."

He cleared his throat. "And you know there's another matter—the reason I came here in the first place."

"My mother's death."

"After the threats on your life, my priority is getting you somewhere safe."

"Yeah, my secret is out. A reporter was at Cedar Trails. If someone digs deep enough, they could learn the identities of others staying or working there."

"I never really understood—how does anyone who needs to hide find Cedar Trails and Mrs. Monroe?"

Jo lifted a shoulder. "She claims that people who are supposed to be there find their way. You already know that Pop brought me."

Interesting. Cole was already leaning hard on the theory that her father had been living in the Hidden Bay region because he, too, had been in hiding for thirty years. Whatever the reasons, whoever her father was, Cole had his hands full with both Jo's present and her past.

He navigated out of the parking lot and away from the airport.

"Pop left his truck there. Didn't say I should take it. Maybe I should—"

"I wouldn't touch it. Leave that to him." All she needed was another bomb. The man had known about the bomb and the timing. He wouldn't have planted it or set it off. Someone else had targeted Jo because of her father. He needed to learn more about the man in order to know who and why. He could figure that out later. Right now, he focused on Jo. She was in a bad place, losing her father again and now her beloved Spruce Hollow.

"Let's talk about your safety and where we go from here. Hawk and Remi have come up with a solution, if you agree. But first, the county sheriff wants to talk to you. After all, your house blew up."

Jo covered her face. Her shoulders shook.

His chest tightened at what she had to be going through. The place was rubble. "Investigators will be looking at what's left. I answered their questions about the bomb and your father's text, which raises more questions." If authorities weren't looking for him before, they were now. "But the sheriff needs to talk to *you*. So I'm taking you there now. Is that okay with you?"

"Do I have a choice?"

"Let's talk about this. Your father said he was sorry for

leading danger to you. You've had three attempts on your life since then."

"I get what you're saying. You think it's related."

Absolutely. "And you don't?"

"I was already in danger when I came to Cedar Trails, but yeah, today has been over the top. I don't believe in coincidence. That's why I need you to find out who my father is. And right now, Cole, please, I just need some space."

Cole drove the rest of the way in silence, leaving Jo to her thoughts. He called the sheriff to let him know they were on their way and would arrive in half an hour. Sheriff Thatcher said he would be there.

So much mystery and intrigue surrounded Jo's life.

Cole thought back to the moment last winter when he thought he was going to die. Bleeding from a gunshot wound to the shoulder, Cole hung precariously on a rocky outcropping as the king tide waves crashed against his perch during the strongest storm in decades.

At that moment, Cole had prayed. He'd asked for forgiveness. He prepared to meet his maker.

He tried to survive and push through until he was on the sand. But he was cold and completely drained. Even special forces soldiers died on mission. He couldn't think he was so special he could face death and win.

He was ready to die.

Then he'd seen her jogging toward him. Dodging breakers and skirting rocks, climbing over outcroppings. He knew then . . . he knew, she was coming for *him*.

He'd seen her from a distance when he'd been surveying the place. And he'd thought her striking. Tall with long dark hair and golden-brown eyes, but he'd been on a mission and couldn't let himself be distracted.

But now . . . he would give anything to let her distract him.

That day on the beach, she'd saved him. She'd assisted him to his feet and said, "Come on. We're getting you out of here."

And he might have been out of his mind, but at that moment, he'd thought he was in love with a complete stranger.

Then Cole had gone and blown it.

14

When Cole said nothing more, Jo closed her eyes and listened to the windshield wipers. She dreaded talking to the sheriff. Why had she so easily trusted Pop? He was her father, for one thing. She'd wanted to learn who her biological father was and wanted to *know* him. He'd been warm and caring and had acted like a father should to his adult child. She'd been eager and ready to forge a relationship. He'd been someone who offered stability in the aftermath of her mother's murder. She'd taken his offer.

Now she was left in a pit of grief and anger. She tried to hide her tears, but Cole might have heard the sniffles. She absolutely had to get her act together, but sometimes tears were warranted. They'd be at the county offices soon, and she needed to talk some things through with Cole before facing the sheriff.

"Something I just don't get," she said.

"What's that?" Cole's voice was gentle and caring.

"He left because he was afraid that he had brought danger to me. And apparently he did. Then he warned us about the bomb. I mean, why not stay to protect me? Why run away when I'm in danger?"

"I can't know, of course, but I suspect that he wants the danger to follow him, and in that way, he'll protect you."

"But can't he see that strategy didn't work? He was gone and yet there was a bomb at my house."

"That's a good point, for which I have no answers. But I'm here, Jo. I'm working with you to make sure you stay safe."

"I know," she said. "But it doesn't make me feel better about how Pop left me to face the danger alone."

"I understand. Part of me wonders if he knew that I was coming. Okay, yeah, that sounded out there."

She gave an incredulous snort. "He didn't like you, Cole."

"What?"

"Sure, he liked you to begin with. But—"

"But I didn't come back. I hurt you, Jo. I'm so sorry. I had reasons, and I want to talk about this and tell you everything." He parked at the county offices. "I'm not sure if now is the time."

"Yeah, it's not great timing."

Inside, the county offices were quiet and nearly desolate since it was almost midnight.

Sheriff Thatcher led Cole and Jo to his office instead of an interrogation room. Jo sank into a chair, and the sheriff offered them coffee, water, or soda. Jo took a Coke.

Then Thatcher sat at his desk and drank from a tall mug. "Normally, I don't keep these kinds of hours, but I wanted to be the one to talk to you. I've hired a new detective—Braden Sanders—but he's out of town until tomorrow. But like I said, *I* want to talk to you." He clasped his hands and leaned forward against his desk. "I'm saying this isn't an interrogation, so please just relax."

Jo appreciated that the sheriff didn't separate her from Cole or make her sit in a small room at a nondescript table while she waited to be questioned as if she was a criminal. Still, she closed her eyes, willing herself to remain composed.

"The property is destroyed."

I can't believe Spruce Hollow is gone.

Considering her father was also gone from her life—by his own choice—losing the tiny house that had been her oasis should be the least of her pain.

"It will take time and probably daylight to sift through the remains. Honestly, we would have suspected a propane leak, except for the bomb warning you received. The WSP bomb squad will be here in the morning. They're part of the Washington State Patrol Homeland Security division, accredited through the FBI."

Oh. "So this is kind of a big deal. Homeland Security. Feds. The big guns, so to speak." Had she expected anything else?

"The acronyms are intimidating. They'll probably send an investigator or two who will write up a report. They'll probably question you and Cole too. I don't know where things will go from there." He studied her, his dark eyes piercing. "Take a deep breath and just tell me what happened."

"I'm sure Cole already told you we were just sitting there and talking when the text came through my cell. Cole grabbed my hand and we ran."

Sheriff Thatcher sat back, his brows furrowing. "Do you have any idea why someone would blow up your house?"

She toyed with the strap of her sling bag. "How can I know? Factor in that Pop . . . well . . ." Jo told him the rest. That she'd gone in search of her father after the cryptic message.

Pop was one of those friendly guys who got along with everyone. He could fool the best of them, she supposed, because the sheriff had always liked her father.

"And then tonight, I saw him. He left and said I wasn't supposed to know him." The words tumbled out through tears. Jo told him everything, including how she met her father right after her mother's funeral. She even shared about Mom's suspicious death that she believed was a murder. The floodgate of pent-up emotions and words had opened wide. So much for keeping herself together.

The sheriff swiped his hand over his bald head. "Well, you've had a real long day. Of course, we'd love to question Ray about his knowledge of the bomb. In the meantime, I'm going to need your cell phone."

"My cell?" She cradled it.

"Yeah. It's part of the evidence in this investigation now. We'll create a mirror image and extract the data. I'll get it back to you as soon as I can."

Jo didn't want to hand her phone over. *What if he calls again?* Sheriff Thatcher would try to ping his cell number, but he wouldn't find her father. "You should know that I've hired Cole to look into my father to find out who he really is."

Cole cleared his throat. "Sheriff, are you aware of another incident yesterday involving Jo on the ferry?"

"I'm aware." He angled his head but said nothing.

"I wonder if that incident is related." Cole didn't look at her when he raised the question.

"What's your assessment?" the sheriff asked.

Jo shouldn't be surprised the sheriff would want Cole's thoughts, given his experience in special forces and now in intelligence and threat assessment.

"I believe it could be related. Jo sensed she had been followed. She was attacked three times after going into Seattle to follow her father."

The sheriff wrote down a few notes. "There are a lot of questions that need answers. If you learn anything in your search for the truth about Ray, please keep us informed. You've already shared that you'd come to ask Jo questions about what happened in Michigan. Please keep me in the loop on all of it, if you don't mind. Let's work together in hopes we can resolve things in a timely manner."

"Agreed," Cole said.

The sheriff leveled his gaze on Jo. "I'm sorry about this, Jo. I was fond of Ray. I've known him for years. It hits me hard. No matter what this is about, I know that he loves you."

Jo had expected a much different response, though she wasn't sure what. She struggled, waffling between believing that Pop loved her and thinking the worst.

"Sheriff." Cole leaned forward. "After the attempts on her life, I need to get her somewhere safe. I have worked numerous security details, so this isn't anything new to me."

"You have some ideas."

"My brother and I have a solution, yes."

Everyone was talking over her head and around her as if she couldn't make decisions for herself. She cleared her throat to get their attention.

The sheriff shifted his gaze to her. "If you need me to put you in protective custody, we can do that."

"I trust Cole and Hawk. I'm in good hands with them. Thank you for your offer."

Without waiting for the sheriff to dismiss them, she stood from the chair and shoved through the door, practically running down the short hall of the county offices. Then she exited into the cool night air and the expected wind and rain.

God, I want to go home.

But she wasn't even sure where that was anymore.

15

Cole rose early and checked the perimeter of the large house that had the outward appearance of a rustic cabin but inside was well equipped with all the necessary modern equipment. Hawk and Remi had spoken with Evelyn Monroe, who'd been able to secure the place from one of her many connections in the region. The house rested on the opposite end of Hidden Bay from Cedar Trails Lodge and sat on a ledge overlooking the ocean, so he only had to worry about three sides. The place was isolated, and the long drive could only be entered via a coded gate a quarter of a mile through the woods. Security cameras were strategically located. He hadn't been told any details about the owner who'd lent the house for use as a safe house.

As for their videoconference with the cold case unit detective in Michigan, he'd had to reschedule with Detective Wilson for ten o'clock this morning. In the end, to solve the mystery behind her mother's death, Cole and Jo might have to travel to Michigan. He couldn't leave her here alone while he was in protection mode, and definitely not until the danger her father had brought ended. Cole was juggling two investigations and a protective detail. All good. He loved a challenge.

But this was all so much more than a job. This was personal to him.

I won't fail you, Jo.

He was *alive* because of her.

Cole stepped onto the west-facing deck that jutted out over the water, fully exposing him to the wind and rain. He took in the view of the waves crashing on the jagged rocks below. To the left, looking south, the crescent-shaped Hidden Bay stretched before him, sheltering the calmer waters within the inlet. At the far end of the bay, he spotted the cliff's edge where the Cedar Trails Lodge stood, but he couldn't see the lodge itself or the steps down to the beach. But it was the view to the right that drew his attention. Here, at the very edge of the north side of the bay, the force of the raw, untamed power of the ocean was on full display as towering waves crashed into the rocks and white spray shot high into the air.

A glance at his watch told him it was time to make sure Jo was up so she would have time to wake up and get her required coffee.

They'd arrived at the home well after midnight. Remi and Hawk had gone out of their way to prepare the place, stocking it with food and making sure Jo had a few clothes to replace those she'd lost in the explosion—at least for now—a mix of items Jo kept at the lodge and things left behind by guests. After learning that Jo's sketches had been lost in the explosion, Remi had even thought to bring the set of sketch pads and art pencils Jo kept at Cedar Trails. While he appreciated her thoughtfulness, Cole almost wished Remi hadn't because Jo refused to go to bed until she'd redrawn some of what she'd lost. Maybe the art was therapeutic for her.

The eyes from the ferry.

Faces from her time in Michigan.

The decommissioned bridge in the woods.

He opened the sliding glass door and headed to the kitchen to grab the poppy seed bagels from the cabinet and the strawberry cream cheese from the fridge and set them out. An alarm sounded from down the hall. A few minutes passed, and then Jo emerged from the hallway. Wearing a T-shirt and sweats, she stretched and yawned.

"Sleeping Beauty's finally awake." Ack. Could he sound cornier?

But he wasn't sure she'd even heard him as she shuffled toward the coffee with a sleep-dazed expression. Last night had been grueling for them both, but especially for Jo. If it weren't for the teleconference call with the detective, Cole would have insisted she slept in. He poured her a mug before she got to it because, despite Jo being a mechanical genius artist, she was the clumsiest person he'd ever met.

Wrapping both hands around the tall sixteen-ounce mug, she guzzled with her eyes closed, not even flinching from the heat. Her long brown hair fell in tangles around her shoulders. He tried to ignore the way his heart was swinging back and forth.

Finally, she opened her golden-brown eyes and blinked up at him. "Thank you."

"You went to bed late. Are you sure you're up for the videoconference call with the detective at ten? Do you need me to reschedule?"

"No. I'll be ready." Her eyes brightened as she moved to the counter. "What have we here?" She grabbed a bagel and started spreading the cream cheese all over. "How do you do it, Cole?"

"Do what?"

"You stayed up late too, watching me sketch. How are you up and making coffee and breakfast, I'm guessing, hours before me?" She bit into the bagel and chewed.

Instead of answering, he just watched her. She didn't seem to mind. Cole averted his gaze.

"Oh, that's right. You're a highly skilled military man." Jo moved to the sofa with her plate and coffee. He moved in behind her and caught the bagel before it slid off.

"Oops. Sorry." She gave him a bashful look. "I mean, thanks for catching that."

Cole was beginning to rethink this entire setup. This place was upscale, and Jo sat on a plush white sofa with a cup of coffee. He hoped they would leave this place in as good a condition as they found it. He was too busy making sure Jo didn't spill her coffee to bother drinking his own as he sank into the much-too-comfortable sofa.

"The sketches are incredible, by the way. They look the same," he said.

"They're not," she said around a mouthful of bagel.

"On purpose?" Dumb question.

"No, by accident." She grinned at him. "I'd been wanting to re-sketch them anyway, to change the shadows and the angles."

"Why? The difference isn't enough to, well . . . make a difference."

"Oh, it is. Trust me."

"I don't get it," he said.

"You will."

"What do you mean?"

"Well, I hope you will. I plan to show the sketch of the face to the Michigan detective. He could recognize him with the changes. Put the face in the database. Something. I know you already sent the image to Allison, but you could send my rework to her. Have you heard from her?"

"Just a quick text update that she had nothing on the face yet . . . or your father."

Cole wished he understood more about the forensic art process or about *Jo's* specific artist process. "So, the bridge. Why'd you re-sketch that?"

"I'm not finished with it," she said.

"What more could you add?"

She stared out the window, drinking her coffee. "More detail."

He scratched a place under his eye. She'd been so exhausted, and still she needed to sketch? "What about the bridge needs more detail?"

She set her mug on the glass coffee table. "I was thinking about what Allison said about Advanced Technologies wanting engineers. She suggested maybe Pop was applying for a job or went there for an interview."

"And that has to do with the bridge how?" he asked. She'd taken Cole out to the decommissioned bridge once, not too far from her home and about a mile up from where the river emptied into the ocean.

"Pop and I went on long walks in the woods. He couldn't get enough of nature, but he always gravitated to that bridge. We'd sit on a boulder overlooking the river, but we never walked out onto the bridge. He told me all about how bridges are built and why this one was decommissioned. He talked about some formula. Strength is greater than or equal to the load times the factor of safety."

Jo held his gaze.

She was onto something.

"When Pop explained it, the whole thing sounded reasonable and made sense. I'm going to butcher it, but basically, the point is to design a bridge—or anything, really—to be only as strong as it needs to be to satisfy whatever the factor of safety is."

"So it's cost-effective and efficient," he said.

"He said to picture a big log, the heaviest, thickest tree trunk that someone puts across a ridge like the one this bridge crosses. An engineer can figure out the very best tree trunk, the smallest one, to get the job done safely. I mean, he kind of talked above my head. That was him simplifying it for me."

"What are you getting at?"

"Cole, who designs bridges?"

Cole waited for her answer.

"Engineers. As I think back on that, I can see it so clearly now. What if he was an engineer? Those skills could lend themselves to his mechanic work at the R&D too. He was just a natural. *Is* a natural."

"Okay, I didn't see that coming. That's a great observation. I'll text Allison and give her this new information. It could help the search for his true identity. Maybe he was a civil engineer before."

"I'd like to know if he knew my mother when he was an engineer or if they met when he had switched to being a mechanic."

"All good questions." He sent Allison the information about Dodge and his knowledge of bridges. "What was the formula again? Strength—"

"Is greater than or equal to the load times the factor of safety. That's all I got. It's a basic engineering equation. Don't ask me more because I don't know. I'm an artist."

"Don't kid yourself, you're a natural mechanic."

"So I can fix a few things. I'd better get ready for our call." She stood, grabbed her mug and plate, and took them to the kitchen.

"I'll clean it up. Just stick it on the counter."

"Okay, thanks." Jo left to dress for the videoconference.

Cole rinsed the dish and mug and placed them in the

rack, then set up his laptop in the office. The house had full cell service and internet, thanks to a satellite, as opposed to the Cedar Trails Lodge, which had none of that and boasted getting back to nature for hard-core nature enthusiasts who still wanted to stay in a cabin rather than sleep out under the stars. He was glad they were here and not there.

Before he got into the videoconference, he grabbed his notebook and skimmed through his notes and potential questions. An email had just come through from Allison regarding Jo's father.

Jo knocked on the doorjamb. "Can I come in?"

"Yep." He waved her in. "You're a key part of this discussion."

She entered and sat in the chair he offered. With Jo here now, Cole didn't want to read the email Allison had sent. He wanted to look at it first before revealing the contents of whatever Allison had learned about her father.

Jo swiped her hands down her jeans.

Nervous? "Are you ready?"

"No, but it doesn't matter." Tension rolled from her. She sighed multiple times. "I left Michigan, left the danger, and now it feels like I'm finally going back and facing it."

"From a distance. You aren't in Michigan." Though it remained to be seen if they would need to go there at some point.

"It's okay. This is what I wanted all along—for the police to take me seriously and investigate Mom's murder."

Cole clicked on the videoconferencing link.

And waited.

16

While they waited for the detective to appear, Jo looked out the office windows. The stormy skies had calmed and remained a flat gray, at least what she could see of the sky beyond the thick marine fog. But the storm inside her chest still raged. Palms sweating, Jo gripped the armrests and stared at the computer screen.

"What's taking so long?" she asked.

"He could be on another call or talking to his supervisor," Cole said. "He'll be here, don't worry."

"Before we talk to him, is there anything that you haven't told me about this investigation?" Because Jo really didn't want any surprises dropped on her while they talked to Detective Wilson.

"I've only read the reports from the past . . . as well as spoken with Naomi Bancroft, my client."

"Your client who hired you to investigate my mother's murder and clear her brother's name." Jo didn't know how she should feel about that. "You hesitated."

"What?"

"You said you read the reports from the past, and then

you hesitated." She shifted to Cole as pain expanded in her chest. "What aren't you telling me?"

Cole looked nervous, and Jo didn't like it. "Cole?"

"You know everything. I was hired to investigate because Naomi believes he's innocent, but she wanted me to investigate your mother too, since she had identified Mason with her sketch. She had a reputation of always being extraordinarily accurate, and that's the reason for her popularity with law enforcement. Naomi believes that Mira couldn't have made a mistake and that, possibly, it was . . . intentional."

Her breaths quickened. "What are you saying, Cole? And be very careful with your next words."

"She had a gift, Jo, like you have a gift. The question coming from my client is why Mira identified an innocent man, nothing more."

"Are you accusing my mother, as if she was some sort of criminal?"

Cole released a heavy sigh. "Absolutely not. I was hired to look into things by someone who believes a loved one is innocent. That doesn't mean he *is* innocent. I'm not trying to build a case one way or the other. And honestly, you should already realize that I'm focused on what is going on with you."

"You figure, work with me and you'll figure this out for Naomi too." Her breath hitched. "Why take the case, Cole? It feels almost like a betrayal."

"Jo, please. I've explained this. I wanted to help you to be free of the danger. I'm looking for the truth, no matter what that is. Learning who killed your mother is key to setting you free."

"From that danger, but now there's my father and his issues." Jo looked out the window. She couldn't catch a break. Right now, it felt like everyone had betrayed her. Lied to her.

Finally, the detective's face popped up. Both Jo and Cole

sat back. She struggled to remain calm after the heated exchange with Cole. With wire-rimmed glasses on a thin face, Detective Wilson appeared to be somewhere in his late forties and looked more like an accountant than a detective.

Cole adjusted the sound. "Detective Wilson."

"Hi, Cole, thank you for meeting me." Detective Wilson smiled. "Please just call me Rick. I don't like formalities in situations like this."

Situations like this?

"Okay, Rick," Cole said. "This is Jo Cattrel."

"Ms. Cattrel."

Jo nodded her acknowledgment. She didn't correct him. He could just address her formally for now. Jo tried to act enthusiastic, but a sense of dread filled her. She'd longed for someone to look into Mom's death, but she was so distracted and weirdly torn since her mind was consumed with thoughts of Pop, especially after last night.

She sat up taller. Mom deserved justice. If only Pop was here now, he would agree, and he would join her in this meeting.

"I'll get right to it, then. When I spoke with Cole, I warned him that you were in danger. I know that you informed the Lansing Police Department early on that you feared for your life and that you believed your mother had been murdered."

"And the police ruled it an accident, but now you're looking into the possibility that she was, in fact, murdered," she said. "Cole told me some of it, but I want to hear from you what changed."

Rick nodded and looked at his notes a few seconds, then said, "Your mother had finished a sketch just before her death. We had never been able to identify the person who murdered a man at an ATM. We couldn't get a clear image of him, but Mira was able to work her magic. But even then, we didn't have a name. Just a face and no leads. That is, until this week. We received an anonymous tip identifying Mason Hyde as the man in the sketch. I'm sure Cole has told you what's going on, since he was hired to investigate."

"He's told me some of it, but I'm still not sure how this connects Mason Hyde to my mom's death. Unless you suspect that he killed her because she'd drawn his likeness."

"I'm getting to that. We tried to find him and bring him in for questioning. We weren't able to track him beyond his address in Michigan, so clearly, he intentionally dropped off the map, which makes him look guilty. But then yesterday, we found him, or I should say we learned of his death."

Jo bit back a gasp.

Cole tensed next to her. Her throat grew tight. Still, what did any of it have to do with Mom? So she sketched a criminal. It wouldn't be the first time. "I'm still not sure *why* my mother was murdered, because I do believe she was, or why *you* believe that I'm in danger from what happened three years ago." There must be a reason. And maybe that reason was the same reason Mom warned her to hide.

"Yes, well, we recently uncovered previously unknown security footage of Mira Cattrel meeting with a man on the night she was killed. If you recall, her vehicle was found overturned in a flooded ditch."

And Mom was already dead when they found her. "And now you believe she was forced off the road?"

"We're looking into the matter again. I should say *I'm* looking into it. So, the man with whom she met before she died is the spitting image of the man in the ATM attack, and the tip led us to Mason Hyde. I wanted to question him about Mira and why he met with her and ask about the fact that she ended up dead moments later."

Jo focused on breathing, slow and steady.

Cole grabbed her hand and squeezed.

"And now you say the man is dead," Cole said.

"Murdered. That ramps up the danger factor in my opinion, specifically for you, Jo."

"But why? He's gone now. Do you think he was coming after me?" She almost shrugged. It all seemed pointless. Her mother wouldn't get justice if Mason Hyde was her killer. "Wait. You don't think the danger was coming from him. I'm sorry, Detective Wilson, but I'm confused. First, what makes you so sure he was the one who killed her?"

"We weren't sure, but their interaction was suspicious."

Their *interaction*? "I'm not sure I like where this is going."

"Don't misunderstand. I'm not saying your mother committed a crime. But you have to admit that it seems suspicious."

And that's part of why he wanted to question her—to find out what was up with her mother. Anger pulsed through her. "She draws his likeness, and he confronts her? Yes, that's suspicious. He confronted her and then killed her. My mother was the victim here."

She was losing it, really losing control, and squeezed Cole's hand so hard she thought she might break it. But he held on.

"What else can you tell us to give us context?" Cole asked.

"I'm wondering if Jo recognizes the man in this image." Rick shared the screen.

"No, why would I? I didn't see everything Mom did. We worked on different projects." She glanced at Cole. Had he seen the picture of Mason Hyde? Probably, since Cole was working for Mason's sister to clear his name. Cole hadn't shown this to Jo, but then again, he probably didn't want to overstep.

The detective waited for her to say more, but she was speechless. What did this guy want from her?

Cole and Jo shared a look. Cole leaned forward. "What are you getting at?"

"The point I'm leading up to is that Mason Hyde was murdered on the ferry and Ms. Cattrel was in the same vehicle with his murdered body as it rolled off the ferry."

17

ole's mind seized up. *What?*

This news slammed him in the gut, knocking the breath from him when he should have been prepared for anything. He tried to keep it together for Jo and in front of Rick.

Why hadn't Rick prepared him for this? Called him immediately. Something. For that matter, why hadn't his client contacted him? This was her brother, after all. But maybe the news was just now getting out that he had been murdered, and she'd only just been informed.

She might very well decide to cancel the investigation. Then again, she might still want to clear her brother's name. All of these thoughts bombarded him at the same moment. Fury boiled inside that the detective hadn't shared this earlier. Then again, Cole got it. Despite his friendly first-name-basis facade, *Detective* Rick Wilson wanted to see Jo's reaction to the news for himself. Maybe he didn't know the details of Jo's experience on the ferry, and even if he'd been able to get information on that from the WSP detective, Rick might not have believed her story. That she'd

152

witnessed the murder of the very man Wilson was searching for in connection with both the ATM murder and her
mother's . . . was in some ways ironic.

Yeah. Cole got it. In fact, he understood it so well, he was
surprised that Rick hadn't knocked on the door of the safe
house, surprising them, to ask his questions face-to-face
and see Jo's reaction to his big-reveal moment in person.

Next to him, Jo's breaths quickened. "I . . . I don't understand. I thought—" She looked at Cole for help.

Don't bring your father into this . . . at least not yet.

Initially, he believed Jo had possibly been targeted because she'd been a witness to the murder. Or at least *seen*
someone standing over the victim. The fact that the killer
tried to drown her in the car with the victim—who they
now knew was Mason Hyde—confirmed that she'd witnessed his murder, and the killer wanted to get rid of the
witness. The danger her father had brought had always
been on the table, and Cole had since shifted toward that
being his main concern.

He sat back. *Think, think, think.* He was usually quicker
on his feet. But this news was the proverbial wrench thrown
into the gears of his multiple theories.

But . . . Mason Hyde? "What was *he* doing there on the
same ferry with her?"

Cole fought the need to scrape both hands through his
hair. To get up and pace the room.

"It would appear that Mason Hyde was looking for you,
Ms. Cattrel, and he found you," Rick said.

"It's a shock, really, hearing that he was the victim. I don't
understand how he found me or why he would look for
me." Jo shook her head.

"If I haven't made it clear, my working theory here is that
after Hyde's face was identified by your mother as the man
caught committing murder at an ATM, he confronted your

mother, and within the hour she's dead. He finally finds you and comes after you."

"You say 'confronted.' What exactly did the video show? I don't need to see it." She wasn't sure she could bear to watch it.

"The conversation looked, well, secretive but also heated."

"And what's his motive to come after me?" she asked. "That aside, it's been a few years. Why come after me now?"

Those questions needed answers, and the best man to provide them was dead. Jo's eyes held the same question as she flicked her gaze to him.

When neither of them said anything more, Rick continued. "Look, I don't know how her death and the danger to you are connected or why. I can't say with absolute certainty that he killed your mother or that he was the source of danger, but I like him for this. Even though, yes, there are still a lot of unknowns, I didn't want to leave you uninformed and take the chance that the danger to you ended with Hyde's death."

Cole had a few questions of his own. "Do you have any leads on Hyde's murder? Have you talked to the detective on the ferry killer case?" he asked.

"The WSP hasn't shared any leads with me. But I believe our investigations are intertwined, and you're at the center of them, Ms. Cattrel. Is there anything you can tell me? What have I missed?"

"This is all a shock to me," she said. "I can't exactly think straight at the moment."

"Understandable," Rick said. "I admit I was stunned to learn this news."

Just how much did the Washington State Patrol investigator share with Rick? It didn't sound like Rick knew about Jo's father, and despite his initial reservations, Cole would share that information now.

"There's another leg to this. The reason that Jo was in Seattle to begin with was that she was on her way to look for her father, who left her a cryptic note that he could have led danger to her. The ferry incident happened when she was returning home from Seattle. You should be aware that since then, there have been two more attempts on her life." Cole explained about the vehicle that tried to run her off the road and then . . . the bomb and her father's warning.

The detective remained composed and didn't appear surprised at the news, even though some of it could have been new to him.

"I share this to let you know that the danger to Jo didn't die with Mason Hyde, if you're leaning that way."

Rick's brow furrowed, and he clicked his pen. Rocked in his chair. "So is it possible that on the ferry, *Jo* was the target, and Mason was in the way?"

Cole liked this detective. But he absolutely hated the direction this had taken. "It's possible."

Rick suddenly sat forward, his face filling the screen. "All of this aside, any ideas why someone would want to harm you, Ms. Cattrel?"

"None. If I knew, we could have solved it three years ago and been done with it." Her voice shook, but she kept her chin high.

Cole squeezed her trembling hand.

Shoot, *his* body shook with anger, so he understood. "Is there anything else on the Michigan side of this investigation that you're looking into that you haven't shared with us?"

Rick scratched his stubbled chin. "If I come up with anything more, we'll be in touch. I hope you'll keep me in the loop."

Cole suspected Rick was holding back. That's what detectives did. They rarely shared everything, if anything, and

Rick had actually shared more than Cole thought he should. Then again, he was just trying to get to the bottom of a barrel full of too many disconnected, floating parts.

"I'd appreciate the same," Cole said.

Rick acted like he was done, then he stared, looked between Jo and Cole. "Jo, stay safe. Keep her safe."

Then he ended the meeting.

Besides heavy sighs and quickened breaths, the only other sounds were the wind battering the house and the waves crashing against the rocks. Cole stood and moved to the window. The marine fog had lifted with the wind. Everything Rick had shared left him more confused than anything.

"This was a lot to absorb," Jo said.

He turned from the window. "Let's get some more coffee and think about next steps."

He really wanted her distracted so that he could read Allison's email, which could have informed him before the detective had knocked him off balance. But it could be about something else entirely.

At the kitchen counter, Jo gripped her mug and stared out the window. In a place like this, the view stole the show.

"I don't get it," she said. "Mom identified this guy as the one to have committed a crime. Then he talks to her in a parking lot, and then she dies." She set the mug on the counter a little too hard. "*Then*, as if he knows about the anonymous tip or that the police have learned his identity and are looking for him, he comes out here to find *me*. *Me*, on a ferry. I never leave Hidden Bay. How did he even find me? Why was he after me? I had nothing to do with any of it. I'm not sure why Mom told me to hide. Why couldn't she at least have told me who I was hiding from and why?"

"This means we're missing something or more than one something."

"What do I do now?"

"You stay safe here with me. We do our best to try to piece this together."

"So let me get this straight. You and Rick have a theory that the danger my father led to me, the person behind it—*the ferry killer*—took out the person behind the danger coming after me from my mother's murderer. Have you ever heard of such a weird case?"

"I've seen stranger things, Jo. I think once we unravel this, it'll make sense. The truth is out there."

And right now, it felt like that truth might just be lost somewhere in a galaxy far, far away.

18

*T*he truth is out there."

And it had evaded Jo for much too long.

Standing on the veranda that partially extended out over the cliff, she took in the tumultuous ocean as she gazed toward the horizon. The Pacific was far bigger, far deeper than her mind could ever hope to grasp. The ocean touched the icebergs of Alaska and the Arctic Circle, and the cold, windy shores of the Pacific Northwest, while expanding to caress the warm shores of the Hawaiian and South Pacific Islands. Beneath her, waves crashed against the rocky shore, a constant soothing sound beneath which lay perilous tides—riptides, really—that stole body and soul.

If Jo looked in the mirror, her face would present as calm, but deep inside, a storm thrashed in her spirit, turmoil that felt like it would rip at her soul.

Mom had tried to keep her safe, and Jo had been fooled into believing that she lived a simple, mundane life. But beneath the surface . . . undercurrents threatened and had now dragged her away. She imagined she was swimming against them, and maybe now she needed to stop fighting and let those tides carry her where they would.

It was the only way to survive. Well, that and prayer. She hung her head and prayed silently.

Lord, help me . . . help me hold on to you through this. Save me.

Then, when she opened her eyes, she saw the words carved into the concrete at her feet.

"He leads me beside still waters. Psalm 23:2"

That was almost ironic. Were these waters *ever* quiet? Hmm. But maybe that was the point. No matter what was happening around her, on the inside, she could still be quiet. Only God could lead her to that place. She looked up at the sky.

"That's it, isn't it, Lord? I'm not there yet. I'm just not there. Help me."

A break in the clouds gave her a brief look into a blue sky and what things looked like far above the storm clouds. That's where her head needed to be right now—above the proverbial storm clouds of this investigation. These inquiries into the pasts of her parents that were now affecting her.

Behind her, inside the lavish home on a cliff, Cole paced, talking to someone on his cell. She hoped he got answers because Jo couldn't take more bad news. Any more shocking news about either her mother or her father would shut her down.

A blast of cold hit her in the face, and she tugged her jacket tighter. She didn't understand it, even after Cole shared his theories. If Pop knew she was in danger, had known about the bomb, then why didn't he stay around to help her? To protect her, even if he believed he'd led danger her way? They could have faced it together and then found justice for Mom. Why had he disappeared into the shadows to leave her to defend herself?

Behind her, the door slid open. She crossed her arms, pressing them against the rail. Cole joined her, and she relished the warmth of his body next to hers. Funny how even wearing a jacket, she could feel it. He put off a lot of heat, plus he blocked some of the wind.

"How are you doing?" he asked.

"As well as you might expect." Or as bad as he might expect.

Jo glanced at him and took in his profile. His dark eyes and thick brown hair. Scruffy, strong jaw. He was handsome and rugged and really listened to her, anticipated her needs and made her heart beat erratically.

She thought back to that day last year on the beach when she feared she wouldn't reach Hawk's brother in time, even though she'd reassured Hawk that she would. She could tell that Cole was trying, but he couldn't make it on his own. He'd lost a lot of blood, and the strength was draining from him. But when he'd seen her, the will to live had sparked back to life in his eyes. Jo had never been the same. They shared a bond like no other. A now broken bond, and she had better get over it and let the past stay in the past.

"Who were you talking to?" she asked.

"Hashing through everything with Allison as well as Hawk. I wanted to have others who are far removed weigh in. They can better see the big picture. I'm stuck in the minutiae."

"You're good at teasing out the answers. I'm glad you're here to help." *Because I don't know what I'd do if I had to go through this alone.*

"Some say, yes." The rain started up again, and Cole scrunched his face.

That look pulled a laugh from her and they dashed back inside.

Jo shrugged out of her jacket and approached the gas fire to warm up. "I looked in the fridge and cabinets. I could make some chili for lunch. What do you think?"

He approached from behind and she turned. He was much too close. "I've always loved your chili. If you're up to it, then yes, please."

What was she doing? This wasn't the time to get all cozy with him, but she wanted to. Oh . . . she wanted to. Was she imagining that he leaned in a little closer? That he felt the same almost irresistible draw too? How could she even think about Cole when she had danger coming at her from all directions?

Frowning, she saw the concern reflected in his face. She'd love to talk to him and find out why he left and stayed away so long, but not now. He had his reasons, and she shouldn't pry. She shouldn't be so needy. They could talk after all this amped-up danger that had her hiding again, fleeing her previous safe haven. Yeah, they could talk about what happened between them, *if* this mess was ever over.

"Listen, there's something I need to tell you," he said.

Oh. Was he going to talk about their broken relationship now? She couldn't. "Not now, Cole. We . . . you and me . . . I have questions, but it can wait. It needs to wait."

His mouth opened slightly. "I . . . uh . . ."

Oh snap. "You weren't . . . Well, this is awkward." He wasn't going to talk about why he left and never reached out to her while he was gone. Wow, she'd stuck her foot in her mouth. She turned on her heels and went into the kitchen. Pulled the ingredients from the fridge and beans from the cabinet.

Cole followed her. *Go away. Just go away.*

He grabbed her hands and turned her to face him. His

eyes were dark and filled with longing, but she looked away. *I can't. Not now.*

Then he lifted his hand and cupped her cheek and, like the fool she was, she melted into that. Her heart responded to him like no one else.

"I want to talk too. I need to explain . . . but you're right. Later. If you'll give me the chance, I promise I'll tell you everything. I've probably already said too much."

She opened her eyes and stared into his. "No, it's not too much. It's reassuring." And here she was, getting much too involved with him. She couldn't let him hurt her all over again.

Jo turned her attention to chopping onions. "You said there was something you needed to tell me. What is it?"

"I'd rather you not have a knife in your hands."

19

At the startled look on her face, Cole took a step back. She'd stopped chopping, and when she turned, naturally, she still held up the knife. Maybe he shouldn't have mentioned the knife, or he could have said it better. Grinning, he gently gripped her wrist and lowered the knife. He'd really meant it in a teasing way.

She looked at the kitchen tool that could be used as a weapon and then at Cole.

"Oh! Oh no. I'm sorry." Then she released the knife on the counter. "Is the news that *bad*?"

He wished he could take the pain away, but there was no way around it. "It's just more to add to everything else."

"Could I just get the chili going first? I have a feeling after you tell me, I might not be able to focus."

He was an idiot. "I'll help you. What can I do?"

"You could pull the ground beef out of the microwave and brown it for me. It should be defrosted now. Are you sure it's all right for us to use this food? Whoever owns this place might wonder when they get back." She twisted her lips into a funny smile. "I mean, I have no idea how a safe house works. Who does this place even belong to anyway?"

"I'm as sure as I can be that the food is for us." Remi and Hawk had assured him the place and the essentials, including food, were theirs to use. "Hawk said it belongs to a friend of Evelyn's, and that's all he knows."

"Of course." She gave a resigned smile. "What would I do without her help?"

What would any of them do? Evelyn Monroe was resourceful. He'd give her that. Together, Cole and Jo worked in silence to make the chili, and Cole wished he hadn't brought up the discussion just yet, but there was never really a good time. Once the chili was assembled and simmering in the pot, they both washed and dried their hands.

"I'm grabbing a soda from the fridge, and then you can tell me the news." Jo sounded emotionally distant, as if she was working hard to compartmentalize everything. If that's what it took to keep her head straight, then a girl had to do what a girl had to do.

On the sofa, they watched angry clouds billowing with a storm rolling in. That reflected his thoughts exactly—a storm was brewing.

"About your dad . . ."

She shifted on the sofa, pulling her legs up under her, then tucked her chin to look at him. "Just give me the news already."

Right. He clasped his hands. "It's not bad. It's just unexpected."

"I'm going to pull my hair out." She glared at him.

"All right. I have connections with intelligence agencies, but we didn't want to use those connections in this case. Allison worked her magic and was able to discover your father's true identity." Cole's throat tightened. "His name is Ransom Driscoll."

Jo shrugged. "It's an unusual name, but you act like that's supposed to mean something to me. Is it?"

With her reaction, he got the answer he needed. "I guess not."

"How did she learn his name?"

"Allison is . . ." How did he express his admiration without giving Jo the wrong idea. "She's good at her job. I'm . . . I mean, CGIS is fortunate to have her. She could be working for anyone."

"You mean like the CIA?"

"Yeah. Like them." And she chose to work with Cole.

Jo was watching him as if trying to read his expression. "So get to it. How did she learn his name?"

"Well, in a nutshell, once I sent her Advanced Technologies, she started running a search in the background. She uses some serious algorithms."

"She didn't tell us that before," Jo said.

"She didn't know. She'd learned about Advanced Technologies but not your father."

"Okay, so how did she find him?"

"In addition to the footage Nick shared with me, Allison gained access to CCTV footage near the building. The day you went to see him, he left the building with someone. He had lunch with that same man—Jim Jordan—a couple of blocks away. Jim Jordan is a major player at Advanced Technologies—a COO, chief operating officer. He usually works out of their California office and was in town that day."

"I don't get it. How did she learn Ransom's name?"

"She used a bit of, let's say, social engineering to learn who Jim Jordan was meeting for lunch."

"And she knows that Ransom's not just another alias how?" Jo asked.

"She was able to confirm that's his real name. Working

from a theory that he could be an engineer, she created an algorithm to search college records from top schools and found him. He has a degree in mechanical engineering from MIT, which confirms what we suspected. She was able to find additional supporting documents as well."

"Then she probably also found what he did after graduation," Jo said. "Where he worked."

"You would think, but she ran into the proverbial brick wall. She hasn't found his work history yet. Not everything is available digitally from thirty years ago, but she assured me she's using all the available tools. She'll keep looking for him. Learning his past could help us learn what's going on now."

Jo released a heavy sigh. "Okay. What next?"

"I want you to be safe. We need to know what he's running from. What brought him to Hidden Bay. What he's involved in that led him to go into hiding, change his name, and then leave when he thought he'd brought danger to you."

Jo stared at the fire. He had a feeling she had something more to say.

"I wonder if Mrs. Monroe would know," she said.

"Why do you say that?"

"She has a reputation among those who know her for helping people. He came here for a reason, and now we both believe that he was hiding in Hidden Bay. Makes me wonder if he was here due to Mrs. Monroe's influence."

He was tracking with her. "Does she know *what* people are hiding from? Did she know what brought you here?"

"I don't know. But it's something to explore. Maybe we should just go and ask her. But I think she's secretive about it all, which makes sense. I doubt we'll learn anything."

"That's an idea." He texted Remi, who worked for Evelyn Monroe and had more access to her. "I'll ask Remi and see what we can learn, if anything."

"Is that it?" Jo asked. "Nothing about what danger he could be in and, by proximity, I could be in?"

"Nothing yet. Allison's digging. This is a start, though."

They sat in silence and listened to the approaching storm. This home was more solid than Hawk's house in Forestview or even the cabins at Cedar Trails. Even so, it shuddered and creaked. But then again, it was on top of a cliff, with a veranda stretching out over the ledge, so it took the brunt of the storm.

Much like Jo. She was taking the brunt of a storm, or maybe it was a perfect storm, stemming from her mother's murder and the criminal activity involving her father.

And perfect storms almost always brought devastating results.

He wanted to search on the name Ransom Driscoll, an engineer, and he probably would, even though Allison's methods were far superior to his internet browser searches.

"Okay, so we know that Pop's name he used in Hidden Bay was an alias. That my mother's suspected killer was on that ferry and is now dead. I'm more confused than I've ever been in my life. Why would someone be after *me*, Cole?"

The only reason Jo would be in danger—that Cole could fathom—based on her *father's* dealings was some sort of revenge.

"So how do we figure this out?" Jo asked. "What next?"

Cole figured that Jo's head would be spinning after the last couple of days she'd had. Even with the experience he had in special forces, he should be prepared for anything, yet he still felt off-balance. Too much was happening all at once. He intended to find out why.

Her mother was gone.

Her suspected killer too, and yes, he needed to resolve what really happened to her. But the one person who was still alive—he hoped—had answers to at least some of their questions.

"I need to remain focused on finding your father." Her father understood the danger she was in. After all, he'd warned her about the bomb. That was serious business, and yet he got on a plane and left her.

"You mean we. *We* need to find him. Because I'll be with you when you do. We're in this together. I hired you . . . not only to find out who he really is but to protect me."

"Your protection goes without saying. Without any official contract." He chuckled inside—they'd never actually signed a contract. What did he care? He moved to sit closer to her.

Her eyes never left him as he sat close and took her hand. His head would explode with everything he felt and wanted to say . . . everything for which he had no words. He had told her he would explain everything, but how? "I'm here, no matter what. Forget the company I work for, it's not about that. You know that, right?"

She slowly nodded, and longing surged through him. More than anything, he wanted to lean forward and kiss her like he used to, back when he knew she wanted it. But that time wasn't now. His throat tightened.

"Thank you, Cole. And you should know that I wouldn't trust anyone else to protect me. I know you're good for that, but you should also know that I'm willing to take some risks if it means finding the truth and living my life without having to look over my shoulder."

Her father had hurt her deeply. Cole liked the guy, when he was Raymond Dodge, but he was beyond furious at Ransom Driscoll for doing this to Jo.

She glanced up from her cell phone. "It's a text from Remi. You'll never believe who is trying to find me."

20

The next morning, Jo had a crick in her neck. Her sleep had been awful, if she'd slept at all. Her mind wouldn't shut down. Now she rode shotgun as Cole drove along the winding two-lane road to meet Naomi Bancroft, Mason Hyde's sister. Mason, previously suspected of killing someone at an ATM as well as Jo's mother, was the victim on the ferry. A dead man. His sister Naomi had contacted Remi at Cedar Trails in search of Jo. Apparently, Jo's hiding place in Hidden Bay was now common knowledge—it was out there.

A few moments after the text from Remi, Naomi had contacted Cole to discuss what had happened to her brother. She still wanted him involved in investigating and wanted to clear Mason's name but wasn't sure how she felt about him investigating while protecting Jo. Regardless, she insisted on meeting Cole and Jo for a conversation she didn't want to have on the phone, claiming she had vital information.

So here we are, on our way to meet the sister of the ferry victim.

And the sister of the man who might have killed Jo's

mother. Maybe this had been a bad idea. Maybe Cole had been right. He hadn't wanted to leave the safe house, but neither could they allow Naomi to meet them at the safe house or at Cedar Trails. She might lead another someone with nefarious intentions to them.

With the windshield wipers working double-time, Cole steered the Yukon north, along the Hood Canal and then finally into the small fishing community. The Hood Canal was the westernmost fjord that was separated by the Kitsap Peninsula from the main body of water of Puget Sound. No Seattle cityscape to view from here, and Jo liked it that way.

The Hood, Line and Sinker bait shop was at the small marina filled with old fishing boats, completely different from the million-dollar yachts moored in the slips across the sound in the Seattle metropolitan area.

Meeting Naomi here had been the woman's idea. On the gray, rainy day, Cole walked close to Jo, his protective demeanor obvious to anyone as they made their way up the short stoop into the shop. A bell rang when he opened the door, and the unmistakable smell of fish and bait hit her. No one was at the counter with the cash register.

Somehow managing to cover and protect her, even as he scouted the place, Cole gently urged her deeper into the bait-and-tackle shop that stocked groceries too. The floor creaked, and the fishy smell permeated the place. Jo loved it.

The bell at the door rang again, signaling that someone else had entered, and Cole ushered her between the aisles to the exit at the back.

"Hey, Chuck," a man said. "How's it going?"

"I hear the blackmouth aren't biting." An older, gravelly voice responded. Must be Chuck.

"That's never good for business."

While the two men continued their conversation, she and Cole moved to the back, where the drinks were tucked in glass-doored refrigerators, and there they saw a reflection of the older man behind the counter—Chuck—talking to another man in jeans and a cap.

"Come on, let's go," Cole whispered. "She's not here."

"We should have waited in the Yukon," Jo said.

A woman stepped from the ladies' room. Her eyes widened.

"It's you." She thrust her hand out to Jo. "I'm Naomi."

Jo shook her hand, and then Cole did the same. Naomi looked to be in her early fifties, and her eyes reflected deep sorrow. Of course Jo was sorry that Mason Hyde was dead, but had the man killed her mother? This meeting had been a bad idea.

Naomi gestured to the back door, then headed toward it. Cole led Jo as they followed Naomi. Once outside, they stood under a large, covered porch. She motioned to an older RV parked a few yards away, close to the water. This was weird, and yet she got it. Naomi wanted to speak in private. In that case, they could talk in the Yukon.

Cole moved to block the woman. "What is this? Why here?"

"I'll explain," she said. "Please."

She opened the door and stepped in first. Cole kept his gun and Jo close. She pressed her palm against her own firearm at her side. Taking the two steps up, she tripped, but righted herself, stumbling inside the musty and dirty space.

"Please, have a seat." Naomi slid into the booth at the small table.

Jo sat across from her, but Cole remained standing.

"Why here?" Cole asked again.

"It had a For Sale sign on it," she said. "I rented it for a day so we could talk here."

"And you didn't feel any other place would be safe?" Jo would have gone a different way.

"No. I also rented a boat for the day and took it across

the sound. I still can't be sure whether anyone followed, but I don't think they did."

Jo shared a look with Cole. That's exactly what he'd done. He'd followed the ferry she had taken.

"You're sure about that?" Cole asked.

"As sure as anyone can be. So, we have to hurry."

"Why would someone follow you?" Cole asked.

"I'm the sister of a wanted man, after all. A deceased wanted man." The last words came out bitter. She leveled her gaze on Jo. "I blame your mother for that."

"Now, wait a minute." Cole stood taller, clearly ready to walk out of this weird meeting.

Jo's throat tightened. "I'm so sorry for what happened, but I don't know what's going on. Please tell me everything. You obviously wanted to talk to me for a reason."

This woman had hired CGIS to investigate Jo's mother's murder to clear Mason's name, and her demeanor reflected her displeasure about Cole working with Jo. Had Naomi brought Jo here to take revenge on her? If so, Cole wouldn't allow that to happen.

"Mason didn't kill your mother," Naomi said.

"Why was he on that ferry?" Jo asked. "Why had he followed me? How had he even found me?"

"He was looking for you, not to harm you. He wanted to ask for your help."

"My help?" Incredulity infused her. "What could I do?"

"Three years ago, his image was flashed everywhere for being responsible for a murder at an ATM—the image your mother had drawn. Mason had to disappear."

"But the police say he met my mother at a grocery store parking lot that night, before she died. So he stalked her. He was angry that she'd drawn his picture."

Frustration and impatience edged Naomi's heavy sigh. "No. You don't understand. She contacted *him*."

"What?" Jo couldn't believe her ears. "How did she even know him or where he lived?"

"You didn't tell me this before, Naomi," Cole said.

Naomi kept her focus on Jo. "He was set up. Your mother claimed she had no choice, but she told him to get out. To leave town and disappear." Naomi shifted forward, vehemence in her eyes. "Your mother is to blame for what happened to him."

Jo felt the need to get out of this place, but she remained sitting, not backing down. "My mother would never have set someone up. And why did he think I could help?" Jo asked.

"And more importantly, how did he even find Jo?" Cole peered out grimy windows. So, he was feeling cagey too.

Naomi closed her eyes and took in a few breaths, then she opened them. "You really don't get it."

Cole growled under his breath and leaned on the table. "You told me none of this. You left me in the dark. I want to know what is going on. Everything. Quit dragging it out. Who is after her, and why aren't you telling this to the police?"

"My brother and your mom knew each other . . ." Naomi pursed her lips, then continued. "You know . . . before."

No. I don't know! "Before?"

"Free—" A bullet slammed into the glass.

Cole covered Jo on the floor as more bullets sprayed the camper. The sound of bullets, of Naomi's and Jo's own screams, was deafening.

21

Cole's heart jackhammered, the pounding competing with the bullets.

Around him, time slowed, seconds passing between each rapid-fire bullet spraying the camper. His thoughts raced through the cacophony.

How am I getting us out of this? I should never have agreed to it.

Lord, help me find a way.

Because right now, the worst-case scenario was going down. How could Cole have let this happen? He started up. Both women were down on the floor.

"Stay here," he said.

"What?" Jo shouted. "No, Cole, you can't go out there!"

"We're all going to die if I don't end this," he said.

Cole would wait until the shooter reloaded, and he prayed they stayed alive that long.

Then . . . the gunfire stopped.

Was the shooter reloading? Coming to check on the carnage? Cole quietly crawled to the door, which had been shredded and remained attached by only one hinge. He slipped out and rolled onto the ground and then up to an older truck. Pressing his back against the truck, gun locked and loaded, he peered around the vehicle, searching for the shooter—or shooters. He couldn't know how many had been involved.

A siren rang out, echoing against the trees and across the water. At least law enforcement was coming, but they usually made their appearance after the fact. He couldn't wait that long. And Cole needed more than one deputy to show up. The report of a firearm resounded much too close, and Cole searched for the source. Still hiding behind the truck, he made his way around to the back.

The bait shop guy—Chuck—aimed his rifle to the south. He fired again, and again, then cursed.

Cole kept his handgun at the ready. Chuck dropped his rifle to his side, then jogged over to where Cole stood by the truck.

"He got away. I might have hit him, but he still got away." Expression grim, he glanced at the trailer and shook his head.

"There was just one?" Cole asked.

"That I saw, yes. Any survivors?"

Without replying, Cole raced to the trailer, threw open the door, which tumbled to the ground, then stepped inside. "Jo? Naomi?"

Jo held on to Naomi, tears racing down her face. "She's been shot. I called for an ambulance."

The woman grabbed Jo's hand, trying to speak. Cole fell to his knees and pressed his hand against the wound in her gut. Fear for her gripped him.

Naomi whispered, "Look up . . ." The rest of what she said was so garbled, Cole couldn't understand.

She closed her eyes. Dead? Unconscious? Boots clomped on the steps.

"Out of the way. Out of the way." Medics stood at the entrance, but they couldn't get in.

Cole pulled Jo to her feet and ushered her to the other end of the camper. He really wanted out that door, but the medics were blocking their egress.

He never should have let Naomi arrange the meeting. He hadn't known about the camper, and when she revealed her plan, he should have refused, but he feared the woman was already spooked and wouldn't share what she knew.

So many what-ifs left his head spinning as he and Jo waited in the small space, hoping for an escape. What was she thinking? He turned her to face him and lifted her chin to look in her eyes.

Just what he expected. The look of pain suffused her gaze and twisted up his gut.

"Why? Why does this keep happening?" she asked.

"Shh." He pulled her to him. He couldn't think of an adequate response.

"Excuse me." A deputy stuck his head through the door and looked around, his eyes landing on Cole. "The sheriff wants to speak to you."

Yet another sheriff. Another law enforcement entity. The list was growing and, at this rate, would soon be a big, tangled ball of law enforcement string. He half expected the feds to finally get involved at some point. Cole led Jo out of the camper and over to the covered porch behind the bait shop. Cole introduced himself and Jo and explained what happened, but he couldn't answer why.

"WSP is already looking into the incident on the ferry," he said, "and I believe Detective Hargrove will be interested in what happened here today."

"He's interested because you met with the victim's sister." The sheriff's grim expression was understandable.

"Yes, sir."

"Chuck informed me he tried to take him out," the sheriff said, "to stop him, but he got away. So we have a dangerous gunman on the loose in my county because you decided to meet here."

"This meeting location wasn't our decision," Jo said.

"Why is someone after you, Ms. Cattrel?" the sheriff asked.

"I wish someone would get to the bottom of that and let me know!" Jo crossed her arms.

Cole sensed she had much more to say but held it all inside.

"Did you get a look at the shooter?" the sheriff asked.

"I was inside for most of it, so—"

"Sheriff?" Chuck called as he exited the bait shop onto the porch, apparently listening in. "I got better than a look. Hood, Line and Sinker might not look like much, but I have security cameras running. I got footage of him."

"I want to see it," Jo said. "I want to know who tried to kill us!"

He hoped they could know if the gunman was the same man on the ferry by just looking at his eyes.

In Hood, Line and Sinker, they all crowded into a small office and stood around a computer screen to watch the footage. The man was dressed in jeans and a heavy jacket and boots. He wore a ball cap that shaded his eyes. Of course. Now they couldn't see his eyes.

But they saw his jaw. The rest of his face. He was in his late forties but appeared fit. Skilled. Ex-military? Interesting.

"Can I have a copy of this?" Cole asked.

"I'll be entering it into evidence," the sheriff said.

"Good, but I'd like a copy, or you can share with the WSP's Detective Hargrove and Detective Wilson at the Lansing Michigan PD Cold Case Unit."

The sheriff narrowed his eyes for a moment. "What is this about?"

"I wish I knew," Jo said.

An idea—a worst-case scenario—kept gnawing at the back of Cole's mind, and he didn't much like it.

22

Jo shivered.

The discussion went on. The questions continued. The rain picked up. And the cold got colder. Why were they standing out here on the covered porch behind the bait shop? The rain came down hard and fast, and suddenly she was back in the camper.

Bullets slamming into it.

Naomi was screaming.

And Cole had covered Jo's body with his. The man had been a human shield. Her chin trembled, and she looked away.

"I have to get out of here." She turned and fled the porch, hurried through the fishy bait shop and out the door.

Splashing through puddles, she jogged to the Yukon and found it unlocked. Then Jo got in, shut the door, and breathed a sigh of relief. Through the window, she saw Cole standing at the door of the shop, concern on his face. The Yukon suddenly came on. He must have unlocked the Yukon for her with the fob and turned it on too. He turned to speak to someone.

She drew in a few calming breaths.

Why is this happening, Lord? I just can't take this anymore.

Cole jogged over to the vehicle, then took his time walking around it. She lost sight of him in the mirror. What was he doing? Then he got in on the driver's side. Pursing his lips, he looked at her, his concern-filled gaze roaming her face. "I know you're not okay. That was rough back there."

"You were a soldier. How do you recover from someone shooting at you?"

The compassion on his face was more than she could take.

"Come here." He leaned toward her and wrapped his arms around her, bringing her as close as he could with a console in the way.

He held her, and she forced back sobs. "Can it just be over already?"

Her question was rhetorical, and the fact that he didn't answer but just kept holding her instead told her that he understood. She just needed to talk. Cole instinctively knew what she needed. When to listen. When to give her space.

And when to hold her. His presence sent all the anxiety running. The sound of bullets in her thoughts died away.

Finally, he said softly, "I'm so sorry this is happening to you."

He leaned his cheek against the top of her head. Jo felt safe and secure in his arms. And she felt cherished.

She didn't want to move, but she eased away. "I'm okay. Thank you for that. I just . . . I needed . . ." *To be held.* She couldn't finish the sentence.

"I understand."

And he did, and that's what she loved about him. Loved? "I know."

Crime-scene tape wrapped the area around the camper—

what was left of it. How had they even survived? "Do we know anything about Naomi?" she asked.

"She's in critical condition. Normally, I would suggest we go to the hospital, but I don't think that's safe. Not for her. Not for you."

"I keep thinking that I could know the reason all of this is happening deep down inside and it's just eluding me. It remains hidden from me. There must be a reason someone is after me."

"And we know more than we did," he said.

"Yeah, like what?"

"Naomi said your mother had known her brother *before*. She told us to look up . . . something. I just couldn't understand her. Could you?"

"I'm thinking on it. It didn't make sense. Free . . . that's all I could understand."

He shook his head. "She knows something vital. Honestly, I wish she had led with that."

"Could the shooter have been after her and not me? Could the ferry killer have been there to kill Mason after all? She and her brother had information." Jo's shoulders tensed.

"Yeah, she said that your mother and Mason had known each other before. But we know that because they met in the parking lot. If what Naomi said is true, your mother contacted him. So they definitely knew each other."

"So, what did she mean by 'before'?" she asked. "Naomi mumbled the word 'free.' Free what? She was cut off by bullets. And I could have completely misheard."

"So let's focus on the before aspect then," he said.

"Maybe it was before some incident that was free, which doesn't make sense, or they knew each other before some point in their past lives." What exactly was her mother's past? Jo hadn't been left with her ancestry handwritten in the pages of a family heritage Bible. She'd simply been told all her grandparents were gone.

"Which means we're missing a lot of pieces," he said. "But we now have a lot *more* pieces. I'll send this new information to Allison."

Jo didn't have to just sit here and wait for the answers to fall into her lap or for Allison to find all the answers. She could at least search the internet at the safe house, even though it didn't always give the correct answers. She'd already searched on her father's real name and never found him. Clearly, Allison was a master at intelligence. Jo had only her art skills.

"So, you talked to the sheriff longer than I did. What did you learn?"

"The sheriff is forwarding the security footage. I'll hold him to it. I left a voicemail with Rick in Michigan to let him know what's happened. I don't know if Naomi told him what she told us about her brother, but she hadn't told me."

"Why do you think she held back?"

"I have a theory or two. One, she might not have known all of it herself. Maybe Mason told her this news not long before he was killed. Or maybe she wanted me to discover what I could on my own without the additional information." He shrugged.

They were still sitting in the parking lot. Two county vehicles remained.

"It's time to get out of here." Cole shifted into reverse and steered them out of the parking lot and away from the chaos. Jo sank down in the seat, wishing she was on the other side of the nightmare.

"Where are we going? What about the house, Cole? Do you think it's still safe? What if this man who's after me follows us?"

"I'll make sure he doesn't."

"How can you be one hundred percent sure he won't?"

"He has a BOLO out on him now. He's on the run." Cole held up his cell. "I have his picture right here. Sent it to Hawk. I sent it to everyone."

"But we can't see the eyes." Even so, Jo was already drawing his face in her mind, completing the sketch by adding the eyes from the ferry killer. Would it be their man?

"We have enough for now, and I have a feeling that his full face will be discovered soon enough. Someone will figure it out," Cole said.

"That's what I used to do, the kind of thing I did with my job. I could—"

"You don't have to, Jo. I don't want to put you through more trauma. We're all watching out for you."

Yeah. Everyone except for her father. *Oh, Pop . . .*

"*I'm* watching out for you."

Jo couldn't help the surge of emotion, but she needed to hide it, so she stared out the window at the harsh gray of a cold March. The clouds and constant rain, the rough water of the Hood Canal, part of Puget Sound, and the woods. Endless miles of Olympic National Forest. At least here, in the Pacific Northwest, the lush forest green brought a sense of hope.

Evergreens might lose their dead needles, but they continued growing new ones and never appeared bare, no matter the harsh conditions. And Jo needed to be more like that. She needed to have that same perpetual fortitude. She needed to be like an evergreen.

All those months and years working side by side with her mother, solving crimes, and she could never have imagined this scenario. And Pop? She'd let herself trust him. Lean into him. Trusting was a risk she had been willing to take, and now she paid the price. At least he'd said goodbye, and she knew, as far as he was capable, that he loved her.

Pop had been Ransom Driscoll.

Before . . .

Was it possible that her mother had been living under a new identity? Where did Jo fit into all this?

Who were my parents . . . before?

Well, her mother was dead and gone, but her father was still alive, as far as she knew. And while Jo drew breath, she wouldn't stop until she got answers. Cole squeezed her hand, drawing her attention back to the moment.

"Are you okay?" He squeezed her hand again.

His tenderness pinged around inside. "Under the circumstances, yes, I'm as okay as can be expected. How about you? You risked your life out there, you know." Again.

"I never should have agreed to meeting her or talking to her inside the camper."

"I don't blame you for what happened. We'll both do better next time." She freed her hand from his.

After all, they weren't together, and it felt inappropriate to hold his hand for too long, especially after she'd laid down the game rules. She had to try harder to ignore the thrumming inside at his nearness. The warmth that erupted in her heart when he looked at her long and hard. And his heroics . . . being willing to step out and take a bullet for her. To dive into dangerously cold water to pull her from a sinking vehicle.

"I hope there isn't a next time in terms of a precarious situation. I mean, to keep you out of danger."

"As long as questions remain, I'm in danger. You're in danger."

"We need answers. So let's get back to the house—as long as no one followed—and talk to the Washington and Michigan detectives and see where we are. Learning who this hitman is could lead us to who is behind this."

She expected the feds would get involved at some point,

if they weren't already, considering the multiple states and agencies involved. "We don't have to wait on that, though. We need to *go* to Michigan."

"What are you thinking, exactly?"

"We know that my father isn't who he said he is. Naomi mentioned her brother knew my mother before . . . so I think . . . is it possible that my mother wasn't who she said she was either?"

Cole didn't answer. Windshield wipers struggled to keep up with the rain as he accelerated the Yukon, steering along the wet road, passing cars, leaving anyone who might follow behind. A man on a mission.

Then, finally, he said, "Anything is possible. And if that's the case, if she, too, was living under an altered identity, then . . ."

"This has to do with them both. It's not two different investigations. It's just one, with one question. What does *their* past have to do with my present?"

23

My thinking exactly.

The possibility that her mother's murder and her father's disappearance could be connected had been at the back of his mind, with each new lead confirming it. Naomi's revelation seemed to lend more credibility—at least in his mind—that there could be a connection.

On the drive back, he had gone above and beyond to make sure no one followed them to the safe house. He'd made sure that no one had placed a tracker on the vehicle. After all, the gunman had been at the bait shop. If he was after Jo and not Naomi, then he could have attached a tracker. Cole and Hawk had arranged to trade vehicles behind a shopping center in Olympia. Cole had driven out of his way for that, but it was worth it. He'd put on a ball cap and Jo had ducked down in the seat as they exited. The plan was that Hawk would wait half an hour and then head in the opposite direction. The two brothers looked enough alike, Cole hoped, that if someone was waiting, they would follow the Yukon.

Cole had seen no vehicle lights along the two-lane road,

then finally, he turned onto the gated drive and steered through the privacy gate, up the drive that cut through a thick, dark forest. It was approaching five o'clock, but the gray, dreary day made it seem much later. He parked in the garage and shut the door behind the vehicle.

Jo started to get out.

"Wait. Let me clear the perimeter and the house," he said. "I'll look at the cameras first."

He viewed the security cameras at the house, and no one had entered or approached. The possibility remained that someone had hacked the cameras, so Cole would clear everything himself for good measure. After he did a quick perimeter check, he moved back to the vehicle. Jo got out.

She stayed with him as they entered the house through the garage. She had her weapon drawn too, as he cleared the house that was a little too large for his comfort when it came to security. But the location met other check marks—it was remote and hard to find or get to.

Cole tucked his gun away.

Standing in the kitchen, Jo rubbed her arms. "When will Hawk and Remi be here with dinner?"

Cole glanced at his watch. "Shouldn't be too much longer."

"How will you get your Yukon back?" She got a glass of water.

"I'll figure it out. It's the least of my concerns." He didn't want to lead anyone here. Still, even Remi and Hawk coming here could be a mistake. But Hawk had been a military guy and was former law enforcement. He would take all the necessary precautions to make sure he and Remi weren't followed. Cole pushed all those thoughts away and focused solely on Jo.

She stared up at him with those big, beautiful chestnut

eyes. Every day seemed to turn into an unending nightmare for her. He didn't know how to stop the madness.

What was worse, exhaustion weighed on him. He didn't have the strength to fight his urgent need to be near her—physically and emotionally. He wanted to tell her what happened, why he disappeared, but that needed to wait because it would only be confusing if he told her in the middle of this muck. Now wasn't the time.

Or was it?

He stepped forward, resisting the urge to touch her cheek and watch the reaction in her eyes. Reach for a tendril of her long, gorgeous hair. He could barely fight his need to wrap her in his arms.

But he could do this for her. She'd said she wanted a professional relationship with him only. Didn't she? But she was sending him completely different vibes. *What should I do?*

"We'll figure this out, Jo." *I promise. I would go to the ends of the earth for you.*

But she wouldn't believe him. Still, the way she looked at him now, he thought maybe she wanted him to say those exact words. He must have been imagining it. Willing it to be so.

And when she leaned toward him, that was all the invitation he needed. He slid his hands over her shoulders and around her back, pulling her fully against him, and held her. She held him. This was right. How it was supposed to be. For the moment, his heart was content. They cocooned each other in reassurance and support, and for his part, he had to admit . . .

He loved her.

God, do you hear that? I love this woman. Please help me protect her. Help us find the truth.

She stepped away and looked into his eyes, and in hers,

he saw longing. His brain shut down, and his heart took over. She was in his arms again, her lips pressed against his.

Cole's heart soared to places he'd never been.

And ached . . . Jo's life was in danger. He couldn't afford this distraction.

She pulled back, and her content sigh nearly undid him. He could hear Hawk's voice, to add to his own in his head. *What are you doing, man?*

Turmoil surged in her gaze, as if she realized her mistake—that she never should have kissed him. And now that she had, could either of them stop what was happening between them again, as if picking up where they had left off before?

A knock came at the back door, then someone stepped right inside. Cole had his gun out, ready to take down the threat.

Hawk stepped into view. Behind him, Remi.

Heart pounding, Cole lowered his weapon. He'd been caught off guard. See? This thing between him and Jo wasn't good. This wasn't the time.

"Whoa, bro. You knew we were coming." Hawk looked between Cole and Jo, then irritation flashed in his gaze.

Remi emerged from behind Hawk carrying a couple of bags of food. "Brought your favorite. General Tso's chicken."

Jo gasped. "Really? Did Brad make it?"

"Yeah. He cooked it up, especially for you." Remi looked at Cole. "Kitchen staff. We just hired him on a few months ago, so you probably haven't met him."

Was her comment meant as a jab at Cole? Hawk had said Remi wasn't happy with him, believing he had hurt Jo.

Jo's smile faded. She must have been thinking the same thing—he had been about to tell her that he loved her and ask for another chance when Hawk and Remi showed up. Remi rushed forward and hugged her. Hawk gave Cole a look that he wasn't sure how to read. Cole decided it was best not to second-guess his brother, trusting that Hawk would speak his mind sooner or later.

Cole opened the sacks of food and pulled out the aluminum containers. "Smells great."

Jo got out the dishes. "Thanks for coming all this way."

Having visitors wasn't normally a good idea, but one, Jo needed the support from her friend, and two, Cole needed the support of his brother. After the day they'd had, Hawk and Remi had come to the house intending to stay tonight. Hawk would assist Cole in providing extra security detail.

Jo and Remi moved to the living area and spoke in too low a tone for Cole to make out what they were saying, but they effectively left Hawk and Cole to finish setting up dinner. Cole plated the Asian chicken and noodles and vegetables for each of them, then set the plates on the table.

Hawk grabbed enough bottled water for everyone out of the fridge.

"Have you learned anything more about today?" Hawk kept his voice down.

"No. I'm letting Allison dig into it. She has the image. Jo mentioned trying to complete the sketch, but she's been through so much already. I can't ask her to do that." But he had a feeling she might attempt it on her own. She had the ability to create extraordinarily accurate images, so maybe he should encourage her to complete the image. He suspected she might attempt to combine the eyes she'd drawn with the lower half of the gunman's face. He'd considered that as well. Allison would reach out to her forensic artist contacts and send Cole something soon.

Hawk's gaze narrowed as he scrutinized his brother. "But there is something else you haven't told me. What is it?"

Cole and Hawk weren't twins, but Hawk's ability to read Cole always surprised him. It shouldn't.

"Naomi told us that Mason knew Jo's mother before."

"Before? Before what?"

"That's what we want to figure out. She then tried to tell us to look something up, but she was incoherent, and we couldn't make out the words. But Jo and I are on the same page in that we think her father's intentional disappearance is related to her mother's murder."

"Wait. You don't think he—"

"No. Not that he murdered her. But that something happened. Mason was on that ferry to talk to Jo, and he was murdered. It's even possible the attack today was meant for Naomi. She and Mason could have been the ones targeted." Cole detailed the rest.

"But the bomb," Hawk said.

"Jo could be in the crossfire of whatever this is. Whatever is going on, I think it's possible that Jo could be her father's kryptonite."

Brows furrowed, Hawk nodded. "I think you're right. She is her father's weakness. She could be used against him, if that's what is going on here."

"She remains in danger no matter the reason."

His back to Jo and Remi, Cole ran his hand down his face. Remi approached and slid her hand around Hawk's arm. Cole couldn't help that he was a little jealous of his brother's ability to finally move forward in a relationship.

Cole wanted that too, but at this moment, he couldn't see a way forward, even on the other side of this danger, especially after the debacle moments earlier. Jo sat at the table, and Cole focused on this moment in time with Hawk and Remi and Jo—the people to whom he was closest in this world.

"I appreciate you bringing dinner," she said. "But . . . honestly, I'm not all that hungry."

"You need to eat," Cole, Hawk, and Remi said simultaneously.

Eyes wide, Jo stared at them. "Well, I'd better try. I get the feeling someone might shove the food down my throat if I don't."

"You're too thin as it is, Jo." Remi smiled. "I figured you wouldn't have an appetite, and I told Brad."

Cole watched her as Remi and Hawk talked about their day—anything to avoid talking about Cole and Jo's day. Remi shared that the storm system coming through had brought spectacular displays at the storm-watching lodge. Then Jo told Remi the best way to fix the door that always got stuck in Cabin 8. But behind all the conversation, Cole suspected they all tried to ignore the growing sense of dread.

After dinner, Hawk and Cole cleaned up the dishes while Remi and Jo sat on the sofa and drank tea.

"Sheriff Thatcher wants to stop by tomorrow and bring his new detective, Braden Sanders."

Cole shook his head. "I don't know about one more person involved or coming to the house, Hawk. Today, after everything else, was over the top. Besides, we already have too many agencies with the proverbial finger in this pie."

"I already told him to come."

"You did that without talking to me first. I'm running this protective detail." Cole dried his hands, then snapped the towel.

"The other option is we go out in the world to meet them."

"Why does he need to meet?" Cole asked.

"Come on, Cole. You're in his county. Jo's house was bombed. Raymond Dodge, a.k.a. Ransom Driscoll, lived here right under everyone's nose. You'll like the detective. He was a DSS agent. In case you're not familiar, that's Department of State's Diplomatic Security Service."

I know what it is. That news perked Cole up. "Really? What in the world is he doing here, then, as a detective in an isolated place?"

"For that matter, what am I doing here? What are you doing here?" Hawk asked. "You didn't think you'd end up here, did you?"

He *hadn't* ended up here. Not yet. He was here right now for Jo. But he didn't point that out to Hawk. "I just don't know if we have the bandwidth to answer any questions and talk more about what's going on."

"I get that," Hawk said. "Is all this as confusing to you as it is to me? My head is spinning, to be honest. And my head doesn't usually spin."

Cole gave him a smirk that said otherwise.

Hawk only frowned at him. "How's she doing?"

"She's traumatized. Who wouldn't be? And she wants to go to Michigan."

Cole got a text and tugged out his cell.

"What? Why?" Hawk asked. "How are you going to keep her safe if you do?"

"Let's just say, while we're here, this is a safe place. But for how long? The quicker we find out who is behind the attacks on her, the faster she'll be safe. She won't have to look over her shoulder again."

"And then maybe you can figure out how to be with her. I see how you look at her. It's obvious that—"

"What's obvious?" Jo moved into the kitchen, Remi on her heels.

"That we need to know more about the reason behind your mother's death," Cole said.

"I'd like to know under what name she knew my father. How and when they met. Naomi said Mason knew my mother before. Before she came to Michigan? Before what?"

"I might have an answer to that." Cole read through

Allison's text. "Mason Hyde spent the last fifteen years working as an engineer at GMC in Detroit, but before that, he worked at Gemini Aerospace. Among other things, they build rocket boosters for space flight."

He watched Jo's reaction.

"So, my father, a mechanical engineer, visited Advanced Technologies, which is involved in various industries, including aerospace. Aerospace, meaning aviation and space flight. And Mason, the aerospace engineer, knew my mother . . . 'before.' Could the past and the present finally be coming together, pointing us in a direction?"

24

So, had her father really worked as an engineer in aerospace? Given what Jo knew about him, things he'd said to her in the past, that would make sense. But they couldn't know for sure. "We can at least look into it and rule it out, if nothing else."

The very idea that her father was a completely different person than he'd let her get to know . . . her mother too . . . The room tilted. Jo pressed her palms against her eyes.

Strong hands gripped her arms. *Cole's* hands. "Are you okay?"

Cole's voice. He was here with her now in this crazy moment. People she trusted were letting her down left and right. People she loved weren't who they claimed to be.

The next thing she knew, she was sitting at the table. Cole had scooted close and looked at her with concern, but he didn't repeat his question. Hawk and Remi waited in the kitchen, but she suspected they watched her too.

"I don't know who my mother was. Scratch that. Yes, I do. She was a woman in hiding. And my biological father, he was hiding too. And whatever or whoever sent Mom into hiding also killed her. Now my life is also threatened, and maybe my sanity. So no, Cole, I am not okay." She might never be okay.

I need air.

Jo bolted from the chair, and it crashed to the floor behind her. She raced to the sliding glass door and threw it open, stepping out into the cold, windy, rainy night. She was running away far too often for comfort. She couldn't get enough air and sucked in the arctic blast. The cold rain bit into her skin like tiny knives.

God . . . this makes me question everything about myself if I can't even trust the most important people in my life.

Cole had followed her out and closed the door. He remained a few feet behind her as she leaned against the rail and looked out into the darkness, listening to the violence of waves crashing against rocks. She let the wind and rain batter her face.

Cole had given her space.

She couldn't even trust her own parents. So what made her think she could trust Cole? He stood next to her and slipped his hand into hers. He bore the brunt of this turmoil out on the ledge overlooking the ocean. He bore it right alongside her. She squinted up at him. Dim lighting from the house illuminated his face. This man weathered the storm with her.

"I won't leave you alone in this." Cole spoke over the storm.

Good. At least he'd clarified. He might leave, because that seemed to be his MO, but not until this was over. She would take what she could get. These were desperate times.

For him, she'd go back inside. He held her hand and tugged her down a hallway and into the study—out of earshot of his brother and Remi. Cole led her to a leather sofa and urged her to sit.

She gladly dropped into it, then he sat close to her.

"Whatever this is, if we aren't misconstruing all of it, it seems painfully obvious to me that your parents were only trying to protect you. That's all it is. Protecting you was everything to your mother. If she never told you about your real father, that too was part of keeping you safe. If he didn't know about you because she didn't tell him, that was part of her plan."

"You say that, but you didn't even know her."

"I say that because I understand that part of her. I knew your father, and I see the actions of a man striving to protect his daughter. He isn't perfect. No one is. And I understand their need to protect you to my bones. For me, it's personal too."

"I feel like I'm paying for their sins, whatever bad thing they did."

Cole's expression grew somber. His breathing quickened. "We don't know that either of them was involved in something illegal."

"And yet, we're making a lot of assumptions already. Seems to me when a man runs and leaves his daughter behind—except, of course, to warn her about a bomb—he has to be involved with something bad."

"You're correct to say we're making a lot of assumptions. So let's just hold off until we have more information."

"There is just one thing that I'd like to talk about. I don't want to make any more assumptions."

"What's that?" His expression told her that he was dreading what she might say next.

"Why, Cole?" she asked. "Why is it personal? You left. You didn't communicate with me for months." Why did she even care, with everything else going on? But she did. "Outside, you said you were with me in this. How can I believe you?"

He sighed. "That's a fair question."

Jo angled to look at his features. The first time she'd seen him, fighting to survive but struggling to live on that beach, she thought he was the handsomest man she'd ever seen. He looked like a dark-haired Ryan Gosling to her. Even now, as she waited for his reply, not knowing if he would completely shatter her heart and her hopes, he took her breath away.

"Where have you been?" The question came out on a whisper.

"You know I got called back to DC to answer more questions. I wasn't so sure I would come out of the chaos that happened last year completely unscathed. And that whole thing made me second-guess myself. I started thinking that I wasn't right for you. Being with you wasn't fair to you. You deserve someone so much better than me."

She'd heard enough and stood. "Stop it. Don't give me ridiculous cliché excuses. You might as well say, 'It's me and not you.' I'm done with lies from my parents. And now you."

Heart in her throat, Jo started for the door.

Cole caught her wrist and pulled her back around and almost into him.

She was powerless to move, despite the pain in her heart. *I'm so pathetic to let him do this to me!*

"Jo." He swallowed. She could see the emotion spilling from his eyes.

She closed hers. She had to muster the strength to pull away. He pulled her fully into his arms. She could not let this happen again.

Then he leaned down and whispered in her ear. "I would do anything for you. Don't you know that?"

Oh, her heart curled in on itself. But she had to be strong, and she took a step back to look up into his dark eyes and pained expression. "I don't know that. I want to believe you. But you promised to tell me, and so far you haven't."

"I didn't come back because I was *protecting* you."

"What? Now you sound just like my father. That's what that was about. You get my parents because you stayed away to protect me?" She'd heard it all and pushed away from him. "I want the truth. I don't care how hard it is."

Cole looked like he was fighting an internal battle that he might not win. He scraped a hand through his hair and paced. "I guess I'm doing this. I'm really doing this. I'm not supposed to do it. But how can I keep you in the dark?"

While he apparently worked through this, his words and behavior scared her. Maybe she didn't want to know after all.

"I mean, when you left for DC, I thought I'd hear from you again," she said. "You could have at least said goodbye and told me you weren't coming back. Hawk didn't tell me a thing. I was just in the dark."

"I know, and I'm sorry. Last year, when I was investigating the helicopter crash that killed my team, I made some enemies. I came across looking like a rogue agent, and unfortunately not everyone believed my story. So I got called back to DC, and while I was there, I was being followed and knew it wasn't safe. *I* . . . wasn't safe to be around. So, I mean, literally, I was trying to protect you."

Well, her anger and hurt dissipated with this new information. "Oh, Cole. I'm sorry. But how can that be? You were cleared of any wrongdoing."

"Officially. Unofficially, it only takes a simple twisting of perception. Come on, you thought I was an assassin too, didn't you?"

Yeah. Until she learned the truth. "So, what happened?"

He got close. Really close. And whispered. "Look at me. I need your complete attention."

Deep concern filled her. He was terrifying her. "You have it," she said. "You've always had it."

She could tell he held back a smile. "I'm not a hero, Jo. I'm a coward. If I was stronger, I would have been more like your father and stayed away. I don't want you to be in any kind of danger. I just can't talk about it."

She stiffened and stepped back, and he pulled her closer. Tugged her to him and whispered in her ear again as if someone could be listening. "I was made to go on an off-the-books mission, okay? I couldn't tell anyone. I was warned not to contact anyone. They relied on my special forces experience, past behaviors of going dark and ghosting others." He sucked in what sounded like a painful breath. "I can't tell you more."

She stepped away. That sounded credible enough, but that wasn't everything. "But . . . when was it over? I mean, when did you finish?" *The mission.* She hadn't said the word aloud because he seemed determined to hide that aspect of this conversation. After all, you never knew who was listening in.

He rubbed his forehead, then dropped his hand, the pain and regret clear on his face. She figured the hurt and anger she felt at his words were equally clear on hers.

"I've been free for about four months." His frown couldn't have been any deeper. "I had to make sure that it was over, and I wouldn't forever be coerced back into secret missions. I couldn't tell you anything. I shouldn't be telling you now. And you'd been through so much. With all my baggage, you had enough of your own problems. I figured I was doing you a favor by staying away. You deserved better. You deserved to be safe. That's when I started my own gig offering private investigations and protection services and partnered with CGIS, based out of Colorado, but I couldn't stop thinking about you. And then I got this idea that I could help you and end the danger that chased you into hiding. I got this absurd idea that maybe if I did that, you could forgive me for going dark on you."

Palms out, he stepped forward.

She stepped back.

"I would give anything to go back and fix my mistakes. I would give anything if I hadn't hurt you. Believe me, I hurt myself too."

And then Cole pursed his lips. He held something back. What had he been going to say?

"Tell me. What were you going to say?"

So much pain etched his features. "Now . . . now isn't the time, Jo. I'm sorry."

"I can't take any more." She left him standing there and rushed down the hallway until she found her room. Not really her room. She slammed the door and pressed her back against it, hating the drama-queen act. She'd asked him for an answer, and he'd given her one, and then she'd thrown it back in his face? She sounded so pathetic.

So desperate.

I should never have kissed him. Because now she couldn't stop thinking about the feel of his lips and his rough face. Jo wouldn't risk leaving her room to step out onto the deck so she could get a good slap of cold in the face. She didn't want to risk facing Cole again. Or, for that matter, Hawk or Remi, who were still here. For *her* protection. How much did either of them know about the reasons Cole stayed away, if anything?

Jo rushed to the bathroom and splashed cold water on her face. Too many conspiracy theories were floating around in her brain, coming from all directions, and she had to make the noise stop.

God, please make it stop.

It was nearing eight o'clock, not really bedtime, but she was exhausted, so she got ready for bed. But she couldn't sleep, so she turned on the small lamp at the writing desk, pulled her tablet out of her bag, and turned it on.

Jo started searching all the information on Advanced Technologies and Gemini Aerospace, but she couldn't gain access to former employees of government contractors. Still, she couldn't help herself and read all about both companies and the various clients they served in the aerospace industry. None of it mattered, really.

Except . . .

Hmm.

Pop had told her that he hadn't married and had no other children, but he'd clearly lied about his life. What else had he lied about? His family?

She didn't have the resources to learn the truth, and despite the way she acted toward Cole, she hoped that he was still in this with her. She hoped his connection—Allison—discovered more about her father, Ransom Driscoll. He was alive, he could tell Jo why she was in danger. He could tell her more about her mother and their life . . .

Before.

25

Cole hadn't slept last night and was feeling it this morning. He'd been tortured by Jo's response to his inability to effectively communicate. If he was a quitting man, he would just give up. But letting go now that he was here and had seen her again, kissed her again, would be harder than he could have imagined.

So much for his grand entrance back into her life. Who did he think he was, trying to save her from the demons that had sent her into hiding?

Any minute now, Sheriff Thatcher and Detective Sanders were due to arrive. At least Sheriff Thatcher had been able to learn more about Naomi Bancroft for Cole. She remained in critical condition. He wanted to ask about those incoherent words, but she was fighting for her life, and that didn't seem important or appropriate. They would keep moving forward with the information on hand.

Cole chugged another cup of black coffee. He groused that Hawk had arranged the meeting without consulting him first. Hawk had assisted Cole when he'd asked, but he wasn't running things and should stop acting like he was on the PSD—protection security detail. But to be fair, Hawk had facilitated a meeting that needed to happen, and Cole was running on fumes. To say he was grumpy this morning was an understatement.

That was mostly because of his messing things up with Jo.

"I don't like this," Cole said.

"I heard you the first ninety-nine times you said it," Hawk said. "What more do you want from me?"

"I fixed it!" Jo stepped from the hallway, grime on her forehead. The heating system had been malfunctioning all night, leaving them a little too cold. That seemed to under-score Cole's last words with Jo.

But the unit kicked on.

She appeared chipper and not at all like a woman who hadn't slept, so he figured their last conversation of the night hadn't bothered her at all. She'd been the one to leave without letting him finish. Well, honestly, he couldn't finish. He couldn't tell her what he'd wanted to tell her. Because he stunk at relationships. He might have pursued her, but sometimes, you just had to let a person fume on their own. When Jo needed her space, she needed it. End of story.

And now, she appeared to be right as rain, but that was because she'd woken up with a problem to solve. Cole could probably have managed, but Jo insisted. He loved seeing how putting her hands to use had set her firmly back in her element. Though the trauma of the last few days lingered in her gaze, a spark of life—the fight—still remained.

He'd spent the rest of the evening talking to his brother about his talent for ruining relationships. He'd actually asked Hawk for his advice, to which Hawk had replied that Cole was brave and could face bullets head-on, but when it came to love and commitment, he was a big fat chicken.

204

Thanks a lot, Hawk. I feel so much better.

Jo didn't look at him. Smiling, she ambled toward the kitchen and tripped on the Persian rug. Stumbling forward, she caught herself. She lifted her chin in a nonchalant air, then shoved hair from her face and set her wrench—Little Jo—on the counter.

Finally, she flicked her gaze to him, and a spark of defiance flashed in her eyes.

This woman. He adored her so much. "Um, Jo. You know the sheriff is coming."

"I know."

"You have a smudge on your forehead. Here, let me . . ." He dampened a paper towel and then dabbed at the smudge.

"Well, how does the rest of me look?"

Good. Better than anyone had a right to look. "Ready to face the world."

"Lucky for me, I don't need to face the world. I only need to face the demons of my parents' past."

"That's kind of a tall order for anybody," Hawk said.

And Jo pulled her attention from Cole to Hawk, just when Cole thought things might be okay. Now he couldn't be sure.

Looking incredulous, she shrugged. "Who would have thought?"

"I hope the sheriff has some information for us," Remi said.

The doorbell rang.

"It's them." Hawk opened the door and invited the sheriff in.

Sheriff Thatcher introduced Detective Braden Sanders. So this guy had been DSS. Cole flicked a quick look at Hawk before zeroing in on the two law enforcement officers.

"Thanks for coming to see us rather than making us come to you," Hawk said. "We're trying to keep a low profile."

"Jo's safety is a priority," the sheriff said. "Here's your cell phone, Jo."

He handed it off, and she looked at it like she hadn't seen it in a month.

The sheriff shifted his attention to the detective. "Detective Sanders has some news as well as questions."

"Coffee, anyone?" Remi gestured to the mugs and the carafe on the counter in a display suitable for her lodge.

The two county officials declined.

"If it's more comfortable, why don't we all have a seat." Hawk pulled chairs from the table, and everyone sat in the living room.

Gray light from the cloudy day barely lit up the room as the house rattled with the wind.

"Let's hear it, Detective," Cole said.

"Is it all right with everyone if I record this discussion?" Detective Sanders asked.

"This isn't an interrogation." Cole crossed his arms. He wouldn't stand for that today. "Or is it?"

"No. But if I ask a question, I want to be able to refer back to the answer."

Cole wanted to tell the guy no. Then again, a thorough investigator was a good thing. "Fine. Record away."

Sanders set his iPhone on the coffee table.

"We're working with bomb specialists from King County, and I've contacted the Investigative Assistance Division of Washington State Patrol. They directed me to Detective Hargrove."

Thorough, indeed. What was this guy doing in a backwater county sheriff's department?

"Preliminary information tells us it was a cell phone bomb. An IED—improvised explosive device—triggered by a cell phone. We suspect the bomb is tied to this guy." The detective tossed a photograph on the coffee table. "Detective Hargrove has ID'd your attacker from the Hood, Line and Sinker." He looked at Cole. "Good work getting the security footage out to the authorities. We believe he's the ferry killer too."

Jo shuddered and rubbed her arms.

Cole sat up. Now they were getting somewhere. "How did you link him to the ferry?"

"We caught footage of our suspect. Same man from the Hood, Line and Sinker attack. Devin Merrick exited a skiff at the marina in Seattle. We believe he got off the ferry mere moments after sending the vehicle overboard. He swam his way to a waiting skiff. Either an accomplice or someone he paid to wait for him. We're still looking for that person. The FBI has taken an interest in Merrick."

"He's *wanted*? How did he board the ferry to begin with?" Cole's frustration wasn't directed at the detective.

"So, the FBI is getting involved?" Jo asked.

"I've talked to the field agents in the local office. They're up to their ears in other investigations but are ready to assist if we need help. I said they're *interested* in him."

"What does that mean, exactly?" Cole said.

"It means they could swoop in and take him, but they'll wait for us to do the dirty work."

Ouch. Sounded like Sanders had some history there.

"Do you?" Hawk asked.

"Do I what?" Sanders retrieved the photo from the table.

"Do you need help? You said they're ready to assist if you need help." Cole would love to get everyone involved if it meant solving this and Jo finally being free from danger.

"Not yet. But I do need answers. Ms. Cattrel, have you ever seen or heard of this man before the ferry incident?"

"What? Of course not," Jo said.

"As mentioned earlier, we suspect he's connected to the bomb at your house." Sanders's voice rose. "And about that, how would your father have known about the bomb? How is he connected to this man?" Accusation edged his tone as if he suspected she was holding back what she knew.

Cole bristled. This felt more like he was interrogating a suspect. Jo was the victim here.

Jo blew out a frustrated breath. "How would I know?"

Cole stood. He grabbed the cell phone and turned off the recording. "I think that's just about enough. You said this wasn't an interrogation."

The man stood too and snatched his phone back. "It's not."

"It's okay, Cole," Jo said. She eyed Detective Sanders. "Detective, those are the same questions I have. If you're looking for answers from me, you're looking in the wrong place. I want to know the answers too, so I hope you find them."

"And you have no idea where your father is?" He said it like he didn't believe her.

Cole wasn't sure he liked this guy.

She sighed. "If I did, I would be there with him, asking him these questions myself, not here answering yours."

Jo stood and walked out of the room and left Sanders staring after her. Cole too. Remi went after Jo.

Cole seethed, but he held it back. He needed this guy on their side of this investigation. Still, he said, "That was about as helpful as a spare tire in a sinking boat."

"It's a waste of time for me to coddle the victim."

"The victim? You weren't treating her like a victim. You were treating her like an accomplice."

"All right." Sheriff Thatcher stood. "Everyone just calm down."

Hawk stood too. Their meeting was coming to an end. At least they'd learned something.

"Look, I won't apologize for my direct questions," Sanders said. "Her life is in danger." He lowered his voice for his next words. "Frankly, she should already be dead."

Cole clenched his fists, holding back his anger. "How dare you?"

"How dare I lay out the raw truth?" Sanders didn't act like any detective Cole had ever met. His background and training made him more like a bulldozer.

Hawk stood between them. "We're on the same team. So how about we work together?"

"I'm good with working together. You keep her safe while I investigate," Sanders said.

Cole shook his head. "She's hired me to find her father." What was he supposed to do about Naomi's investigation with her in the hospital? She was still recovering and hadn't responded to his texts. But that investigation was intricately connected to Ransom Driscoll as well as the danger from Michigan, so with or without Naomi's go-ahead, he was in it.

"How effective can you be when your attention is divided?" Sanders asked.

Cole walked to the window to stare out. This guy was unbelievable. But he wasn't wrong. "Okay, look. Like Hawk said, we're on the same team. If you learn anything, please let me know."

"I do know something." The detective's features seemed to soften. So he *could* be a nice guy. "I'll let the sheriff tell you. I need to take this call."

Sanders stepped away from them—as far as he could get in this house. Cole half wondered if he was snooping and was of a mind to follow him, except for what the sheriff said next.

"You ever wonder what a man who leaves does with the assets he leaves behind? Dodge-Driscoll owned the R&D for over twenty-eight years."

"I don't know, let someone else run it until he comes back?" Cole couldn't keep the frustration out of his voice. "Or leave it to his daughter?"

"He sold the business to Evelyn Monroe."

The eccentric woman who owned the Cedar Trails Lodge and facilitated helping people who wanted to disappear?

"And what is *she* going to do with it?"

"She's already done it. On behalf of Jo's father, Monroe put most of the money from the sale in a trust in Jo's name. And she set the rest aside for Jo to have cash on hand." Sheriff Thatcher handed over the paperwork. "I was supposed to deliver this, but I trust you to see to it that she gets it."

Cole looked at the documents from the Whitlock and Burnham Law Offices out of Olympia and a separate envelope that he suspected held the cash. "Why didn't he just give the R&D to Jo?" He dropped his hands. "She's a handy person. I think she would have enjoyed working there. Or at least he could have let her make the decision to sell it or keep it." What was he saying? After what her father had done, Jo would probably never go back there.

The sheriff shrugged. "My guess is he believes she is no longer safe here and wanted her to have the money. Maybe to hide again?"

"No. Jo doesn't want to hide anymore. She wants to know who murdered her mother and why her father is hiding." And this time, he didn't take her with him, like he did three years ago, after the funeral.

While he had the sheriff alone, he might as well ask him. He gestured toward Sanders standing in the large formal dining room across the way. "Where'd you find this guy anyway?"

Hawk got closer. "I'd like to hear that too. I heard he was DSS. Is he former military?"

The sheriff arched a brow. He gave them a look that said he wasn't going to talk about Detective Sanders. "You might not like his direct ways, but you'll come around."

That remains to be seen. "So. Jo's dad has communicated

210

with Evelyn Monroe. Can any of this tell us where the man himself is?"

"No. You're welcome to talk to Mrs. Monroe, but I doubt you'll learn anything more."

"Well, this might all be good and well—like he's looking out for her—but he needs to know that she has a price on her head, and that's because of him."

Sanders returned from his call and apparently heard part of their conversation because he said, "I think he knows. He warned her about the bomb and just seconds before it went off, which means he's in direct contact with the bomber, who we believe is Merrick. We find Merrick, we find her father. We find her father, we find Merrick."

"How can you be so sure?" Cole asked.

Sanders tilted his head, looking at Cole as if confused about how Cole couldn't see what he saw.

"I get it," Cole said. "But there are too many unknowns to be sure about anything. Once we find either Merrick or Driscoll, we can learn who is behind the threats and the danger."

"Exactly. Someone hired Merrick to kill. Someone threatened Driscoll. I suspect that same person is behind Mason Hyde's and possibly Mira Cattrel's deaths."

All connected.

All leading back to one person.

26

What? He left me money?

The sheriff and that obnoxious detective had gone. Jo shouldn't have left. She should have remained and grilled him with her own questions. And now this from her father? A bundle of cash, and then a trust on top of that?

She lifted her hands, refusing to take the two envelopes from Cole. "I don't want it. What am I supposed to do with it? Hide again? Disappear somewhere else?" Anguish filled her. She didn't want to look at Cole, but she couldn't help searching his gaze for something . . . she didn't even know what.

"You can think about what you want to do. You have enough money to probably do anything you want, within reason."

"Right. I'm sure I can't buy an island if I wanted." She cracked half a smile. And she could feel more confident about paying Cole. He never said how much he charged, and she hadn't asked. Shoot, she hadn't even signed on the dotted line. She'd been impulsive. Desperate. But she'd find a way, even if she didn't use *this* money.

Still . . . she plopped on the sofa and looked at the gray skies through the picture window. "What was he thinking? Why would I want his money? He knew I was in danger, and he left. I don't want his money. I wanted—I needed—*him*. He knew there was a bomb, and he . . ."

"Warned you," Cole said. "Jo, I know you're angry with him and this dilemma that he's left you in. What I'm about to say doesn't come close to comparing to this predicament. For years, I thought that my dad preferred my brother over me, all because I overheard something. I was an adult. Dad was long gone before I learned the truth. I heard everything out of context. I'm just saying that, until we know more, you should withhold judgment. I can't know what your father was thinking, but I suspect that he's putting distance between him and you to try to draw the danger to himself and *away* from you, his daughter. I know he loves you."

"Is that right?" Jo hated the sarcasm coming out. "Look. I'm sorry. I'm letting my frustration at my dad get to me. The way Detective Sanders sounded like he thought I was complicit in a crime didn't help. But I didn't mean to take it out on you." Still, right now, she was angry and resentful. All negative emotions. *Lord, help me let them go!*

Cole was right, though. Pop had probably left to protect her. "Thanks for sharing. I know he loves me. This is all just hard to swallow."

"You can think on it. In the meantime, I've booked us tickets to Michigan."

"Michigan?"

"You said we needed to go, so we're going."

"When are we leaving?"

He arched a brow. "Late tonight."

"The red-eye?"

"Getting to the east from the west is never easy." He

patted his shoulder. "Don't worry. My shoulder makes a good pillow."

Jo grumbled under her breath and went to the bedroom to pack a few things. This should be a quick trip, except there was nothing quick about traveling from one side of the country to another. She had no idea what she might find. Then again, she knew what she was looking for and hoped to glean some clues or at least more questions.

Her father had left her money when all she'd really wanted were answers. So she had to get them on her own. If she found him, maybe this time she could ask more pointed questions and force him to give her answers. But instead, she'd have to get answers from her deceased mother.

She paused and looked out the window as the wind shook the strong house. That's how she felt—she'd been a solid structure, and the foundation had been ripped out from under her. She'd made the mistake of trying to rebuild by trusting Pop, and again she'd been toppled.

Her mother's past and her father's past were somehow entangled, and even after all these years, the danger was closing in. Jo wasn't sure why she was caught in the middle.

She exited the room and moved down the hallway, noting the whispers. Jo could learn more if she waited and tried to listen. Eavesdropped. But she hated hearing something she wasn't meant to hear, and so she made some noise. "Y'all are whispering. You must be talking about something you don't want me to hear."

Hawk, Remi, and Cole glanced up from the kitchen table. Remi was the one to get up and move to her. "No, of course not," she said. "I'm not exactly sure why we were whispering. Maybe we just didn't want to disturb you."

She shrugged it off and sank onto the sofa. "Well, I'm all packed. So, what were you talking about, really?"

Remi sat too. "I need to get back to the lodge, that's what. I don't want to leave, but you know how it is."

"You've already done so much. This is your busy storm-watching season. You need to be there. Honestly, *I* need to be there. The fact you can make that place work without me kind of hurts." Jo's heartfelt smile held the pain of her words.

"Oh, don't think that way. You've done a great job training other staff. Dylan isn't as handy, but he'll do in a pinch. We miss you. But your safety is more important than anything." Remi leaned over and hugged Jo. This time she whispered. "Cole's worried about taking you to Michigan. We were discussing the possibility of Hawk watching you or Cole moving you to a new and safer place far away. Like some island somewhere."

Remi leaned back and smiled, sending a message with her eyes that said, *Don't give me away, or I'll never be privy to their private conversations again.*

Understood. Jo nodded. *Message received.* She and Remi had forged a deep friendship at Cedar Trails Lodge, especially with their shared traumatic experience last year. If she ended up leaving the lodge because Pop thought she wasn't safe here, then she would miss Remi. The only way for her to stay in Hidden Bay was to end the danger. For that, she had to walk through the rising torrential water. The Scripture from Isaiah floated through her heart and mind. *"When you pass through the waters, I will be with you."*

God was with her. She knew it. And he'd sent her friends here, in this new life she'd lived for three years. They were with her too.

She stretched. "I'm hungry. What's for lunch?"

Remi laughed. "I'll let you and the boys figure that out. I have to get back to the lodge."

"I'm taking you," Hawk said. "They're heading to the

airport tonight, so there's no need for me to come back. Unless you want me to house-sit." Hawk glanced at Cole. "Do you?"

"You're good. Go. Be with Remi. Make sure all is well and no more reporters or anyone suspicious shows up looking for Jo or her father, especially our guy, Devin Merrick. If he shows up, call the feds. After all, they supposedly have taken an *interest* in him."

"Yeah, well, let's just say that I might want to get some answers from him first," Hawk said.

Cole gave his brother a sly grin. "We think alike."

And they weren't even twins.

Later that afternoon, Cole put his and Jo's luggage in the back of the vehicle Hawk had left for them. He'd spent the rest of the day on his computer researching, and Jo sketched a few pictures of nature to relax. They'd need to head out soon to SeaTac—Seattle-Tacoma International Airport—because it would take about three hours, at least, to get there, and they needed to check in an hour and a half ahead of the flight.

For dinner, Cole microwaved frozen beef-and-cheese burritos. Jo was all for having zero mess to clean up and keeping it easy. She suspected that once they finished eating, he would ask questions. If she started talking now, she'd lose her appetite.

So they talked about the weather. They both agreed, too, that Remi and Hawk looked great together as a couple. They talked about when the two might get married and then what their kids would look like. Crazy to think they talked about such a romantic topic when she got the feeling Cole really wanted to avoid the hard discussion they needed to have about them. Whatever was left of them. Was there even a "them"? She didn't know.

She'd wanted to know why he left her high and dry, and he'd told her. She thought that understanding why someone had left her could ease the pain. But the news he'd shared hadn't washed away the hurt. And with that small hope that rose in her, that she and Cole could be together, she could be setting herself up for more heartbreak. She and Cole weren't exactly a perfect match like Remi and Hawk seemed to be.

Those thoughts rambled around inside her head while their actual conversation revolved around safe topics until finally, her appetite left her. A fourth of the burrito remained, and she tossed it, rinsed the plate, and put it on the rack. Cole joined her and put his plate away too.

Then he crossed his arms, leaned against the counter, and peered down at her. "Now that we agree on how nasty the weather is but how magical it makes this place, and we both agree that Hawk and Remi are magical together and that they're good for each other, let's talk about the topics we've been dancing around."

"Okay." She'd let him ask the questions.

"What's in Michigan?" he asked. "I mean, besides the obvious. Anything else you can tell me?"

"Pop selling his shop and giving me the money reminded me about the boxes of stuff in my apartment back in Michigan."

"What happened to your stuff?" Cole asked.

"I'd given my landlord the rent money I owed and told her I was leaving because I was in danger. I left in a rush. Left everything behind. When I contacted her again, I learned that she'd hired a service to clean it out. She didn't waste any time getting it ready to lease. But fortunately, my friend Becky had stopped by and got some of the boxes.

"I'd told her everything, and she convinced me to listen to my mother's instructions and urged me to leave. I was on the run, and so I never looked back. I'm hoping Becky still has those boxes. I hadn't asked her to do that, but now I'm glad she did."

"Didn't you contact her?"

"I decided it would be safer for everyone if I waited. Eventually, I would ask her to send the boxes to me if I thought it was safe. About another year passed before I tried her cell number, and it belonged to someone else."

"You mentioned she'd moved in with her parents. Did you try to call them?"

She released a slow breath. "No. I started to, but then I stopped myself. They didn't need more drama in their lives. I didn't really need the boxes."

"But now you feel the drama is worth it. If your friend still has the boxes, what do you hope to find in them?"

"What someone was looking for at my apartment."

"Okay, it's worth a shot. We can meet with Rick—Detective Wilson—and then we need to get out of there and get to a safe place. Stay on the move. If we find nothing new, we might consider heading to Nevada where Gemini Aerospace is headquartered and where Mason Hyde worked."

"That's a good idea. Has Allison learned anything about my mother's true identity yet?"

"After me, you'll be the first to know."

———

Hours later, Jo tried to get comfortable in the slim window seat of the flight to Michigan. She was the lucky one to get to look out the window at utter darkness. Now and then, she spotted a star above. Sometimes a few lights grouped together indicating a small town, but the flight across the northern states was completely black at night. Maybe she should take Cole up on his offer of a sturdy shoulder on which to lean her head and sleep.

ELIZABETH GODDARD

Instead, she rested her head against the seat back. She didn't feel like leaning or relying on anyone while she traveled through the dark of night, stalking the danger before it caught up to her first.

27

Jo hated the red-eye and loathed the three-hour layover in Philadelphia before they finally touched down in Detroit. Now they were in Michigan, and the blue skies belied the cold thirty-five degrees. They rented a car, and Cole stopped around 11:30 a.m. so they could grab an early lunch and coffee up before their drive to Lansing.

"Thanks for this. I need coffee if I'm going to function. That was a rough night." She dug into her scrambled eggs, then looked up at Cole. "You?"

"Same. Do we know where we're going?" he asked.

"You know, you don't have to pretend I'm controlling this investigation."

"I'm not pretending. I'm letting you take the lead. I don't know what I don't know."

"After the rough night with little sleep, I can't begin to understand what that means." Other than she was in trouble if she couldn't understand.

He snorted a laugh. Cole. Actually snorted. Then he finished off his eggs and bacon. "You'll figure it out."

Done with lunch, this time Jo took the driver's seat because, as Cole put it, she knew her way around, having grown up in Lansing. She drove northwest from Detroit toward Lansing, which would take them about an hour and a half and put them in Lansing around two. Much later than she wanted to start the fact-finding part of her day, but flying across the country was never easy.

She and Cole talked about life in general terms. She shared with him about her life in Michigan. How she'd gotten her BA in studio art at Michigan State University, then had worked and trained with Mom on the forensic side of things.

Cole got a text and read it. "Detective Sanders is asking to meet."

"I guess you'll have to break the news to him," she said. "Did he tell us we needed to stay close? You know, because sometimes the police tell people not to leave. He didn't say that, did he?" Because she couldn't afford to get on the wrong side of the law for any reason.

"I don't think he'll be happy," Cole said.

"As if you really care. I got the sense you didn't like him," she said.

"What's not to like? He's thorough. He's invested. He doesn't hold punches." Cole sounded matter-of-fact, just like Detective Sanders.

"Then why don't you like him?"

"Same reason you don't," Cole said. "I think we'd probably be best friends under different circumstances."

"Seriously?" She didn't get the feeling Cole had many friends. But she obviously had him wrong on several points.

"Possibly." Cole texted. Replying to Sanders?

"What did you text him?"

"Can't meet today."

"That's it? You didn't add that you could talk on the cell phone after you're done with appointments, unless it's something urgent, in which case you can call him now?"

"No need," he said.

"Well, try to wait to call him until after we meet with Becky and then Detective Wilson," she said.

"My thoughts exactly."

Finally, they arrived in Lansing, and Jo drove them to Becky's neighborhood. She navigated down Maple Street and parked in front of Becky's parents' house. Mr. and Mrs. Stobbe. Becky was still single when Jo left. Did she have a boyfriend now? Engaged? Or had she married while Jo was in hiding? A pang hit her chest. Maybe Jo had found new friends, but she'd left old ones behind. It wasn't fair.

"I looked it up, and they still live here." She got out and Cole joined her.

"No one followed us," he said. "But if they somehow know that we're here, they might guess where we're going. Allison tells me that Merrick is resourceful enough to potentially find out we bought tickets and what flight we were on."

"*Now* you tell me a guy who plants bombs and who the feds are after could have known I was flying to Michigan?" But really, she'd suspected as much.

She took the two steps up onto the porch and then, at the door, rang the doorbell. A few moments passed, and then the door opened to reveal a woman in her late fifties.

Mrs. Stobbe's eyes widened, and she gasped as her face lit up. "Jo? Oh my goodness . . . Jo!" She stepped forward to embrace Jo. Then she held her at arm's length, tears filling her eyes. "Well, don't just stand there, come on in. You and your friend."

She followed the woman inside but gave Cole a glance. He was looking over his shoulder. He was as bad as she was, but for good reason. At least no cars had passed or parked since they'd arrived.

"Can I offer you tea?" Mrs. Stobbe asked.

Jo shared a look with him again. "No, actually, I wish we

could stay that long. We have an appointment with a Lansing detective. When this is all over, I'd love the chance to visit and catch up. Actually, I'm looking for Becky."

Mrs. Stobbe's expression dropped.

Jo's chest tightened.

"Oh, Jo, you don't know."

"Know what?" Her breaths quickened. She blinked back unshed tears.

Mrs. Stobbe grabbed Jo's hands and held them.

"Becky passed on. She's with Jesus now. Oh, honey . . ." The woman pulled Jo into another hug, more concerned for Jo than her own pain, since Jo was only now learning about her daughter's death.

Jo closed her eyes and tried not to break down in front of Mrs. Stobbe, but she couldn't help the shudders. She resisted sobbing. At the moment, it was beyond her to grasp this news. How could she have missed that when searching for Becky? An obituary hadn't even come up. Jo should have been more diligent. Maybe she hadn't wanted to stalk her friend, or she was more afraid of what she might find.

Jo stepped away from Mrs. Stobbe and wiped at her eyes. "I'm so sorry to hear this. I . . . I didn't know. I missed her funeral. I missed *everything*."

"Now, don't you blame yourself. Becky explained that you'd had to leave and hide. That you were in danger. She missed you terribly, and she hoped that one day you would reach out to her again, and now here you are."

"And Becky's gone. Can I ask . . . ? No, never mind. I shouldn't ask."

"You want to know how she died."

"Yes." Jo hung her head.

"Sit, Jo, please. I'll get you a cup of tea."

Jo did as Mrs. Stobbe directed her. Looked like they were having tea after all, but this news had shocked her. She could berate herself later for not trying harder to keep in touch with Becky. For not searching the internet for her friend to make sure she stayed out of the news, but the thought of doing that seemed entirely too morbid.

As for Cole, he remained standing and peered at the pictures. While she waited for Mrs. Stobbe to return, she glanced at the images on the wall, taking in a young family and their daughter and her two siblings. Becky's family. A bigger framed photograph stood out on the fireplace mantel. Becky was so young and beautiful. Cole acted like the news of her death disturbed him too. He hadn't even known her. But maybe it was enough to watch things unfold and learn that Becky had died.

Mrs. Stobbe returned with a tray of tea and chocolate chip cookies. Cole moved to sit next to Jo. They had just under two hours before their meeting with the detective.

Jo lifted the cup to her lips, embarrassed that her trembling hands were causing the china to clink. She sipped at the hot liquid. She'd always been a coffee girl, but she wasn't going to turn down the tea. Besides, she'd had enough coffee.

"The chamomile tea should settle you a bit," Mrs. Stobbe said. "Becky died of a rare form of cancer. A brain tumor."

I didn't know. Why didn't she tell me? Because I disappeared.

Jo tried to prevent her lips from quivering. Mrs. Stobbe's concern for her nearly undid her.

"Oh, Jo, please. Becky wouldn't want you to be in so much pain."

"I didn't know. I could have been here with her if I hadn't been a coward and run away to hide."

"Now you listen to me, young lady, Becky thought you were brave. That you were a hero. She would have told you, but she didn't know how to reach you. And at the same time, she said that she wouldn't endanger your life by even trying to find you. She loved you. She told me that if I ever saw you again, to make sure you knew not to blame yourself for not being here. Becky knew you well enough to know you would try."

Mrs. Stobbe forced Jo's chin up. Forced her to look her in the face. "Now, you promise me that you'll do right by Becky and stay safe. Stay hidden for as long as you need. Promise me."

Jo didn't want to promise, but how could she refuse? "I'll try."

Mrs. Stobbe gave a wan smile. "And I love you too, dear girl. You were my Becky's best friend. You've been through a lot. Don't you spend one second carrying another burden."

Mrs. Stobbe drank from her own teacup. Chamomile for her too? "Now, you said you don't have much time. I won't pry, but what can I do to help since Becky isn't here?"

"I don't think there's anything you can do." The news had left her completely distraught. Why hadn't she prepared herself for the possibility?

"But what would you have asked Becky?"

The woman was persistent.

"Mrs. Stobbe," Cole said.

He probably suspected that in her current state of mind, Jo had lost her ability to ask the question, the reason they'd come here. And he would be right.

"Jo shared with me that Becky had taken some of her boxes from her apartment after she left. She had planned to hold on to them until Jo returned. Do you know where they are?"

"Becky had moved out after you left, Jo, but then she moved home when she got sick, and we kept her room the same. The extra boxes are up in the attic. I don't know if the things you speak of are up there. But you're more than welcome to look."

"I'm going to get some fresh air while you search for your things." Cole stood. "I'll give you some privacy. Are you okay to do this?"

Jo stood too. Could she do this? She had to see this through. They were here, and she wouldn't get another chance. She wished Cole would just join her. "Uh . . . really, it's fine . . . you don't—"

He held his hand up. "I need to make a call."

With the look he gave her, it finally registered. He was in protection mode and wanted to check things outside. Maybe he'd heard a noise.

"Oh. Okay." She rubbed her lips together. "I'll let you know if I find anything interesting."

And she hoped that *he* didn't find anything interesting. The last thing she wanted to do was bring danger to Becky's parents. They'd certainly been through enough, losing their daughter.

In three years, Jo had lost too much.

28

Cole's reasons for going outside were twofold. His heart broke when he'd watched Jo learn the truth about her friend. He should have looked Becky up ahead of time to protect Jo—emotionally, that is. So they could have been prepared for this. The other reason was that he wanted to reassure himself they hadn't been followed.

If Merrick had somehow figured out where they were going, they were in a position to get ambushed again. They'd been here with Mrs. Stobbe longer than planned. He was a fan of sticking to the schedule. But he couldn't have known that Becky Stobbe had passed away. He wasn't sure how that information had been lost on Jo as well, but maybe it had to do with the fact that she'd worked at the lodge for so long. Cedar Trails was a place where there was no internet or cell service. People quickly lost their need to constantly look up information on everything and everyone.

He pushed aside the morbid thoughts and focused on checking the perimeter of the house. Nothing in the quiet neighborhood appeared suspicious. He pulled his jacket tighter when snow started falling. Honestly, he'd expected the ground to be covered in the white stuff when they arrived.

Cole made his way around the back of the house that had a good forty feet between the neighboring houses, which was more distance than usual. A tall wood fence defined the backyard and separated the neighbors' yards. He found his way into the fenced-in area and held his cell to his ear so Mrs. Stobbe wouldn't become suspicious that he was scoping out her place. Of course, he could always just explain that he was Jo's protection, but neither of them wanted to leave Mrs. Stobbe disturbed or afraid.

Still, Jo's murderous pursuer didn't seem to have any qualms about taking down someone who was a witness to his crimes or who stood in the way. Nothing out of the ordinary jumped out at Cole, but he remained on guard. Stepping back into the house, he caught Jo coming down the stairs with a box.

Mrs. Stobbe emerged from the kitchen.

Jo shook her head. "I only found one box. I thought she'd taken several."

"Oh dear. I'm sorry. Was there something specific you were looking for? This has to be so hard on you." Mrs. Stobbe lowered her voice. "Is it . . . safe now? I assume that you're back and whatever danger you were in is gone."

Cole cleared his throat. Now would be a good time to open that door.

Jo glanced between him and Mrs. Stobbe. "Well, not exactly. Cole is my protection."

"You mean like a bodyguard?"

"That's exactly what I mean," Jo said.

Mrs. Stobbe appeared disturbed at the news and pursed her lips. She could be considering her own safety.

"We should get going," he said. "We'll take the box with us, if you don't mind."

Nodding her agreement, Jo handed him the box, he presumed so she could hug Mrs. Stobbe, and he took it.

Mrs. Stobbe wrapped her arms around Jo. "You come back to see me when you can. Promise?"

"I promise." Jo stepped out of her arms and offered a sad smile.

A fist gripped Cole's heart and squeezed.

"Please take care of yourself," Jo said.

"Mrs. Stobbe, please contact either me or Jo if anyone else comes by to talk about Jo or Becky." Cole handed her his business card.

She pressed her hand against her cheek. "Am I in danger?"

"I don't believe you are," he said, "but it doesn't hurt to remain cautious."

"I understand." Mrs. Stobbe walked with them to the door. "Be safe, Jo. I'll be praying for you."

Jo was breathing hard by the time they were back in the rental vehicle, and this time Cole drove. He entered the address for the Lansing Police Department so the map system could direct them.

Then he steered away from the curb. "You okay?"

"I didn't think that we could have brought the danger here. I mean, if someone was tearing through my apartment searching for something, maybe we shouldn't have come."

"We'll let Detective Wilson know about our visit. In fact, I think we'll just open the box while we're there with him, in case we find a clue. Does that sound okay to you?" Cole still wasn't sure what she hoped to find besides photo albums and memories, like she'd said.

"It could all be for nothing," she said. "Anticlimactic. I'm starting to second-guess our trip here."

Twenty-three minutes later, he parked.

Detective Wilson met them at the entrance, glanced inside the box for good measure, then guided them through the police headquarters to his office. Filing cabinets lined the walls. Cold cases? His desk was covered with documents and files. Probably just as many digital files stored away as well. He was just one lone investigator, but at least Mira's case had been reactivated.

Jo sat down and put the box on the desk. "Thanks for letting us open this here, Detective Wilson—I mean Rick. I have a question. It just hit me, really, so I hope you don't mind." She glanced at Cole. "My mother's death was considered an accident by your department. How is it suddenly a cold case when it was never a case to begin with?"

"Ah. Good question." Rick adjusted his glasses. "Fortunately, that's easy to answer. When a case is deemed an accident and then new information comes to light, it's redesignated. Since this happened three years ago, it is now a reactivated cold case." He scrunched his face. "I hope that doesn't sound confusing."

"No, it's fine. It makes sense. Sort of," Jo said.

Rick eyed the box she'd brought. "What's in that?"

"I don't know. It's a box I left behind. My friend Becky Stobbe"—Jo's voice cracked—"kept it for me. If you don't mind, I'll just look through this box before we get started."

"Sure, I'll grab some coffee and water." Rick left them alone.

Jo hesitated, then pulled the top open to reveal knick-knacks wrapped in newspaper. A small jewelry box. No, wait. It was a music box with a little ballerina.

Jo looked at it with love. "It plays the theme music from the movie *Anastasia*—'Once Upon a December.' I loved that movie. Mom got me the box. It's hard for me to fathom that, even then, she was probably living in hiding under an alias." Jo sagged. "I never knew my biological father growing up, and now, I guess I never really knew my mother either."

"That's not true, Jo," Cole said. "Your mother is *who* she is, no matter her name. No matter her job or where she lived. She loved you and built a life to support you and protect and nurture you. Look at you. You followed in her footsteps. If you think about it, everyone has a life . . . a different life, even . . . before they get married and have kids. You know? Just ask people who are into genealogy."

She reached to the bottom of the box and pulled out two thick photo albums. His mom used to keep those physical photo albums too. Where were they now? Did Hawk have them stored somewhere? Did people still do that? He didn't know. Jo held one of them against her chest, unshed tears in her eyes.

This had been a rough trip for her. Cole hated that.

"She was great at scrapbooking our life together," Jo said. "Took lots of photographs of our vacations and every birthday."

Finally, Jo started flipping through the pages to look at the photographs. "What am I doing? I can do this later."

Jo had hoped to find something that had the potential to explain her mother's death. While that was disappointing, he was relieved nothing else showed up to hurt Jo. She tried to force the photo album back into the box, and an envelope of more photos slid out.

Frowning, she snatched them up. "I haven't seen these before."

Rick returned, gripping a couple of mugs of coffee. Under his arm, he held two bottles of water.

"Let me help." Cole grabbed the coffee mugs and set them on the desk.

Jo thumbed through the photos. "These are . . . I don't know where this is. They're old. Before me."

"What are we looking at?" Rick leaned against his desk and peered at the photos too.

"I found them in a box of my stuff from my apartment.

I don't remember ever seeing these before." Jo gasped. "I don't believe it."

"What is it?" Cole asked.

Her hands shook. "Cole, this is it. This is what I was looking for. I didn't know what I would find, but this has to be important."

"Again, what are we looking at here?"

"It's a photograph of Mom with Pop." She peered closer.

Cole looked closer too, and Rick moved to stand over Jo's shoulder.

"Where are they?" Rick asked.

"And who are the other people with them?" Knowing could get them somewhere.

"I think I recognize one of the men, though I can't be sure," Rick said. "This could be a much younger version of Mason Hyde."

"I think you're right," Jo said. "Mason worked at Gemini Aerospace, and we don't know where Pop worked, but they are all three in this picture, along with two other people I don't recognize. This could be a personal picture or a work-related picture, in which case Mom also worked with them."

Cole shared a look with Jo and Detective Wilson. "This is just more confirmation that it's all connected."

"To their past," Jo said. "I still don't know how any of it has to do with me."

Cole was certain now if he hadn't been before. Jo was kryptonite. She was leverage. Her father was still the key, and they needed to find him. If Naomi was able to answer questions, they could possibly find out more from her.

Rick shook his head. "I hate to tell you, but since we spoke via the videoconference, I've had another case take priority, and I can't give this as much time as I wanted."

"We're just now getting somewhere with this. How could this not be a priority?" Cole asked.

"I figured I'd tell you when you got here that we tracked down Hyde's vehicle. Pulled it from a lake ten miles north of Lansing. After the case was reopened, I dug through the original report that concluded your mother had lost control of her vehicle and it overturned in a flooded ditch. I located the vehicle at a salvage yard and took another look and found what someone missed before. Red paint on a black vehicle. We pulled OnStar records from three years ago and were able to locate Hyde's vehicle in the lake. The damage to his vehicle confirms the collision with your mother's." His voice grew tense, his features tight.

"So, you believe Mason Hyde really *is* to blame?" Jo asked. "His sister believes he was set up. He knew my mother before, and this picture shows us that too. Something happened before. We have to find out what it was."

Rick sighed. Removed his glasses and cleaned them with a tissue. "I'm inclined to agree with you, but since we have evidence that points to the suspected murderer and that man is now dead, my boss told me to consider the case closed. Again."

"What?" Jo gasped.

"There's a lot more going on here," Cole said. "You know that."

"This is my nightmare all over again. The police didn't listen to me right after she was killed, and then I was in danger and had to run and hide. I'm still in danger because of whatever happened. The threats are still coming, even after Mason has died. What about the fact that he was murdered?"

"I hear you. But he was murdered in Washington, and authorities there have taken the lead. You no longer live in Michigan. So there's that. His case is connected to yours. Again, Washington." He put his glasses back on and lifted his palms. "I'm not saying that it's not still on my radar, but I can't put much time into it. If you learn something new, something that can move the blame from Mason Hyde—the suspected murderer who, by the way, also had motivation—then I can try to convince my boss we need to reactivate it. But for now, as far as the Lansing PD Cold Case Unit, we're at the proverbial dead end."

29

A dead end.

Jo was feeling like that herself as the plane touched down at the airport in Seattle. Could a person suffer jet lag when they hadn't left the country? Just flying across the contiguous US of A had done her in. Fortunately, last night they'd stayed in a hotel near the airport in Detroit. Their flight had arrived at SeaTac just after lunch. Even though she'd gotten a good night's sleep, she was still dragging.

Honestly, she thought Cole had been considering a flight from Michigan to Nevada, to Gemini Aerospace, where Mason Hyde had worked, but he didn't change their tickets. Just as well since her head was spinning like the worst kind of amusement park ride.

Mom and Pop and Mason Hyde in the same photo.

Cole led the way out of the airport, and she could barely keep up with him as they walked across the skywalk to the parking garage. "How do you have so much energy? You're like that Energizer Bunny."

"Don't call me a bunny. Ever. Especially a pink bunny."

He slowed and grinned down at her as he opened the back of Hawk's F-150, which Cole had driven to the airport.

Once they were settled inside the truck, he drove out of Seattle-Tacoma International Airport and then around the Olympic Peninsula until he finally steered up the drive to the safe house. At least they'd gained some hours on the flight west, but then lost them on the drive to the safe house.

The garage door hung open, and Cole's Yukon was parked inside, along with Jo's Land Rover. Hawk emerged from the garage and waited.

She yawned as Cole parked behind her vehicle. "So, your brother is going to stay with us again? I don't want to take up so much of his life. He and Remi need time together. And, I mean, how long is this going to go on? We can't live like this forever. Besides, I can't afford to pay you for protection forever."

Cole turned off the vehicle and released a sigh. "Relax, Jo. A lot has happened over a short period of time. It hasn't even been a week. Okay, we're one day short of a week. But we're making progress. Michigan was a good call. We have new information that could lead us to finding out what happened decades ago."

"And why my life is in danger."

He grabbed her hand. The look he gave her reassured her that he was in this until it was over, just like he'd told her. "I'm not doing this for the money. So get that out of your thoughts."

Except, well, she wanted this to be a professional working relationship. *Right. You kissed him!*

And if she reminded him of their professional agreement now, she couldn't stand to see the disappointment in his eyes. And in her heart. She was kidding herself.

I'm so into Cole.

I'm so in trouble.

Might as well prepare for the eventual heartbreak—a double heartbreak. She still had to process through what he'd shared before about his reason for not returning. He had sounded like he sincerely regretted it, and he wanted another chance.

Hawk assisted Cole, bringing the luggage into the house.

"You didn't have to wait here, Hawk," Cole said.

"You know I did. I had to make sure the house is clear and safe for my favorite brother and his friend in need. I didn't want you to be exhausted and get here to have to clear the place. And besides, my presence scares off all the monsters."

Jo couldn't help but smile at that. If only. Still . . . "But for how long?" she asked. "Eventually, this Merrick guy could find me here."

"Let's hope we can find him and take him down before it comes to that," Cole said.

"Get some rest," Hawk said. "You look terrible. Sanders is coming by in the morning."

Again? Not what she wanted to hear. "What time?"

"Eight thirty." Hawk moved into the kitchen. "Remi sent food if you're hungry. Eat. Sleep. Recover. And Jo, she sent some more of your art supplies over. Clay, pencils, canvas, and paint."

"Wow, that's sweet of her. She must think we're going to live here for months." The thought dragged her spirits down even further. "Where are the supplies?"

"In the study."

Jo left the brothers and moved down the hall until she found the study. This wasn't her home, and she didn't want to make a big artsy mess here, so she wouldn't paint or sculpt, but she could sketch some more. She already had her sketch pad. The thought energized her, so she grabbed the pad and the pencils and positioned the chair to look out the window at the glory of God's creation. This room was positioned so that she got a great view of both the ocean and the forest. Since it was only 4:30, she could still watch the crashing waves and see the lush Olympic National Forest to the southeast.

The view moved her deeply. It was almost spiritual.

She flipped open her sketch pad to find the verse she'd written there.

Before the mountains were born or you brought forth the whole world, from everlasting to everlasting you are God.

Psalm 90:2

There was that word again.

Before.

Interesting. Jo once again watched the waves crashing and then looked out to the horizon—where the gray waters met the leaden skies. Where the ocean ended and the sky began was almost indiscernible.

Emotion thickened in her throat.

Nature inspired her, but she hadn't known just how much until she'd lived in the Pacific Northwest. One could find beauty anywhere, of course, but this place, near the designated wilderness coast, amped up her appreciation. Now, instead of people or the caricature sketches she'd drawn for the lodge, she wanted to sketch and paint nature.

As she looked at the box of clay . . . she wanted to sculpt nature instead of facial reconstructions.

An image of Mom working on a facial reconstruction drifted across her mind. She closed her eyes to capture the memory and hold on to it, thinking back to those last few days before Mom died. She'd smiled and been happy. They'd had a good life. Everything had been normal.

Then her mood had dramatically shifted. Something had happened, but she wouldn't share anything with Jo.

"Jo, you all right?" Cole stood in the doorway, his voice pulling her out of the memories.

"Sure, I just need a moment," she said.

He moved the rest of the way into the room and looked at the sketch pad, then smiled. "Feeling inspired?"

"How can you tell?"

Angling, he peered down at her, so much understanding in his gaze, and maybe even . . . something deeper, something more. No. She had to be wrong.

"I hope you'll get some rest," he said.

"I will, I promise." Eventually.

He left her to her own devices then. Left her to think of the scent he'd left behind and the emptiness now that he wasn't in the room. This tough special forces guy, the quiet professional who could rescue, protect, and defend. He could also show such gentleness and compassion that it nearly made her weep.

She drew in a breath and refocused on her last thoughts of Mom. Something there was nagging at her. Bugging her.

I have to get this. God, please help me see what I'm missing.

She looked at the clay again, closed her eyes, and remembered Mom.

Who were you?

Like Cole said, Mira was her loving mother, and she shouldn't have died at sixty. Jo should have had many more years with her mother. Instead, she was killed. Murdered. Who had wanted her dead and why? Mason's sister Naomi made it sound like he'd been framed, and it all had to do with before.

Before . . .

Whatever Mom had been involved with before, she'd been a forensic artist for as long as Jo had known her, and she couldn't fathom her mother doing anything else. But what had she been doing right before something had upset her? Had she received a call at home? Seen someone? Jo had been caught up in her own world, oblivious.

She squeezed her eyes shut. *Think.* Figuring out what had set Mom off to make her afraid so that she warned Jo felt utterly futile. Opening her eyes, she moved to the box of clay and pulled out the big block wrapped in plastic. Peeling back the plastic, she pressed her hand against the clay, Mom's preferred material for forensic reconstructions. Jo hadn't sculpted since she'd left Michigan because she didn't want to remember—

Suddenly, an image flashed in her mind.

Mom's last reconstruction. Her mother had stared at the image and become visibly shaken. She'd gotten on her cell. Jo hadn't connected the face to her reaction. Jo searched through her photo library in the forensic album where she and Mom kept their work for reference. She'd kept it all on her personal cell. Right or wrong. She didn't know. She didn't care.

Scrolling through the images—and there were many over the years—she didn't find the ATM murder image loaded that looked like Mason Hyde, which was odd, but she found the last reconstruction and enlarged it on her smartphone screen.

Her heart might have stopped at the image.

I know this face.

30

After Hawk left, Cole opened up the fridge to look at the food Remi had sent from the Cedar Trails kitchen staff. She was feeding them too well. Or was it Brad? He'd have to meet this guy on the other side of this chaos. Brad was always making Jo's favorite food. She'd never mentioned him, but did Brad have an interest in Jo? A sliver of jealousy carved through him. Jealousy that maybe Jo had found someone else? And why shouldn't she? He hadn't exactly left her with good feelings about him. And he couldn't deny that he was jealous of his brother, who had found the perfect woman. Cole couldn't be happier for Hawk. It was about time.

Jo emerged from the hall, her face flushed as she rushed toward him.

He shut the fridge door. "What's wrong? What happened?"

Her eyes were wide and bright. "Where is it?"

"Where is what?" He moved to the counter.

"I need to look at it." Her words came out breathless, as if she was in full panic mode.

"Whoa, just calm down and tell me what you're talking about." He gently gripped her shoulders.

She drew in a long breath and visibly calmed. "The picture. The photograph of my parents together. The one that included Mason Hyde and two others. I gave it to you, didn't I?"

"It's in my laptop briefcase. I'll get it."

"Thank you."

"Did you remember something?" He hurried over to the sofa. Hawk had brought their suitcases in, but they hadn't put them away yet. He flipped open his briefcase on the sofa and pulled out a file folder, then handed it to her.

She opened the file and tugged out the photo. She peered at it closely as she moved into the kitchen for more light.

"That's her," she said. "It's her." She glanced at him, her eyes flashing with both excitement and fear.

"It's who?" He pressed his palms against her biceps. "Calm down and explain."

Tears burst from her eyes. "I'm sorry." She swiped them away. "This is so convoluted."

"Why don't you sit down and catch your breath?" He pulled out a chair for her and she eased into it.

Without asking, he grabbed her a Coke from the fridge, popped the top, and handed it off. "Drink this."

She stared at the soda, hesitating before finally taking it, then she took a few sips. "The clay that Remi sent. It reminded me of Mom. She'd finished a facial reconstruction, someone who had been dead for thirty years, and that's when Mom started acting weird. I hadn't thought about it before, but I'm certain of it now."

"But what does that have to do with this picture?"

Jo slowly stood. "Because the facial reconstruction she

242

completed was of a woman—she was never identified, as far as I know." Jo pointed at the picture. "This . . . *this* is the woman."

Cole stared at the image of the woman. Two women, three men. "How can you be sure?"

"I'm positive. I'm sure. I remember the image."

Cole considered it. Jo's mind could be putting this woman's face in her memory. "Is there a way for us to get the image she created of the skull?"

She sagged. "You don't believe me."

"I didn't say that."

"But . . . you're right."

"About what? I haven't said anything to be right about."

"I mean, even if my mother did re-create a face from the skeletal remains, it's subjective. It's one of the most controversial techniques in forensic art. Take a look at this picture." She whipped out her cell and scrolled through the images to show him a picture of a sculpted face.

He stared at it. "It's very similar, I'll give you that." He wished he could sound more certain for her sake.

She stared at the image and then again at the photograph.

"You could definitely be onto something. You said it was subjective, but it works, though, right? I mean, missing people are found using this method, reconstructing from their remains, aren't they?"

"Yeah, and that's the only reason it's still in use. Because it *has* worked at times. Mom preferred it. She relied on information from a forensic anthropologist. Like age, sex, and ancestry."

"Okay, is it possible that your mother, the artist, somehow created this woman's face? A face that she knew because she obviously knew the woman in the picture." Cole shrugged. He had no idea how this stuff worked.

"It's possible," she said.

"We need to look at the reconstruction and find out who the woman in the picture is. For all we know, she is alive and well. But if she's missing, that will tell us something. But . . . Jo, if your mother recognized this reconstruction, she would have told the police, right?" That was just another reason why it made no sense to him.

"She didn't. That's just it, Cole." Jo stood and paced the kitchen. "She didn't. The police had the image she created, the sculpture, but they had no name to go with it and were still searching for an identity. Even with all the science and technology, DNA, many remains never get identified. So maybe you're right. Mom didn't tell them because this skull wasn't the woman in the picture. I'm jumping to conclusions in my desperate need for answers." Jo looked up at him, her gaze searching for reassurance, begging him to get on board with this.

"Then again, she was upset. I'm telling you that's when she acted strange. That's when she told me if something happened to her, then I should run. Right after she finished this—I think she must have recognized this face. It was a few days later that we argued. I was furious and left. I never saw her again."

"Okay, so timeline here. When did she create the incriminating image that identified Mason Hyde?"

"She worked on that right after this sculpture. I'm telling you, something was upsetting her."

Cole moved back to the fridge and got out the plastic containers of food. He'd been starving and ready to eat when Jo had rushed in with this new information, but now his appetite was fading.

"Okay, so let's talk this through. What if the skull re-creation *is* the woman in this picture, someone your mother knew? What are the chances that she would be the one to re-create her face? I don't know. That just doesn't make sense to me."

"It's strange." She hovered over the containers. "This smells good. What is it?" Jo opened one of the container lids. "Lasagna. My favorite."

"Your favorite?" Okay, so that stung. Brad knew, but Cole didn't.

She looked at him. "I'm hungry, aren't you?"

I was. But now . . . ? How could she eat at a time like this? But yeah, she should eat, and he would join her. "Let's eat and we can talk this through."

He grabbed a small plastic bin, took his turn nuking the lasagna, and ate right out of the personal plastic container. Who needed a plate anyway? You just had to wash it when you were done. Or not.

He sat at the table and ate, but he didn't taste the food. He had a feeling Jo's mind was consumed with what they had just learned. If it was actually true. They really needed to confirm the reconstruction identity if possible. He tugged out his cell and called Detective Wilson in Michigan and left a detailed voicemail about what they needed. It was after normal work hours in Michigan, and he hadn't been sure the man would answer. He had a life, after all, Cole hoped.

"And we need an ID on the people in the picture, specifically the woman. Regarding the skull, we need to know how, where, and when that body was discovered." He ended the call. Like Rick was working for Cole. He'd already emailed Allison all the information, including an image of the picture. They needed to know who the people were, regardless of the facial reconstruction.

Jo had finished her lasagna. She must have been ravenous. Then she grabbed another soda. She was going to be wired tonight, even though she had to be running on fumes. She started in on the peanut butter cookies.

Even more wired.

"Okay, let's say—" she stopped and stared at him. "What? Why are you looking at me like that? I need the sugar. It'll let me think. You should try it."

At the counter, he snatched his own cookie. "Please, continue. You were saying?"

"So, Mom knew this woman and knew something had happened to her, and then when she suddenly sees that she has re-created her, then of course she is freaking out."

Cole had a thought. A crazy thought, really. "What if . . . okay, just hear me out. This is going to sound nuts."

"Nothing you can say right now will surprise me," Jo said.

He frowned but continued. "We discussed before that something had to have triggered your mother to start acting strange, and then she warned you that if something happened to her, you should hide. So, what if the skull was deliberately put in her hands to re-create? As some kind of warning."

Yeah. Ridiculous.

"I was wrong," she said. "That does surprise me. Hmm."

He'd have to think on it some more. "It's all conjecture. Forget I said anything."

"But it fits. It fits. Don't you see?" Jo asked. "She was upset, so upset. Cole, I think you're onto something. I like the way your mind works, but on the other hand, this is morbid. I mean, I've read a lot of mysteries, and this falls into line with some of the darkest ones. I should have been the one to come up with that."

"Seriously, Jo, I'm glad you weren't." Because this was truly dark.

"Let's talk this premise through," she said. "Going out on that limb with you because, as they say, truth is stranger than fiction. So, someone arranged for her to re-create the skull so that she would be scared? So that she would be warned. Warned about what?"

"Still, how is that a warning?" he asked.

Jo stopped in front of him and stared up. Her eyes full of determination. Of fire. "To let Mom know that she was no longer safe—she'd been found! That's it!"

Jo rushed around the space as if giddy with excitement, but this was such a morbid topic.

"I think we're both jumping to a *lot* of conclusions," he said. "We need a lot more information to land on this theory." Still . . . "Naomi said that Mason was framed. Mason is in the picture, along with your mother and your father. I've seen this before. Someone could be eliminating loose ends, killing people, even after decades. Could that same someone have forced your mother to frame Mason through the forensic process? I hate to say that out loud. I don't mean to indict your mother in this."

"No, it's okay. I mean, you're right, this is all conjecture. But it's a plausible theory."

He wasn't sure about that, but it was a start. "Then, after framing Mason, she died."

"She was murdered." She stared at him, long and hard. "And now he's dead too. Also murdered."

He was concerned that none of this was accurate, and they were both getting worked up for nothing. "Let's take this one step at a time."

"You don't think it sounds possible? You're the one who came up with it."

Yeah, I know. "It sounds . . . out there."

"Cole. Seriously. My life is *out there* right now. Nothing makes any sense, except for this."

Cole couldn't take that from her. Not now. Not yet. Not when it seemed to energize her and give her hope. But he couldn't imagine a body being dug up in Michigan or planted there to begin with. Someone would have to already know where her mother was, if it was a warning. And what a morbid, disgusting warning. He'd find out how and where the body or the skull was discovered. That would tell them something.

But if her theory was anywhere even close to the truth, then they were dealing with a very sick person. And his fear for Jo's safety just shot through the roof. They needed to know what the incident was that trapped Jo in this dangerous space. The windows rattled with the wind, startling them both. Jo jumped closer to Cole.

"It was just a gust of wind." He took the opportunity to pull her in even closer. Holding her calmed his nerves, soothed his soul.

"I don't know, Cole. That sounds like tapping. Creepy tapping."

"And why would anyone be out in this weather, tapping on the window?" Why not shoot them where they stood in the kitchen?

He pushed her behind him.

31

She was accustomed to the creaks and groans a structure made when it was quiet and during a storm, so she shouldn't have overreacted.

"I'm just tired. It's fine. I'm not scared of the wind." *I can't be.* Her nerves were getting the best of her. Her adrenaline was crashing. That was all. She started to move away.

"No, wait." He ushered her deeper into the kitchen. "Wait right here. Do you have your firearm?"

"No." She opened the drawer and pulled out a butcher knife. At his frown, she said, "It could work in a knife fight, okay?"

The wind rattled the windows again. Was one of them open? She didn't remember the wind causing such a chilling noise.

"This is some kind of storm coming in," Cole said. "I still think it's the wind, but it can't hurt to check."

Cole left her alone in the kitchen for an infuriatingly long time.

Where are you, Cole?

Oh, for crying out loud . . . Jo wasn't going to stand here

and wait for the boogeyman, who might have already gotten Cole. She'd started forward when Cole emerged from outside, bringing wind and rain with him.

"You were outside?" she asked.

"How else was I supposed to check?"

"You left me alone in the kitchen with only a butcher knife?"

"It was just the wind. And I got a text. I need to check it." He pulled his cell out of his jacket and peered at the screen. "It's from Allison."

Putting the knife down, she tried to relax. The morbid talk about the skull had set off all her nerves—the monster-house, scary nerves—making her impatient. "Well, what does it say?"

"I've asked Allison to search on a connection between your father and Mason Hyde, since they were both involved in the aerospace industry and your father recently met with someone in that same industry after leaving you the message and just before he disappeared. It's just one angle to explore, but I think it's the strongest connection we have. Allison has gone as deep as she can go online. She had hoped to find images of them together that might include the others in the photo and help us identify them. Not all records are available digitally. That means we need to go old school."

"Old school?"

"Yes. There's a museum in Seattle at the King County International Airport Boeing Field—the Museum of Flight." He stared at his smartphone. "It includes everything about the businesses and technology of aircraft and space. The Pacific Northwest has played an important role in the aerospace industry since the beginning. Looks like it has recently been dubbed the 'Silicon Valley of space.'" He glanced up at her, his eyes bright with anticipation.

Her brows shot up. *Really?*

He shrugged. "When you consider that more than half the satellites in low orbit were manufactured in Washington, and hundreds of companies are part of the space cluster, many of them supplying NASA, it makes sense. But we're getting ahead of ourselves. We need to go to the archives at the museum to confirm we're on the right track."

"Archives? Does that mean card catalogs and microfiche?" *Please, no.*

"Your guess is as good as mine."

Jo plopped into a kitchen chair. "This seems so hopeless right now."

He sat in the seat across from her. "I've had experience investigating complex cases, and this feels complex to me. I get the sense it involves something much bigger than we can imagine. Trust me, I've honed that instinct."

"But you can't know."

"That's why we leave no stone unturned. Investigations take time," he said. "Days. Weeks. Months and years."

That elicited a smile. "Okay. I'm feeling so much better now."

A laugh erupted from him, then he grew somber.

"What about Naomi?" she asked. "Are you reporting any of this in your investigation about my mother back to her? She wanted to clear Mason's name, remember?"

He released a heavy sigh. "I received an email from her today. I have a feeling a family member sent it. It simply said she released me from the investigation. She'd wanted to clear his name, but the stress of it is too much while she focuses on healing. Again, I can't see Naomi giving up, especially after being attacked so brutally."

She didn't know how she was supposed to feel about or react to that. "Did you respond?"

"I reassured her that I would clear his name and told her to focus on recovering."

"You're a good man, you know that?"

He lifted a shoulder. "I just try to do the right thing, though sometimes it's hard to know what that is."

"Like saying you would clear his name when you can't be sure he didn't kill my mother?"

"I'm reasonably sure that Naomi was correct. This was a setup."

Jo frowned. That meant her mom had committed a crime. "Naomi said Mom warned him to disappear."

"She did say that." Cole stared at the floor as if in thought.

Or maybe this felt as awkward to him as it did to her.

"Well, I guess the museum it is," she said. "We just keep chipping away until we find the truth. I hope we can find images of everyone in that picture with Mom and Pop. She must have tucked it into my photo album for a reason. Instead . . . instead of in *her* photo album." Jo shrugged. "Maybe she wanted me to find the truth if something happened to her. That photo could be why someone broke into my house."

"You could be right, Jo. The photo is incriminating in that we know of three people in the photograph who are dead—if we confirm that woman is the reconstructed skull," he said.

"Besides your father, the other man—if he's still alive— could also be in danger. And for whatever reason that danger has transferred to you." He stood and paced the kitchen. "Which means following the clues provided by that photo, visiting the museum, could be the most dangerous thing we've done yet."

"We're going, Cole. End of story. It's better than sitting around here and being bored, waiting for answers to come to us." She stood and then closed the distance without realizing it. "I mean, unless you just want to sit around here and be bored with me."

Oh man, am I flirting? Because it definitely sounded like flirting. Wrong time. Wrong place.

His crooked grin sent warmth straight through her. They were an odd couple, except they weren't a couple at all. But she wanted them to be. The more she thought about his explanation of why he hadn't come back, and the regret and sincerity in his voice, the more inclined she was to accept it and forgive him. To move on and forward.

With him.

He stepped closer and twirled a strand of her hair around his finger. "I could never be bored with you, Jo." The words sounded strained. "Don't you know that?"

No. No, I don't. "A couple of days ago, you didn't finish what you were going to say. What were you going to tell me? I should have stayed and let you finish."

And just when she thought he might tell her, he leaned forward and kissed her on the forehead, then backed away. "Get some sleep. We have an early morning meeting with Sanders and what looks to be a long day."

"And I'm still recovering from jet lag." But she left him with a smile on her face because she felt like, finally, they were getting somewhere.

Visiting a museum that might actually tell her what happened . . . *before* . . .

Instead of sleeping, she sat in bed and sketched images of her mother and her father, separate and then together. Another image of the unidentified woman. Jo imagined her mother creating the reconstruction of the skull and then stepping back to look at her work. The shock that could have rolled through her at that moment when she recognized the face.

Jo closed her eyes. What had Mom thought? Had her

first thought been that someone had found her? That it was a warning? Cole was right. They needed to know more about where the body was found. Where and how. Jo didn't believe in coincidences, so it was hard to fathom that her mother would happen to process a skull of someone she knew. Still, it was within the realm of possibility. Add to the equation her reaction and the danger that followed, and Jo was convinced the reconstruction was part of it all.

Seeing that skull had prompted Mom to finally tell Jo the truth about Dale and about her biological father, though she hadn't told Jo his name. Weirdly, Mom had claimed she didn't know.

She didn't know who Jo's father was?

Her mother was a liar. And yet, maybe to Mom, the lies had been worth it if it meant protecting Jo.

Well, look at me now, Mom.

Mason Hyde was dead. Mom was dead. Pop was on the run from danger—and certain death. The woman in the photo was dead, or so that was their working theory. Was the other man in the photo still alive? Jo wasn't in the photograph, but she'd inherited the danger because, what, she knew something? Something so terrible, so horrific, that her pursuer needed to silence anyone connected to the knowledge? Jo had no idea, and she was apparently in danger by proximity.

Knowledge was power, as the saying went.

Or, in this case, the appearance of knowledge was deadly.

32

The next morning, Cole offered Detective Sanders coffee and then brought him up to speed. They sat at the table in the breakfast nook. Listening, Jo stood at the kitchen counter slathering cream cheese on her bagels. Cole thought it best to give Sanders the information about the skull and see if he came up with a similar theory rather than hand-feeding him the theory that her mother had been warned with the skull reconstruction.

Sanders sipped on coffee like they were old friends and frowned. "Have you heard from Michigan yet on where the skull was found?"

"I talked to Detective Wilson this morning," Cole said. "He said this was a new twist and one he'd never heard of before. He almost sounded hesitant to look into the details about where the skull had been discovered, but he knows we'll just go around him if he doesn't stay involved."

Sanders clasped his hands and leaned forward. "Let me be clear. You won't need to go around me."

Cole wasn't entirely sure why Sanders would be so

invested, but maybe he was like a pit bull and had no intention of letting go.

"In my past work experience," Sanders said, "I was involved in a case where several people were eliminated due to their connection to one event. Without knowing more, I almost get the feeling this has the markings of that kind of case."

Although the detective hadn't mentioned the possibility that the skull was meant to be a warning to Mira, Sanders was tracking with them. The detective intrigued Cole. He wasn't the kind of man to hold everything too close. Detectives usually didn't like to share their information while working an investigation. But maybe in this case, Sanders knew it was a give-and-take. And he respected Cole, that much was clear. In some areas, Cole likely had more resources than Sanders. There was the law, the rules and systems that were put in place. And then there was the human factor. Cooperation and collaboration would get them much farther than a "turf war."

"I agree with your assessment," Cole said. "The only thing that doesn't fit is Jo. She doesn't know anything, so why has she been targeted?" He raised the question for Sanders, but Cole believed she was a means to an end. Someone wanted to get to Ransom.

"Are you sure she doesn't know something?" Sanders asked.

"Excuse me?" She dropped her cream cheese–covered knife and it skittered over close to Cole.

"I'll get it." He bent down to pick it up before a sticky mess ended up on the floor.

Jo slid into a chair across from Sanders and glared at him.

"Are you sure you don't know something?" Sanders asked her. "You could know something without knowing that you know."

Similar to what Cole had told her. *"I don't know what I don't know."*

"My world was rocked with the death of my mother and the threats to my life. Everything was taken away from me by some kind of turbulent current hidden beneath me, there all the time, but I didn't know. I didn't see it until it pulled me under and away from everything I've known and loved."

Way to let him have it, Jo. She was getting fed up, and Cole didn't blame her.

"But you have the picture now," Sanders said. "You know that much. That could be enough."

"I don't know what it means, though. I don't know who the additional people are or what their connection is."

"I think you're getting there," Sanders said.

"I had planned to take her to the archives to learn more about the photograph." Cole tapped his fingers on the table. "But I'm not so sure we should go to the museum today."

"What are you saying?" Jo stood. "We're going, Cole. You can go with me, or I'll go without you."

"Your parents gave up their lives and started new ones to hide whatever the secret is. It's too risky."

"Why the sudden change of heart? What changed your mind?" She continued without giving him a chance to reply. "It's riskier not to learn the truth. Their truth, their danger, that has pursued me for three years." Jo folded her arms, standing her ground.

"I'll go too," Sanders said. "It's part of my investigation. I can help protect her."

Did Cole need or want help? He could contact Hawk to assist. "It's out of your jurisdiction."

"But part of my investigation. Look, a bomb happened here in my county. I've been coordinating with the WSP detective and, for my part, getting the answers behind that bomb in the rainforest means I have to sink my teeth into it." He leaned closer. "I'll follow you. Having an official vehicle could come in handy. You and Jo can talk things out in the archives. I won't hover. I'll be there to keep a sharp eye out."

Cole had to think about it. He didn't want Sanders causing any roadblocks. Then again, Sanders could suspect that their man, Merrick, would show up, which is what Cole feared.

"Listen, that picture could hold the key," Sanders said. "It could be the most important piece that ties it all together."

"Exactly why this could be the most dangerous leg of the investigation," Cole said. And why he was having second thoughts about taking Jo into yet another situation where they could be ambushed.

"I'm going, Cole. I'd love it if you came too." Jo had made her case.

Fine. He didn't know Sanders all that well, but he had a sense about people, and the man was a determined investigator. "Okay. We're heading out in an hour. Meet us south on 101 at the turnoff to Forestview."

"See you in an hour." Sanders let himself out.

An hour later, Jo adjusted her sling bag over her arm. "I'm bringing my sketch pad. You never know when the muse will strike, and sketching can help me think."

Cole grabbed his firearm, set the security alarm, and they exited the house. He texted Sanders that they were heading out and would see him in a few minutes. They got into Jo's mean-looking Land Rover this time. Cole hoped the police presence Sanders provided would deter any followers.

"That guy rubs me the wrong way," she said. "I wish he didn't have to join us."

"Ever hear the saying 'There is safety in numbers'? He's offering his help, and we're taking advantage of the fact that he's also part of this investigation."

"I wish we hadn't shared what we're doing with him," she said.

"Really? Because we need all the help we can get. He could just as easily have taken over and insisted he would continue the investigation at the museum."

"No, he couldn't," she said. "I need to be there. I'm the one connected, and I'll find clues he couldn't find."

"I agree. And Detective Sanders is in it with us now. You should give him a chance." Like Sheriff Thatcher had said, *"You'll come around."*

"Cole, is he going along for protection?" she asked. "Are you worried that *you* won't be enough? Because if that's it, I'll tell you right now *you* are absolutely all I need."

He didn't know how to respond to that. Had she really meant to say those words? And if she had, had she meant them in the way that he really wanted to take them? His heart was in his throat now, and he had no coherent response.

If Sanders wasn't following them, Cole might have pulled over onto the shoulder or into a parking lot and kissed her with everything in him. He knew now, without a doubt, that . . .

You're absolutely all I need too.

33

In the lobby of the Museum of Flight, Jo bought tickets. Yeah. With the cash bucket Pop had left her. The plan was to take the self-guided tour through the museum, and then they would make their way to the archives. Detective Sanders had secured them the required appointment in the archives. As it turned out, having him along worked out to their advantage. Due to the nature of their investigation, he was able to expedite the process and get them right in while retaining their firearms.

I guess he isn't so bad after all.

They slowly made their way through the business and technology sections of the museum, which she found only mildly interesting. All she could think about was her ridiculous words.

"You're absolutely all I need."

She'd been referring to protection, and she'd wanted to encourage him. But when the words came out, they seemed to mean something different. Something more. That Cole was all she needed—after God, of course. Hearing the words out loud, though, she felt the truth of them all the way to her bones. And she couldn't take them back. Besides, he'd gotten a call from Detective Rick Wilson in Michigan and had put it on speaker, so she hadn't been able to add to the words, even if she had wanted to.

As she took another step forward to the next section, she tried to focus on the exhibits and ignore her thoughts about her feelings for Cole. Detective Sanders had stayed behind as she and Cole inched their way around the displays. Sanders was on his cell. Maybe his uniformed presence would help deter any danger that could occur in a museum.

As for danger in the museum, given what they'd learned earlier today from Rick, nothing would surprise her.

She thought back to the call.

"I dug around like you asked and notified the investigator that we might have possibly identified the remains, except we didn't have a name yet. I asked about the circumstances of the discovery."

"And?" Cole had asked.

"Seems someone discovered it on their property, dropped it off in a plastic bag with a note that said they didn't want any trouble."

"What do you make of that?" Cole asked.

"The property owner didn't want the law digging around on their property, but if it helped a missing person's family find closure, then they were happy to help. We need to identify the person dropping it off, though, and this isn't the way things are done. We absolutely need to look at the property to learn more about what happened. Could be that more bones are found." Wilson had sounded beyond frustrated. "But none of that happened like it should have three years ago when the skull was left for Mira."

"Any cameras to identify the person dropping it off?" Cole asked. "How deep did they look into it?"

"They did their duty, Cole, no need to question that. It

was a dead end, no pun intended. The skull was sent to forensics, and Mira was the primary artist we used on facial reconstruction. Mira didn't mention that she'd known the woman and had appeared in a photograph with her. I think the woman could be the same one in the reconstruction. But there's the chance we got this wrong and it's not her."

"Jo, you all right?" Cole's voice startled her, pulling her back to the moment, to the museum.

Sanders stood with them now, and both men stared at her.

"Did you remember something?" Sanders asked.

"Me? No." Just lost in thought. "Let's get busy."

"I'm not sure why we need to walk through the museum," Sanders said. "We could head straight for the archives."

As they approached the next section, Jo knew why. "Context."

"Context?" Sanders angled his head.

"Even as a forensic artist, context and perspective can make all the difference. We go into the archives with the right perspective about what was going on here during the time we're going to search on."

"Makes sense to me," Cole said. "No need to waste time talking it over."

Cole led them forward to the aerospace section, which included the history of flight and old airplanes, then they got to what Jo considered the relevant stuff. Space flight. The history of NASA. Her heart pounded as she studied the images on the wall, read the exhibit information, and even stood next to an Apollo mission model. She lost her ability to breathe for a few moments when they came to the exhibit of the space shuttle orbiter full-flight simulator, where astronauts had trained for their missions.

Could Pop really have been involved with this somehow? Or was she searching in the wrong place? Images of various prominent figures took up an entire wall, none of whom she recognized.

"So, this next section is about rocket science. What else?" Cole asked.

"We need to find where my father worked," Jo said. "And Mom, if she worked with him."

"Hard to do without knowing the name of the company," Cole said.

"I have a feeling we'll find it today," Jo said. They continued to walk through the exhibits. Jo started feeling overwhelmed. Pop the mechanic. Pop the bridge-fixer engineer.

Pop . . . "Oh my."

"What is it?" Cole asked.

"I'd forgotten. I don't know if it means anything."

"Just tell me."

"Back in his office at the R&D . . . he had a shelf with die-cast model cars. And . . . a rocket. And . . . an orbiter, I mean a space shuttle." Her knees grew weak. "This is it. We're onto something."

He frowned.

She sagged. "You aren't tracking with me, are you?"

"I mean . . . you could be right, and I hope you are. It's almost time for our appointment at the archives, so let's head that way," he said.

"Cole," she said. "His repair shop was the R&D. What does that mean to you?"

He hitched a half grin. "Okay. I'll give you that. R&D means research and development."

"Exactly. Going through the museum like this helped just like I thought it would." Jo was finally getting it. "It helped me to see things about Pop. Little things here and there. Now I can attach a deeper meaning to them, and they fit well into this aerospace backdrop."

As she followed Cole to the archive entrance, she could

hardly believe any of this. She teetered between feeling excited and betrayed. Cole gave their name to the woman at the reception area, and she reviewed the appointments on her computer screen.

Sanders sidled up to them. "I told you I would give you privacy in the archives. I'm going to stand guard. I'll remain here at the entrance." Sanders leaned closer to Cole. "I'm getting a feeling and one that I don't much like."

Cole shared a concerned look with him. "Okay. We'll be in the archives room."

Well, that wasn't much comfort. Was she really in danger here? Then again, if coming here meant they were close to learning the truth someone did not want them to discover, then she was glad for Cole's presence and the added protection from Detective Sanders.

Inside the archives, they met with the librarian, Cindy Jaynes, a woman in her fifties with auburn hair. After Jo and Cole explained the era they were interested in researching, Cindy searched, then retrieved the microfiche. She showed them how to use the machines and offered her assistance if they needed anything more.

"We're working hard to get the files digitized, but it's painstaking and time-consuming. We'll get there one day." She smiled. "Well, I'll let you work. I'm helping other patrons today as well. Just find me if you need me." Cindy left them to it.

Jo sat at one microfiche machine and reviewed the aerospace information from thirty years ago. She requested a span of five years on either side of the thirty-year mark. Jo took the first few years, and Cole took the last. This was going to be exhausting.

Skimming, skimming, skimming.

Skimming while not entirely sure what she was looking for besides anything that might lead her to her father's work in aerospace. Mason Hyde's work, and he'd worked with Gemini. That information could be in here as well. They searched for photographs or any information regarding either of her parents. Names. Activities. Events.

It's a start.

And could take hours or days, for which they'd need to get special permission. At the possibility of learning the truth, she was gripped by both excitement and terror.

Who were you, really, Mom?

And who are you, Pop?

If only either of them had told her the truth. Her heart pounded, and she pressed her hand against her chest.

Just calm down.

She hadn't found anything.

Yet.

Jo skimmed through the images of employees at an aerospace company called Resonant Solutions, responsible for rocket boosters, until her eyes grew tired and nearly crossed. An ache grew between her brows.

And . . . *there.*

Finally. A black-and-white photograph of a man she recognized standing next to a desk, smiling for the camera. The image was part of an article on rocket engineering. What she'd been searching for.

Oh my . . . "Cole." Her whisper might have been too loud.

Cole rolled his chair back from the privacy booth next to her. She waved him over. The booths were spaced far enough apart to give privacy so that he had to roll in his chair over to her booth, then he peered closely.

"It's him. It's Pop," she said. "Ransom Driscoll, just like Allison said."

"If *that's* his real name," Cole said.

"Oh, come on, he didn't have a reason to use an alias

back then. Though, I mean, we don't know his reason for using one now, even."

"Right. He didn't use an alias until something *happened*. Time to find out what that was. I'm just going to go back to my cubbyhole and search on his name."

Now that she'd found her father, she could potentially find her mother too, and the unidentified woman in the picture with her. She held on to so much hope, but what if she came up empty?

No, this was happening. Pop was a mechanical engineer who had worked for a rocket booster company. A rocket engineer. Wow. She could hardly fathom that. Then again, she could look back on their previous conversations and it made sense.

But what happened? "Why isn't Pop still a rocket engineer? Why didn't he stay working with Resonant Solutions?"

"Well, one thing, it was absorbed by Advanced Technologies," Cole whispered over her shoulder. She hadn't known he'd come back. "So that also connects him to Jim Jordan, the COO of Advanced Technologies, with whom he had lunch."

"What are you doing?" she asked.

"Checking in."

"Look at this article. This is everything. Pop worked with Mason Hyde for a decade in structural mechanics." Her throat closed off completely.

"Space Shuttle Solid Rocket Motor Project." Cole scrolled to the bottom of the article. "Look. The *Liberty* orbiter is in this picture."

"Resonant was one of the many NASA contractors," she said. "The *Liberty*, just one of several orbiters, including *Enterprise, Columbia, Challenger, Discovery, Atlantis,* and *Endeavour.*"

"Where did I see the *Liberty* before?"

"In the museum. We literally just read about the *Liberty* disaster that happened in 1995, almost ten years after the *Challenger* in 1986, and eight years before the *Columbia* tragedy."

Oh . . . she pressed her hand over her mouth. He worked on the NASA contract. She couldn't breathe. "Thirty years. This is it, then. If we're looking for an incident, something that happened *before*, the *Liberty* disaster could be the incident we're looking for." Pop was there with the company, and then bam, the *Liberty* malfunctioned, exploded, killing six astronauts. He started a new life in Forestview. Less than a year after the incident, Jo was born in Michigan.

"Go. Go find my mother. Search through this event."

The thought that she was finally onto something, finally going to get answers, overwhelmed her. Tears streaming, frantic, she searched for her mother through the employees listed on the project. In total, tens of thousands of employees across multiple contractors worked on the space shuttles. But Jo kept her search close to her father's department, or she'd be at a loss, unless some of the records were digitized and she had a name she could search.

There. Mom's face smiled back at her. "Cole!" she practically shouted.

He was at her side again. "Shh. We're not the only ones here." He glanced over his shoulder. "We are now. It's almost closing time. We need to wrap this up. We can come back if we need to."

"Sanders is keeping guard, remember?"

"Exactly. He's too far away to help."

"But you're here. Look." She pointed.

She couldn't stop the tears from streaming down her cheeks. "She's here, hugging the unidentified woman in the photograph. Mom's name is Myrna Carter, not Mira

Cattrel. I still don't have the woman's name." She pointed along the screen as she read. "We're getting somewhere. I can't believe this. We need to get copies of this. Find the librarian. Oh . . ." Her heart palpitated. "They both worked on the—"

"*Liberty*."

"I'm just so proud of them. Why would either of them hide and leave behind their lives? Live separate lives?" Painful emotion clogged her throat. "They worked with NASA, for crying out loud."

"The reason remains to be seen." Cole sounded distant.

Through blurred vision, Jo continued reading about the shuttle's explosion killing all astronauts on board. Inquiries and investigations occurred for weeks and months afterward. And yet here they were, searching the microfiche archives to find information about Pop.

"I've got him. Looks like the gang—your mother, father, and Mason—worked under Troy Martin. I found his picture." Cole pulled up the man's picture on the screen for Jo.

She sucked in a breath. "Everyone in that picture is accounted for, except for Troy and this woman."

"We know the company and the situation, so I want Allison to track the employees down. See where they are now. That's asking a lot because Resonant employed almost an entire town in Nevada. Probably still does but under the new name of Gemini."

"Since both Mason Hyde and my mother were murdered, and my father has gone into hiding, do you think there could be other Resonant employees who disappeared or died under suspicious circumstances?"

"I hope not, but we'll find out." He quickly typed a text. "Letting Allison know all the names. She has enough and can put it all together for us. If she weren't human, she would be AI. She's brilliant."

Jo sank back and stared at the screen as she scrolled. "I can't find any references to Pop after the incident. Mom either. They could have been fired."

"Lots of moving parts here. Employees come and go. Contractors too."

"I get it. Even with over half a million people employed in the industry, many of them engineers. Physicists and the like." The weight of this news pressed against her, weighing her down. "This must be what 'before' means."

"Before?" He angled his head, lifting his gaze from the cell.

"Naomi said her brother knew my mother 'before.' And her garbled word makes sense now. She said 'free.' What if she meant the word *freedom*? To look up freedom. What's another word for freedom?"

"*Liberty*. Before the *Liberty* disaster." Cole said it for her.

"Yes."

"And after?" he asked. "Might be another disaster if we're not careful with what we've learned." He leaned closer. "I think we're onto something, and it's highly volatile, dangerously explosive information."

"We don't have all the information. We just know that *something* happened, and now we might know what it was. But there is obviously more to this."

He nodded and started taking pictures of the information on the screens. Was that even allowed? Not that it mattered to Cole. Not to her either. They needed images of this stuff.

"We'll ask for copies of everything, now that we have enough information to ask, but I don't want to wait for it."

Jo scrolled through and snapped images too.

"Is there anything else we need to know?" He stood and looked around with his protective, on-guard demeanor. "Because we probably need to get out of here."

"I'd like to stay as long as possible. I don't want to leave only to think of something I could have looked into. I'm going to read everything I can about this."

Cole continued taking pictures. Looking over his shoulder. Watching the exits. He was getting nervous, and that was making her nervous.

Jo kept reading, and all of it made her cry. The tragedy, losing all those astronauts. Had Pop gotten fired? Mom too? Then she read about another tragedy surrounding the Space Shuttle Solid Rocket Motor Project. One of their employees—the unidentified woman with Mom, Pop, and Mason in the picture she'd found in Michigan—had gone missing . . . *thirty* years ago. Jo couldn't breathe. Her name was Helen Martin. The man in the photograph—Troy Martin. Helen Martin was his wife. "She was missing," she whispered.

Oh God, oh Lord . . . this is no surprise to you.

Her heart pounded erratically.

Mom found you, Helen. Mom found you because someone intended for her to find you.

But who was behind her disappearance? Who was behind sending Mom the skull?

Caught up in her devastating thoughts, she hadn't realized that Cole was there, crouching next to her so that he was at eye level. "We've learned enough," he spoke in low tones. "We need to hand this off to Sanders completely."

"What? No. Why?"

Cole stood and started pacing. He scraped his hand over his mouth, rubbed it. The lights flickered. Cole froze.

Jo slowly stood. The microfiche screens went out.

And so did the lights.

34

Cole's hackles raised as he reached for his firearm. Gripping it, he motioned for Jo to get down on the floor.

"Maybe she forgot we were here. That's me just hoping," Jo said.

"Not likely. Keep quiet and follow me." Cole ducked as he crept forward so their heads couldn't be seen over the partition walls.

"Where are we going?" She whispered the question.

He turned and put his finger to his lips, then continued forward, making his way through this maze of a library, with old-fashioned card-catalog shelves, books, documents, and microfiche. If he headed for the front door, they could be ambushed. Where was his backup, Detective Sanders? Maybe Sanders wasn't aware of what was going on inside the archive room, or maybe he had been taken out. Only two egresses were available if they didn't go out the front. Three if you counted crashing through one of the windows. The entire south wall contained windows. Regardless, any effort to escape was a risk if this was another attack on Jo.

And he couldn't know that for sure either.

He couldn't know which exit was being covered. Maybe all of them. He didn't for one minute believe that the librarian had forgotten them. She would have come back to make sure they had left and had returned the microfiche. Tidied up the workspaces before shutting off the lights and locking up.

At least light from the windows filtered into the room, but it didn't chase away all the shadows.

Lord, help me get her out of this.

He continued creeping toward the well-lit Exit sign, then pulled her into the shadows to watch quietly, except Jo misstepped and knocked a chair against the counter. His heart hammered at the sound. He braced for a reaction.

Gunfire echoed off the walls, the sound reverberating through his skull. Bullets pinged the partitions, barely missing Jo's head.

Jo instinctively ducked. Whimpering, gasping for breath, she covered her head and moved to crawl under the desk, but he redirected her, urging her to crouch and rush ahead of him toward the wall and to safety, protecting her with his body.

He handed her his cell, then whispered in a barely audible tone, "Text Sanders that we're under attack." Just in case the guy hadn't heard the shots fired.

As if the man wouldn't already know, if he was worth the weight of his law enforcement badge. Cole grabbed a couple of pens off the counter and slid them across the floor to the exit to see if he got a reaction.

Nothing.

Merrick—and Cole strongly suspected their murderous stalker was behind this attack—wouldn't be fooled. Cole needed to get Jo to safety and go on the offense. She handed his cell back and he read the text from Sanders.

I'm coming.

Anger boiled in his gut. Cole weighed his options. Until help arrived, he could wait the gunman out, but anyone entering was in danger. He handed off his additional firearm to Jo and urged her into a dark corner behind a partition. Motioned for her to stay.

Then he turned to face the enemy and hunt their pursuer. He'd learned to blend in and move quietly during his time in special forces, but he was stalking a man with the same skills. Today at the library, Cole had taken some time to look into Merrick's background via his cell. Merrick had been Army too. He'd found an image showing his unit and showing him shaking hands with an engineer from a military contractor. And when Jo had found Troy Martin, Cole learned the connection.

A window shattered, allowing blustery, cold wind into the room, along with rain.

The actual archives were back in another room—an environmentally controlled room. But this violation could have a negative effect on the collection. The shattered window was meant to be a distraction, and he zeroed in on finding the shooter.

His skin tingled, alerting him to a presence behind him. He turned to face the muzzle of a gun. Lunging, he thrust the man's arm upward.

Gunfire resounded.

The bullet meant for him went into the ceiling, then they battled for control of Merrick's gun, which took all Cole's focus. Muscles straining, Merrick grunting with the effort, Cole let instinct take over so he could win this. Protect Jo.

But if he killed Jo's pursuer in this fight, they would get no answers from his dead body. In his peripheral vision, Cole caught sight of Sanders.

Straining to overcome his opponent, he ground out the words "Get. Her. Out . . ."

"You're in more danger than she is." Sanders rushed forward to assist Cole.

The shift in focus was all Merrick needed. He abandoned the gun, reaching for something else—something faster and just as deadly. A blade. He thrust the knife at Cole who twisted away, losing his grip on Merrick, though he'd seized the gun. Still holding his knife, the guy slipped behind the tall shelves and jumped out the shattered window. Cole ran after him, ignoring Sanders's shouts.

Sanders could protect Jo.

Cole refused to let the man who posed imminent danger to her escape. He jumped through the window and landed on the soft earth in a crouch, then sprinted after Merrick in the cold rain. Merrick raced up the slippery sidewalk, then crossed the busy street. Cole followed, dodging cars, ignoring honks and cursing shouts. One vehicle continued forward, blocking his path, and he slid across the hood.

"Sorry!" he shouted, but he couldn't let the man get away.

He couldn't let Jo continue to be threatened. Her life endangered. Breathing hard, he sprinted. This guy must have been a sprinter in college or the Olympics. Cole might die trying to keep up with him.

The man approached a drawbridge. Traffic had stopped at the lights. Cyclists and the foot traffic paused too. The drawbridge had already started lifting, but that didn't deter Merrick.

Would the bridge operator stop the process? Could he? Cole had no idea.

"You can't make that. You're not going to make it!" Cole shouted, but he, too, continued forward.

The bridge became unnavigable, and Merrick appeared

to only now realize his mistake. He turned to face Cole instead. Brandished his knife. He'd lost his gun at the library.

Cole still had his. "Give it up, man. You're done. It's over. Police everywhere are looking for you. I know you're working for Martin." He wouldn't make promises. He wasn't a lawyer. But bring this guy in, and he could roll on his boss's crimes.

"You got me all wrong," Merrick said. "I don't know what you're talking about."

There was that aspect too—he'd been hired to do a job. But Cole doubted that was the case here, given the connection. And with the words, vessels were lining up to pass under the drawbridge as it continued lifting. Cole was no fool, and he started backing down the ever-increasing angle of the lifting drawbridge.

Knife in hand, Merrick suddenly ran toward him. Cole realized that law enforcement vehicles had approached. Officers had accumulated at his back. He lowered his gun.

"Look, put the knife away," he said. "I don't want to shoot you. I don't want either of us to get shot."

The man suddenly veered toward the rail, surprising Cole with his intention.

"No! Don't!" Cole shouted.

Merrick jumped over before Cole had even finished shouting.

Oh, for crying out loud.

"You think that's going to stop me? You're in for a rude awakening. I'm not afraid of the water."

But that wasn't true.

He'd hated it ever since the helicopter crash. He'd hated it after being stranded on the rocks with the king tide coming toward him. The ocean had nearly taken Jo from him. But Merrick had been the one to send her off that ferry.

And Cole would end this.

For Jo.

It was now or never. His cell phone was going off. Text alerts and rings. Yeah, that was about to end.

Cole raced toward the edge, peered down to make sure this wasn't a suicide jump, then gripped the rail and jumped over too.

Into the darkest fear he'd ever known.

35

Jo stood under an awning, shivering, even with a blanket over her jacket. Police cruisers were all along the street. A couple of fire trucks too.

Fear for Cole squeezed her throat. Detective Sanders stood near and spoke to the WSP detective. She couldn't even think of his name right now. Nor could she make out their words with all the street noise.

The wind and rain.

Sanders moved closer, leaned in, and said, "I wouldn't worry. Remember, he was special forces. He's been trained to survive the most extreme circumstances."

If only she could trust Cole's training and skills. She'd sensed that he struggled with water. Oceans, lakes, and rivers. And for good reason. He'd been through a lot of bad that was associated with large bodies of water, not the least of which was last week, when he'd pulled her out of Puget Sound. She could have died. He'd risked his life to rescue her. In the past, he'd never said much about his fears, but she'd seen his reaction every time she mentioned wanting to go on a long walk on the rocky beach, which she absolutely loved. Cole was as strong and as sharp as any man she'd ever met, and he hid his fears well. He was determined to overcome them.

"I don't understand, though," she said. "How did he end up in the water?"

"Police say he jumped in after Merrick."

"But why? Why would he do that?" He risked his life. He could have waited for a better chance to catch him. Her fury over his decision nearly overshadowed her fear for him.

Sanders's gaze was intense. Unnerving. "I understand completely. The man has been trying to kill you, Jo. Cole couldn't let him get away."

"We would catch him eventually. He didn't have to take the risk."

"Eventually? He might never get a better chance to take him down. He didn't want you to remain in danger."

Jo looked up at Detective Sanders. This close, she noticed a small scar along his face beneath the five-o'clock shadow. What had he been through to get that? She hadn't liked him at first. But he was a man who didn't back down, and in that way reminded her of Cole, who appreciated his skills. "What would you have done? Would you have jumped in?"

"It's hard to say. I don't know the exact circumstances. But then again, if someone was pursuing someone I cared about, then I would move heaven and earth to stop them."

Metaphorically, of course. Was Cole trying to move heaven and earth?

Her knees shook at the thought, and her heart melted almost completely. *Cole . . . come back to me.*

Please.

What were you thinking? That was all she needed, to trust this guy, then have him disappear on her. What was *she* thinking? He'd gone in the water to get the man who'd persistently tried to kill her. No matter her fear of heartache, she couldn't stop her feelings for him.

I'm in love with you.

She hoped, she prayed, for a chance to tell him. She didn't even care why he'd stayed away for so long. Maybe she was foolhardy, but maybe Cole was afraid too. Maybe he was afraid Jo would reject him.

What was she thinking? She needed to be more concerned about his safety. She glanced around the law enforcement presence. Some of the vehicles were leaving. A crowd had grown but was now dispersing since the spectacle on the bridge had ended.

In the gathering, a familiar face stood out.

What? Wait. Jo started forward. "Pop!"

What was he doing in the crowd? And where did he go? The bodies merged as the crowd lost interest. And Jo had lost her father.

Where did he go? Jo dropped the blanket and tried to catch up. She weaved through the dispersing mass and caught up to a man in a gray raincoat, then grabbed his arm. "Pop?"

He turned to glare at her. It wasn't her father. "I'm sorry, I thought you were someone else."

Rushing forward, ignoring the rain and cold and the fact that she was cutting people off, she came to the street corner. Which way had he gone? To the right, or had he continued across on the crosswalk? Traffic was flowing, and she couldn't so easily cross now. She couldn't have imagined Pop's face. He was staring right at her too. He was trying to reach her, but she had been standing near law enforcement, and Pop clearly did not want to be found by them—or at least he hadn't wanted to make his presence known and then, once again, bring danger her way. But what a joke. Danger had never left her alone.

Jo started moving again. She would find her father today.

Sanders caught up and moved into her path, blocking her way. "Where are you going?"

"I saw my father. I *know* it was him. He's here! We have to find him. He knows what this is all about." Still, he'd walked away from her. He was there and then he left. Why would he walk away? Maybe he was trying to get her a message. He could text her, couldn't he? Did he consider that mode of communication too dangerous?

"And that would be too risky for you." He grabbed an SPD street cop passing by and explained the situation.

"You have a picture?" Sanders asked her.

"Sure." But she hadn't wanted to get Pop in trouble. She'd wanted to talk to him on her own terms. She pulled up the image and showed the cop. Sent it to Sanders, who sent it out to others who could search for her father.

She pressed forward. "I'm going to search for him."

Sanders caught her arm. "While Merrick is still out there, that would be a bad idea. Cole trusted me with protecting you. You have two choices. I can take you back to the safe house, or you can wait in the police headquarters for news about Cole."

"We can't leave. Cole is going to show up eventually. He'll wonder where we are." And Pop was here too.

"He'll be furious with me if I don't protect you. You look exhausted, and it's freezing out here. I think the safe house is where we need to go. Did you learn everything you needed in the museum?"

Sanders was being reasonable, and Jo didn't want to listen, but he was right. Exhaustion pressed down on her, along with a hefty dose of fear. As for the museum, she could always come back and even search the digital archives now that she knew more about what to look for. But they had definitely learned a lot. "For now, I guess."

"Listen, what would Cole want you to do?" he asked. "After all of this, he'd want you to be safe. I'll take you back and wait with you. I can work with Hawk to coordinate protection, and we'll let you know as soon as there is any word on Cole."

But what about Pop? Admittedly, she wouldn't see him again today if he didn't want her to. She allowed Sanders to escort her back around the corner, and they walked toward their vehicles. She glanced over her shoulder. If Pop wanted to talk to her, he'd just have to find her again.

As for Cole . . .

"What if he doesn't make it?" There. She said out loud what they both feared.

Sanders wrapped the blanket around her again and pulled her under an awning and out of the rain. "You can't think like that."

"Then where is he?"

"He's tracking down your attacker. Hunting him."

"Along with the entire Seattle PD? Someone would have found one of them by now." Tears spilled over her cheeks. She was simply too exhausted, and the cold was eating away at her composure.

Sanders pursed his lips into a grim frown. Yeah. He was thinking the same thing as Jo. Cole hadn't made it. She pressed her hands against her eyes.

Oh, Lord, please, please help him. Let him be alive out there somewhere. I can't take this anymore.

"Okay. We're done standing out in the cold. The best thing we can do for Cole is get you back to safety." He urged her out into the weather again and to his county vehicle—a Ford Interceptor.

"What about my Land Rover?"

"Let's leave it for him. He'll find his way back."

I need to believe that.

But Detective Sanders sounded as if he was trying to convince himself.

36

Shivering, breathless, Cole crawled up onto the banks of the river. His limbs were almost worthless.

This might have been a huge mistake, except he was far too close to capturing Merrick to just let him go. He couldn't run away or swim away. Cole was on him.

Can't lose you now.

He scrambled to his knees and then got on his feet. Sluggishly, he tromped forward to the old abandoned industrial warehouse.

Before crawling from the water, Cole had seen Merrick slip inside.

I have so got you now.

Once this guy was incarcerated . . . no more bombs. No more attacks. No more . . . anything. He'd learned vital information. The only person from Jo's photograph who was still alive, other than Driscoll—Jo's father—was Troy Martin, founder and president of Resonant. After selling that company to Gemini, he'd earned millions before moving to be installed as CEO for another aerospace contractor.

And this guy, Merrick, was connected to Martin.

Cole hoped the water would adequately drain from his gun before he had to use it. He gulped in air and moved his body to get the blood flowing and warm up his core. He cautiously approached the old aluminum structure and, standing against the wall, listened. But the rain pounded. The wind still blew.

He heard nothing to indicate that Merrick moved around inside the warehouse. Merrick had been limping when he came out of the water, so Cole assumed he was injured. Merrick also had at least fifteen years on Cole. Still, he wouldn't underestimate this man's abilities. They'd both been trained by the most elite training force in the world—the US Armed Forces. Cole would use every advantage he could get.

Would Merrick expect Cole to go through the front door or a side entrance? Didn't matter. Cole wasn't going in the front, so he'd better find another door, or a window, into the structure that appeared ready to collapse. The posted signs said it had been condemned.

He found a side door cracked open and he quietly slipped in. Once inside the dark building, he waited until his eyes adjusted to the limited light filtering through the windows. Cole's limbs were still a little numb, and he was moving slower than he would have liked under the circumstances. So he waited in the dark, in the quiet, for Merrick to make his move.

Was he even still inside? Or had he run out the back door? The hair and skin on his arms rippled, and he ducked, saving his head from a blow. Cole dropped to his back and aimed his gun.

Merrick lunged at him with a knife.

Cole fired.

Merrick dropped.

But he wasn't dead. *Please, don't be dead*. He had to be

wearing a bulletproof vest. But this had been point-blank. He dropped to his knees next to the wounded man. The vest hadn't spared him from the blunt-force trauma, and now he saw that a bullet had pierced his chest.

And Merrick *hadn't* worn a vest. *What?*

"Why'd you make me do it, man?" Cole asked. "I told you on the bridge. It's over. You could have come in." He felt the man's pulse. Thready, but still alive.

He kicked the knife out of reach. Cole tugged his cell out, but it was dead. He found Merrick's cell in the pocket of his waterproof jacket. Cole fished it out. Yeah, he was messing with evidence, but a life was at stake. Using the cell, he called for emergency services.

The guy mumbled. Cole used the flashlight on the cell so he could see his face. His bloody teeth. The guy was actually smiling?

"Glad to be taken out by you," Merrick said. "You're a worthy opponent."

Dude, this isn't a video game. "The thing is, I shouldn't be your opponent. We fought on the same side. What were you thinking?"

"Doesn't matter."

"Maybe not right now. Hang in there. Help is on the way."

"I'm checking out before then."

Cole hated to sound crass or like he didn't care, but . . . "Tell me what I need to know to save the girl, man. You were once a soldier. Let the good side of you be the voice that speaks now. Why did Martin hire you?"

That would depend on how deep this guy had to reach to find his way out of his mercenary role.

"My uncle . . . he has a way of getting what he wants. He's worth billions, you know. The only person who could take him down is Jo's father."

"Then why didn't he take him down?"

"Uncle Troy would kill anyone who tried to take him down. The ones who knew about it."

"Your uncle or you? You killed Mira, didn't you? And what is *it*? And what does Jo have to do with this other than she's Driscoll's daughter?"

"He . . . needed to *find* him. Draw him out. The woman he loved. The daughter he didn't even know. He had accomplished that. I didn't know about my aunt. That he killed her. Not until this week. I figured it out, but I was already in it up to my neck. In it with him. Like you said, it's over now, at least for me. I might as well check out."

Draw him out so he could kill him. That's why Driscoll put the distance between him and Jo, but it wasn't enough. Did Jo's father have a clue that she'd continued to be targeted? Seething, Cole pressed harder, blood seeping through his fingers. The light grew dimmer as it grew colder and darker outside.

"You're wasting your time here," Merrick said. "My uncle knows where she is, man. He knows. You'd better get to her."

Closing his eyes, he said nothing more. Cole feared moving Merrick would only cause more damage, so he did his best to staunch the bleeding. He'd caused it, but it had been Merrick's life or his own.

"No! No, no, no." He punched the ground. Where were emergency crews when you needed them?

37

As the county vehicle approached the safe house, Jo's chest tightened with her rising panic. She might have fallen asleep from exhaustion along the drive that took almost three hours.

But now she was wide awake. A couple of outdoor lights illuminated the house along the coast.

What was she going to say to Hawk? *I let your brother run after the killer. I left Seattle, left him behind . . .*

She closed her eyes and tried not to berate herself— because really, what could she have done to stop him? It wasn't like he asked her opinion before he jumped out the window and chased after the guy. Cole had made his own decision. He'd made his choice. Still, his determination to stop Merrick revolved around protecting Jo.

She hadn't heard anything yet about Cole—had he survived, or was he . . . gone? She tried not to think the worst.

Please come back to me, Cole.

As if she had any right to him.

Sanders steered up to the house and parked behind Hawk's vehicle. Hawk rushed from the house.

"Anything on Cole?" he asked.

Detective Sanders shook his head. Hawk pressed the heel of his hand against his forehead and turned his back on them. Sanders escorted Jo inside the house.

A few lights were on as she dropped her bag on the sofa. The place felt . . . empty . . . without Cole. Sanders proceeded to tell Hawk about the events. He wasn't there inside the library with them, but Jo had told him what she and Cole had learned. They believed they understood the event that had tied her mother and father and Mason together. Sanders had contacted the Michigan detective about identifying the skull and confirming the identity—Helen Martin. Pieces of the investigative puzzle were coming together, and yet Jo still had so many questions.

She left Detective Sanders and Hawk to talk and make calls in their search for Cole as well as answers.

Jo moved to the windows. Dusk would soon turn everything obscure.

She could hear the waves crashing but would have to step out onto the porch to see them. Clouds billowed and raced across the sky. The weather in Seattle was no match for the raw and terrible beauty here. The glorious and yet painful experience.

She stepped outside onto the deck, shutting the door behind her.

Who knew if either of the two men would discover she'd left the house? Or maybe they would and give her space— that's what Cole would do. Then eventually, he would join her outside. Stand next to her as if bearing the burden with her.

She spoke to the wind and rain. The storm and the sea. But mostly to God.

"Lord, I've lost so much already. I'm still gutted from what happened to Mom. I've had two fathers leave me. Just walk out on me. Now I can't lose Cole too. I just can't. Please keep him safe and . . . bring him back to me. He doesn't belong to me, I know he doesn't, so maybe if you can't bring him back to me, take him somewhere safe. If I never see him again but I know that he's safe, that's okay. That's fine. Just . . . whatever part of him I held on to for myself, Lord, I give that over to you. Please . . . just keep him safe."

She said the words out loud, though only God could hear them over the storm. She thought back to the beach around this time last year, when she'd rescued a dying Cole from the rocky shores during a king tide . . . the riptides almost took him. Had they taken him this time for real?

Where are you?

Because if he was alive, if he was okay, he would have called Hawk. She couldn't keep thinking this way and had to ignore the fear gripping her, the ache in her chest . . . *God, please keep him safe.*

If he's even still alive.

She almost dreaded the moment that Hawk would let her know he'd heard something. She feared it wouldn't be good.

"Jo," Hawk said.

And here he was, to tell her the news.

"You need to get back inside," he said. "It's too cold."

Hawk pressed an arm around Jo and tugged her from the rail, then led her back inside. Soaking wet. She hated dripping all over the floor.

"Cole will have my hide if I let anything happen to you."

She lifted her gaze, hopeful.

He smiled. "Yes, I heard from Cole. He's okay."

She sagged. Almost leaned into Hawk, but she kept her composure. "Where is he?"

"He's on his way. Cole says you're in danger, so we're going to move again when he gets here. Sanders left to get a new safe house ready."

"I've always been in danger. I don't even know why."

The way Hawk looked at her, she suspected *he* might know.

"Well?"

"Cole learned some things, though I don't know what it all means. It sounds like your father might know."

Yeah, of course he did. "And someone is after me to get to him. Is that what you're saying?"

"It's possible."

"And likely." Tired. She was just so tired. "I'm just . . . I'm going to change."

His expression one of relief, he nodded. "Pack up all your stuff so we can be ready to leave here for good. I can help you pack up the art, or Remi and I can come back to get it later."

"And go where? This is a safe house, isn't it?"

"Just be ready. I'll warm up the soup Remi sent."

Jo headed for her room, and in the bathroom, she took a long, hot shower to warm up.

Then, after thick and creamy homemade chicken noodle soup—compliments of Brad at the Cedar Trails kitchen—Jo needed time alone. Wasn't like she could sleep, but she didn't want to sit in the big spacious living room with Hawk. He was pacing. Calling people. On his laptop.

What was taking Cole so long?

So she moved to the office to wait.

She sat in the office and listened to the waves and just sketched whatever came to mind, but her heart was so heavy, all the images were morbid. Still, she could put the puzzle pieces together. She sketched the various faces she'd seen today in the images, along with the space shuttle. Drew great streaks across the page to depict the orbiter traveling through space. Jo set that aside, then opened up her tablet and searched on the man in charge of Resonant's space shuttle team—*Liberty*. Along with her father, he was the only one in the photograph still surviving. The only one, along with her father, who had not been murdered.

Pop, why didn't you just tell me? That would have been so much easier.

Maybe she and Cole needed to pay Troy Martin a visit and ask him the hard questions.

The house shuddered. Jo got up to look out the window. Darkness had settled in. No stars lit up the sky. She heard the ocean's turmoil as the wind gusted so hard an eerie wail blew through the walls.

Jo imagined she was in a gothic novel, sans the romance. She'd given up romance. All she cared about was Cole returning from his attempt to stop a bad guy who'd come after her.

While she waited for him, she could do her part, though, and so she continued to research, intending to read about Martin's role at Resonant and his new role in a high-level position at another aerospace company. His mug was in a few pictures, and it was like looking at age-progression photographs. He looked familiar. She might have even seen him before. That fact gnawed at the back of her mind. She'd seen so many faces, though, she could be mixing them all up.

But then she quickly got sucked into reading about the *other* space shuttle tragedies—the *Challenger* and *Columbia*—and the investigations surrounding them. In the case of the *Challenger*, engineers had tried to warn those in charge of giving the go-ahead to launch. In fact, one engineer in particular had feared for his life. His testimony as a whistleblower would be damaging to those in power.

Jo's heart pounded. Could that be it?

Mom and Pop . . . had been whistleblowers? Or at least

they'd tried. Or maybe they'd felt too threatened to even come forward. She didn't know. Maybe she was jumping to conclusions, but this sounded reasonable.

She set her tablet aside. She had to tell someone. Plus, she could ask Hawk if he'd heard anything more from Cole, who was supposed to be on his way. Jo bolted from the chair and opened the door, padded down the hallway to an empty living room. Hawk's laptop sat open on the table.

"Hawk?" *Where'd you go?*

A door was banging somewhere.

Back and forth.

Back and forth.

She crept through the house and found the door to the garage open. Cold air rushed inside.

Chills crawled over Jo. She backstepped. *I need to get my gun.*

The power went out. Jo froze, then hearing a noise, she tugged her cell from her pocket and lifted it to shine the flashlight in the face of an intruder who stepped through the open doorway.

She instantly recognized him—the face she'd been working on since Michigan.

"You."

38

*Y*ou'd better get to her."

Merrick's last words to him.

Cole couldn't get to the safe house fast enough. He wished he had his own personal helicopter like Hawk. He wished he had asked Hawk to fly his helicopter and come and get him. Jo could have ridden along too.

At least while he drove to the safe house, Sanders was working on getting a *new* safe house and, at the same time, putting out the appropriate warnings to law enforcement channels to find Troy Martin, whom Merrick had accused while confessing his own crimes.

The WSP detective had loaned Cole a burner cell and assured Cole that he would keep him updated. In the meantime, Cole had tried to call Hawk again, but in this part of the Olympic Peninsula, the cell wouldn't work. At least he'd been able to reach his brother once and warn him. Hawk knew to remain on guard and vigilant and to be ready to move.

Fear churned in his gut.

He steered up the rough drive. The power was out. In

fact, no lights were on inside, that he could see. No security lights lit up the grounds. That could be from the storm, or something else entirely. The trees he could see within the circle of light from his vehicle swayed back and forth. At least the rain had slowed.

A rare flash of lightning silhouetted the house against the cliff. Cole parked behind Hawk's vehicle.

He was still here? Why didn't he answer? His brother's lack of response jacked up Cole's internal warning signals. He left the lights on and hopped from the vehicle with his handgun out—locked and loaded. Approaching the house on the cliff, he felt like he was in a creepy novel. Even creepier at the moment because the power was out.

Gun ready, he skirted around Hawk's vehicle and then forward. He didn't want to get shot by his brother—friendly fire—approaching the way he was, so he texted Hawk.

I'm here.

And heard nothing back. But that didn't mean anything. Or it could mean everything. His pulse skyrocketed. Two people he loved were in that house.

Or *had* been in that house.

Lord, please let Hawk and Jo be alive and well in the house.

Cole could be getting worked up for nothing. Sanders could have secured a safe house and Hawk taken Jo to it. Still, Cole had heard nothing from Hawk or Sanders. They would have informed him of the move. Something else was going on here.

The garage door was open, which wasn't in keeping with security protocol. Illumination from his vehicle gave just enough light that he could see where he was going. He cleared the garage, found the breaker panel. The main circuit had been flipped. He switched it back on and then entered the house through the garage door. And he could also see that he was alone.

Or . . . maybe not alone.

Inside the house, a few lights had come on, and he continued in clearance mode, leading with his loaded gun. Hawk's laptop remained open on the table. Not like Hawk. Panic crept up Cole's spine and tightened around his throat. Pulse racing, he cleared the rest of the house as quickly as possible.

Jo wasn't here. Her bag remained on the bed. Unpacked.

Hawk wasn't here. But his vehicle was still outside.

This was. Not. Good.

A noise drew him around, and he aimed his handgun, then quickly lowered it. "Hawk?"

His brother stumbled forward, holding his head. "I'm sorry."

"Hawk!" Cole rushed forward, then ushered his brother to the sofa. "You're hurt. What happened?"

"I don't know. Someone hit me in the head. Jo . . . where is she?"

Fear gripped Cole's chest and squeezed. "She isn't here."

"Then you'd better find her. I'll be fine." Hawk fumbled around and found his cell, then dropped it.

Heart pounding, Cole grabbed the cell, got Sanders on the line this time. "Hawk's hurt. Jo is gone. Get here. Send backup. Send an ambulance. Send everyone. We have to find her!"

He ended the call. He didn't have time to talk. "Where could he have taken her?"

"Who?"

"Troy Martin."

"You know it's him?"

"I don't, but someone must have taken her. And Merrick said his uncle was after her. His uncle, Troy Martin."

"Okay. Okay," Hawk said. "This is all my fault."

"Now isn't the time, Hawk." Jo was gone. It didn't matter who was to blame. Cole paced. "I've got to find her." But, God help him, he didn't know how.

Where are you?

And when he found her—*Lord, help me find her*—he would never leave her again. She'd have to kick him to the curb if she didn't want him around. But Cole couldn't stay here and wait. He would get out there and actively look for her.

"Come on, Hawk. I'll take you to the lodge. You're not staying here alone."

"But what about all those emergency people you called? I'll be fine. I need to guard the place. The evidence someone was here."

"You're not thinking clearly. That doesn't matter anymore. He has Jo. That's all that matters."

Remi rushed into the house. "Hawk! Why haven't you answered my calls?" She moved to her fiancé. "What happened? Where's Jo?"

"He took her," Cole said.

"Who took her?" Remi asked.

But Cole wasn't answering her questions. He exited the house and got back into Jo's Land Rover.

Think. I've got to think. He had to think like a space-shuttle engineer turned mechanic. If Martin had her, he would use her to draw her father to him. So Cole had to think like Ransom Driscoll, who never did anything without a reason. Everything he'd done had a reason behind it.

Cole just couldn't see it . . .

Until now.

296

39

In the cold, dark space of Pop's office at the R&D, Jo tried to escape the ties on her wrists and legs. She'd suffered so much already. *Why did I let him take me?*

When he'd walked through the door at the safe house, she instantly recognized him as someone she'd seen in Michigan. A random guy on the sidewalk. Someone who hadn't registered in her mind as anyone but a stranger. She'd sketched an image of him. Troy Martin had aged more than she could have imagined from that original picture of him with her parents, Mason Hyde, and his wife—Helen Martin.

He most certainly was the one to send Mom the skull. That he had the skull was enough to confirm to Jo he was the one to both murder his wife and hide her body. Helen had gone missing and had never been found. But this man had known exactly where her body was.

Jo should not underestimate how far this man would go.

He was holding Jo, waiting for Pop. He wanted to trade her for her father. How did he think he could get away with this? What if her father just called the police? Then again, she had a feeling that her father had already experienced just how nasty this man could be, and a call to the cops would risk Jo's life. He would probably make the trade. Still, what if her father showed up to trade himself for her? Then what? Like Martin would let her live. She knew too much. Right. Finally, she knew something.

Footfalls alerted her that he'd come back from wherever he'd gone. She'd hoped to get out of these ties and escape before he returned. But she had made zero progress.

"The secret's out, you know. You can't get away with this." Why did she bother? This guy was some sort of rocket scientist and thought bringing her here was a good idea.

He paced the greasy, exhaust-filled space. Growled, then scraped all the model cars off the shelf. And stomped on them. The space shuttle and rocket were missing.

He was losing it. Really losing it. And Jo shouldn't antagonize him, but man, she really wanted to. She wished she had her wrench, Little Jo.

"So, what was with the skull you sent to my mom?" Though she knew, might as well get the whole story if she could. "That was your *wife*. Did you kill your own wife?"

He turned and walked toward her, anger and fear twisting his face, then he relaxed. Composed himself and looked at her like he knew what she was trying to do and he wasn't falling for it. He wasn't going to tell her what she wanted to know. Wasn't going to monologue like the villain in every superhero movie.

She said nothing more. What could she say?

His pacing picked up.

Pacing, pacing, pacing.

He growled again. Dug through Pop's drawers and found duct tape.

Great. She'd done it now. She'd asked one question. Okay, maybe two. He tore off a piece and then grabbed her cheeks, pinching hard to make her cry out—but she refused to give him that satisfaction—then he plastered the tape across her closed mouth.

I will not cry.

But she really wanted to. She was ready for this to end and wished it had never started. She should have fought, but he claimed that all he had to do was press a button and Hawk would die. He might have been bluffing, but the risk was too great. She would find another way out of this.

Except . . . well, Hawk. That button—real or not—remained a risk.

Jo held on to hope that Cole had arrived at the safe house by now and had already found Hawk alive and well somewhere. He could be looking for her even now. But how would he find her? This place was probably not on his radar and would be the last place he would think to look.

"He's not coming." The man kicked the desk, then her chair.

"I'm here." Her father emerged from the front of the shop.

"Pop!" But the word was indiscernible with duct tape covering her mouth. Tears streamed from her eyes. Her father had shown up. Now they could both die together. He should have stayed away. She twisted and turned, fighting the ties.

Her father stepped into his old office, looking like his old self—the one she'd known anyway. He was in coveralls. He looked like he'd been working on building something all day. Where had he been after she'd seen him earlier in Seattle? All these questions she wanted to ask him, but she had been silenced. Could this Martin jerk give her a few moments with her father?

There was still so much more she wanted to say to him before they were both silenced forever. She forgave him the instant she saw him, believing with all her heart that all could be explained. He'd done it for her. He'd left for her sake. She knew that now.

"You wanted me. You have me. Now let her go."

"I want you, but you know what else I want. Now, where is it? Give it to me now."

Pop stepped forward. He never looked at her but kept his gaze pinned on Martin. He looked haggard—more worn-down than she'd ever seen him—and at the same time intimidating.

"Once she's free."

"You don't hold any cards, Driscoll. You never did. Give it to me now, and I'll let her walk out. But refuse me, and I'll set the bomb off. It's under her chair." Martin showed the trigger device. The same device he'd shown to her, threatening to kill Hawk. He was bluffing. There was no bomb under her.

I mean, I don't think there is.

Oh, I hope there isn't a bomb.

"You wouldn't blow yourself up," Pop said. "You killed your own wife to keep the secret that you were using substandard materials that could not hold up under the pressure, the forces of acceleration, eventually killing people. The *Liberty* blew up because of you. I warned you it would happen. Helen tried to talk you down, and you killed her."

Pop looked at Jo. "I knew that your mother was next, Jo. If Martin lost the NASA contract due to his ineptitude, he lost the company. He lost everything. He was willing to kill anyone who stood in his way. Your mother and I had no choice but to disappear. I wish I would have stayed and fought. But Martin owned the town, and he owned the chief of police, his brother."

"And you were just a lowly engineer," Martin said. "If you had stayed, you'd be dead, and I wouldn't have to be here now. But here we are."

"Yes, here we are. You're not going to blow yourself up after all the trouble you've gone to."

"You called my bluff. But I *will* shoot her in the head." Martin produced a gun, whipped it out faster than Jo could have imagined. And pointed it at her temple.

Jo half wished her father was a sniper rather than an engineer so he could just take this man out from a distance and be done with it. No one else was going to do it. No one else would save them because there was simply no place to perch and see inside this space.

Pop tossed the model space shuttle to Martin, and he caught it. "What's this?"

"Everything's inside."

All this time, the space shuttle must have had a small data card in it.

Martin smiled. "Smart man. Now, walk with me." Pointing his pistol at Pop, he gestured for him to step outside into the back.

"We had a deal. Let her go."

"Oh, I'm setting her free. And then you'll be so distraught that she died in a fire that you throw yourself off the bridge. I call that poetic justice. I should have left you to pursue your interest in infrastructures."

Pop looked at her, his face twisted in anguish. "Remember what I told you—"

"You don't get to stall." Martin fired the gun in Jo's direction. He missed, but she thought that might have been intentional.

She tried to scream against the tape on her mouth, even though she hadn't wanted to give Martin that satisfaction. Pop sent her a hard stare, looking as if he was trying to communicate with her through his eyes, then disappeared out the door with Martin.

What? What had he been going to say? *"Remember what I told you."* What did he tell me?

A small explosion resounded at the back of the office. So Martin had set up a bomb after all. One intended to burn the place down. Fire quickly spread up the walls.

I'm not going to die. I cannot die here. God, I don't want to die.

Jo hopped the chair toward the door. Even if she had to hop outside in this chair, she'd do it. In the early hours of the morning, surely someone would call the fire department, and they'd have this out in no time. They'd put it out before she got burned up, if she couldn't escape.

Right. This place would burn fast. She couldn't wait on anyone to save her.

God, help me!

The chair tipped over. Not good. This would take her longer. She pushed and tried to slide toward an escape while at the same time trying to break free of her ties. If she could break part of the chair, she could escape. Why hadn't her father, whom she knew to be supersmart, come up with a better plan? One that couldn't so easily leave them both vulnerable. Of course Troy Martin, a man who would kill his wife, had no plans to leave either of them alive.

"Remember what I told you." Well, obviously Pop couldn't just speak plainly in front of Martin, so he must have sent a cryptic message that could somehow help her out of this situation.

What was it? Time was ticking. Fire was spreading, and she hadn't gotten free yet.

The flames spread fast and the smoke thickened. The door was only a few yards away. It might as well have been ten miles.

40

Flames consumed the R&D. Cole slammed on the brakes and parked, then jumped from the Land Rover. He raced to the shop.

God, please don't let Jo be inside. But he feared she was inside with her father and that someone had set the place to burn down. In his mad search for Jo, he'd thought about her father's shop. Cole might find clues there, so he'd driven through Forestview. He'd been praying for a signal, a sign, or a clue . . . something. Anything. But he hadn't expected this—the worst-case scenario he could have imagined.

Sirens rang out with the approaching volunteer fire truck, which had gotten here entirely too late. Cole raced around the back. He kicked open part of the fence that was warping under the heat and hoped Jo had found a pocket, some place that wasn't burning. Behind the structure, flames licked the skies, and the heat prevented him from going in. He searched for a way he could get inside, while he was dying on the inside.

"Jo!" He should have told her he loved her when he had the chance.

What have I done? He shouldn't have chased after Merrick. He should have stayed with Jo.

God, please let her not be inside. Please . . .

Anguish gripped him.

His knees buckled.

"Cole?" A shout came from behind. He twisted around to see her beyond the old salvage cars and parts. She was halfway up the privacy fence. "Cole!"

She jumped down and he raced toward her, grabbed her up into his arms, and held her tight. Cole would never let her go.

I love you!

Jo pulled away and gripped his arms. "Cole, we have to go. We have to save Pop! Follow me." She raced back to the fence, and he followed.

"What's going on? What happened?" he asked.

"Help me over this."

"We could just go—" He glanced back at the part of the fence he'd kicked in, but it was on fire now. "Never mind." He clasped his hands together, and she used the extra step to pivot over the top of the fence.

Cole climbed over and dropped down into a patch of ferns.

The fire still raged, but the fire truck was here to put it out, and Cole would leave them to it. If the rain started up again, that would help. Someone had obviously used accelerants.

He couldn't have been more relieved that Jo was safe. But this wasn't over yet. She took off running in the early morning light.

"Where are we going?"

"To the bridge. Martin is trying to make it look like I died in the fire and that Pop was so distraught he threw himself from the bridge."

"That old bridge."

"What other bridge would I be talking about? We have to hurry. They could already be there by now."

He'd never seen Jo run so fast. Cole kept up with her, followed her. She knew the way. He had to focus on avoiding trip hazards in the dense foliage. He could barely see as it was.

Jo didn't shout or call out after her father. Which was good. If Martin had a gun on him and tried to force him over the bridge, their silent approach would be the advantage they needed. The rush of the river grew louder as they drew near.

Jo suddenly stopped and pressed behind a tree. Breathing hard, she tugged him with her. "They're on the bridge. Cole, you have to take a shot. You have to take Martin down before he kills Pop."

"I thought you said he would try to force him off the bridge."

"He'll try, but Pop isn't going to jump. He wants the bullet to prove that he didn't commit suicide, that someone shot him, so there's an investigation into his death that will lead to Martin."

"Stay here." Cole crept forward, formulating the best way to get Ransom off that bridge and safely away from Martin. The river beneath the decommissioned bridge covered the sounds as he moved.

But neither could he hear the exchange between Jo's father and Martin. He didn't have a rifle with a scope, and it was far too dark for him to try to shoot the gun out of Martin's hands. But he didn't want to kill the man who had so much to answer for.

Cole got up on the bridge behind Martin. "Put the gun down, Martin. It's over."

"Stay out of this," Ransom said. "This is between Troy

and me now. Step off the bridge. I want Troy to know first-hand what it feels like when your life is being held up by substandard materials and engineering and too many careless mistakes."

Gunfire rang out at the same moment Ransom dodged the bullet Martin intended for him. Ransom moved from the bridge and hid.

Cole could not shoot someone in the back. "Drop the weapon, Martin."

Cole rushed forward.

"Cole, don't," Jo said behind him, her voice shaking. "Just step off the bridge. Come back to me."

"Jo, please. Stay back. It's too dangerous." What was she thinking?

"You're in imminent danger if you stay on that bridge."

Ransom appeared on the far side, but he hadn't stepped back on the bridge.

No way was Cole allowing Troy Martin to walk away. Cole closed the distance to Martin, who had put his gun down and lifted his hands up. He expected this guy to fight tooth and nail for his survival. After all, he'd committed heinous crimes to save himself. Cautiously, he approached, prepared for anything. Martin turned, an evil smirk on his face. He held a detonator in his hand.

"I'd rather die than let you take me."

Cole didn't believe that for one second. He'd destroyed too many lives to save his own skin.

But Martin pressed the trigger in his hand. An explosion rocked the bridge, destroying the north end. A loud crack resounded, and the boards beneath him shuddered. Cole braced for the rest as he looked down.

A horrific sound met Cole's ears as the bridge crumbled beneath both him and Martin. He tried to grab Martin, but the man twisted free at the same moment Cole grabbed at anything that wasn't crumbling and falling beneath him.

Jo screamed. She'd come out onto the bridge too and now grappled with the rickety beams, barely hanging on.

"Get off the bridge, Jo." This from Ransom Driscoll on the other side. "This bridge isn't stable. You've always known that. I warned you never to get on it. Now, please, just focus on getting off. Both of you."

Cole glanced down at the rushing river. "I can't let him get away."

"Cole, you can't go after him," Jo begged.

"It wouldn't be the first time this week that I've jumped into the water to save someone." Yeah, and it had been a near miracle that he'd survived. But he would do it again if necessary.

"Son, he isn't worth saving. You can't save him anyway. Now I'm begging you to save my daughter. I'll go after Martin. If he's still alive, he's mine." To Jo, Ransom said, "Get off the bridge, Jo. I'm telling you right now."

41

The bridge shifted as more of the supporting beams that held it up collapsed. Jo's grip slipped, and she held on with one hand now. Moisture bloomed on her palms. *I don't want to die because of this bridge.*

All this time Pop had taken her to this bridge, he hadn't been contemplating how to fix it. Had he been contemplating the possibility of this moment when he would face off with his enemy?

"Jo, hang on. I'm coming." Cole gasped out the words.

She reached up and pulled herself forward. "I've got it. I've got it. Just . . . you get off this bridge. Don't you dare go after him. Pop is right." She pulled herself farther, gaining traction with her feet, and glanced back at Cole. He was still hanging precariously. How could she reach him? Her heart might just break at that look on his face.

"Come on, Cole. You can do this. Pop is right too. That river has already taken Martin out to the ocean."

Could he survive that? Only God knew.

She finally climbed up onto the ridge and off the bridge. Heart pounding, limbs shaking, she sat up. "Cole!"

He wasn't going to make it. This wasn't right. She'd found him on that beach a year ago, and she'd been able to save him then. But the rail from which he hung wasn't going to last much longer. She couldn't get to him. He couldn't get to her.

The metal twisted and Cole dropped farther, hanging precariously. Jo held back a yelp. Her pulse skyrocketed. She couldn't lose this man.

Despite the twisting railing, Cole started up, climbing toward her. Jo could meet him halfway. She had to help him. If she could just grip one of his hands *and* pull him onto the remaining structure. She inched toward him, now fully on the bridge again.

"What are you doing, Jo?" Pop called from across the bridge. "What's left of the bridge isn't going to hold you both."

Finally, she lay flat and gripped Cole's hand.

"He's right, you know," Cole said. "You shouldn't be out here."

Even so, Cole squeezed her hand and used it to maneuver toward the part of the bridge that remained intact though still unstable, crawling from where he hung over the rushing Pulsap River, which flowed right into the ocean only a mile or so away.

Breathing hard, Cole climbed onto the bridge and turned onto his back to catch his breath.

Jo grabbed his hand. "Let's get off this bridge."

He rolled to his knees to climb to his feet.

The bridge shuddered and collapsed beneath them. Jo and Cole tumbled toward the river, along with chunks of the old bridge. Pop called after them.

Jo screamed. Heart pounding, she prayed. *Jesus, Jesus, Jesus!* And that they would hit water and miss the rocks.

And above her, Pop stood looking down from the ledge, anguish on his features.

Fear gripped her. Tried to paralyze her. She'd already faced certain death in the fire. Had she survived that only to perish in the river?

The river current would be vicious. She had to prepare for that. Fighting it through flailing would only increase the risk of dying. She had no time to be afraid. Jo dragged in a breath before she hit the icy cold water. She plunged deep, the shock engulfing her. Beneath the surface, the river twisted her body, tumbling her around, over and over. She fought to get to the surface as the current swept her away.

Finally, she breached the surface and frantically looked around to get a read on her surroundings. Any big threats coming up, above and beyond the river itself. She looked for Cole.

"Cole!" Jo shouted.

She had to stop fighting the river and let the current carry her. Jo turned flat onto her back, her feet pointed downstream. A violent undercurrent would drag her under. She had to find a calmer part of the river and then she could swim at a forty-five-degree angle toward the riverbank, except this was a canyon that would take her all the way to the ocean and spit her out.

And the river never slowed.

Calm never happened.

She'd be washed out to the Pacific. Her limbs were already growing numb.

"Jo!" Cole appeared near her, shouting over the rapids. "We can do this. This will open up into an estuary. Swim out of it. Can you do that?"

"Yes!" *Can you?*

The river grew wider and more brackish toward the ocean. Only problem was the south side of the river remained an unbreachable ledge, but the north bank opened up. Jo's limbs were so numb, she couldn't even be sure she was still swimming as Cole urged her forward.

"We can do this," he said. "Come on."

Finally they crawled up onto a sandbar. A little bit farther, they would reach the shore.

Jo rolled onto her back, much like Cole had done on the bridge. The misting rain made sure she stayed wet after crawling from the river. "We have to get out of this, Cole. We both probably have hypothermia. The wind isn't helping."

"Okay," he said. "Give me a minute."

"How did you know?" she asked.

"How did I know what?"

"Where to find me?"

"I didn't. But I wasn't going to sit at the house and do nothing, so I started searching. Detective Sanders put out an APB and closed the roads. Troy Martin only had so many ways out of the Olympic Peninsula. I thought about the R&D and that maybe there was a clue there. I saw it burning as soon as I steered through Forestview. It was a hunch, nothing else, but then the fire sealed it for me. I knew he must have taken you there so he could wait for your father at his old shop. There must have been something there he wanted."

"Pop's die-cast collection. He gave Martin the space shuttle. My guess is that it had a small data drive in it. The die-cast models saved my life."

She thought back to that moment in the shop when Martin had escorted Pop out and left her to burn. Pop had given her his last words to remember something he'd said.

Her body against the concrete, she was face-to-face with those ridiculous model cars. Some crushed underfoot by a madman. Then she knew what Pop wanted her to remember. Something he'd said referencing the model cars. *"The smallest details can have the biggest impact."* That was it, then. That phrase defined his life over the last thirty years. Those small details had been ignored and caused a disaster. And that phrase had defined her life, her way out of the burning shop. She'd been able to cut off her ties with the sharp edge of the smashed die-cast Lamborghini.

Cole started to get to his feet, yanking Jo's attention back to their sandbar.

"I don't believe it," he said.

"What?"

"He's alive. He made it."

Jo rolled to look in the direction Cole stared. "That's him limping away, isn't it?"

"I can't let him get away, Jo."

Cole started, but she grabbed him and wouldn't let him go. "He won't get away, Cole."

He stared at her long and hard and then dropped to his knees next to her. "You're right. Now that the cops know who's to blame, there's nowhere he can hide. I just . . . I want you to be free to live your life. Free . . . to love."

She sat up. "Thank you for that. Thank you. I'm free now, but ask me what I want. Go ahead."

He drew closer to her, his face so near. Anguish filled his features. A gust of wind caused the sand to pelt his face, and he squinted to look at her. "I'm almost afraid to ask. But . . . what do you want, Jo?"

"I need to know, Cole. What *else* were you going to tell me when you explained about being away for so long? You never finished."

"I should have," he said. "I don't know why I held back. I love you, Jo. It's as simple as that. I love you."

That was all she wanted to hear. "I love you too. Please don't ever leave me again."

He quickly grabbed her up into his arms and kissed her thoroughly, warming her up. Forget hypothermia. After kissing her breathless, he released her. "I'm never leaving you, Jo. I think I loved you the first moment I saw you coming to my rescue."

42

Whop, whop, whop.

Cole held on to Jo and turned to look north, where a helicopter landed. Hawk jumped out, along with Detective Sanders and two deputies. Hawk wasn't flying that thing with a concussion, was he?

Interesting. Who'd given them the heads-up? His arm around Jo, they walked along the sandbar until they were near the water. "I really hate having to get wet again, but we're not going to make the beach without going through the water. At least we have a ride back."

He suspected that Hawk had some blankets in that bird as well.

"You ready?"

"As I'll ever be."

Holding Jo's hand, Cole walked with her through the thigh-deep water to the shore. The icy cold shocked him again, but he could weather any storm, any kind of shock or dangerous waters, as long as he had Jo by his side.

A vehicle appeared on the beach, heading from the north. Jo's Land Rover? "What? Who's driving—"

"Pop. He must have raced back to the shop. I don't know how he crossed the river, but I bet he was the one to call for help too. Oh, I bet I know. He probably was able to maneuver a tree trunk via some kind of leverage and then crossed. That sounds like him. But how did he get my Land Rover?"

"I took your Land Rover to the shop. Left the keys inside in my panic. Come on." Cole picked up the pace, and the Land Rover stopped near them.

Cole opened up the back to climb in, expecting Jo to get in the front with her father, but she climbed into the back with him.

"I have the heat cranked up," Ransom said.

Hawk hiked toward them, and Cole lowered the window.

"We got him." He peered into the vehicle at Ransom. "You're planning on hanging around, aren't you? You have a lot of questions to answer."

"Sure. I only meant to protect Jo."

Hawk jogged back to the helicopter where they were hauling Troy Martin. Hawk wasn't even an aerial deputy anymore, but his skills and his bird obviously came in handy.

"Are you in trouble, Pop? Did you commit a crime?" Jo asked.

"Not as far as I know. Look, Jo, I can't tell you how sorry I am about everything."

Cole spoke up. "Why don't we talk about this back at—"

"The lodge. Cedar Trails Lodge. I just want to be back with friends and family. I consider everyone at the lodge my family."

"Cedar Trails Lodge it is." Ransom steered them along a forest road and then finally turned onto the road to Cedar Trails Lodge.

Jo squeezed Cole's hand and then got out of the vehicle. Remi was waiting and hugged Jo, then dragged her inside her personal cabin. Cole and Ransom followed. Remi wrapped them each in a thick blanket.

A fire was going in the fireplace, and they had the choice of drinking hot apple cider, hot chocolate, tea, or coffee. Remi was the best hostess, but after all, she ran a lodge.

Cole settled on the sofa next to Jo and wrapped his arm around her shoulders. She gripped a mug of coffee in her hands. It was over, finally over. But he could tell by Jo's pained expression she wasn't done.

"You'll have to tell the police everything, Pop. You know that. But I want to hear it first. You owe that to me, don't you think?"

Ransom Driscoll hung his head. "It's a long and complicated story. I told you some of it in the shop, just in case that was my last chance. Your mother and I, and Mason, worked with Troy Martin. He was the founder and owner of Resonant, which employed most of the small town of Griffin, Nevada. Your mother and I were two of fifty or so engineers. Resonant was one of hundreds of NASA contractors. We developed and supplied only a few of the more than 2.5 million parts for the *Liberty* shuttle. Even today, the orbiters are considered the most complex flying machines ever to be built. But that's beside the point. Myrna was best friends with Helen Martin."

Jo sat forward, and Cole dropped his arm. He wasn't entirely sure this was the best way for Jo to learn everything, but it wasn't his place to stand in the way. And they needed answers.

"I was project manager, and I repeatedly tried to tell Troy we had issues. Big issues. But he refused to listen. Myrna . . . she should never have told Helen, but she thought maybe Helen could talk sense into her husband. But NASA was already threatening to use other contractors, and Troy didn't want to lose his company. Not to mention destroy an entire town, should Resonant lose the NASA contract."

"That's a lot of pressure," Cole said. "On all of you."

"Myrna knew that Helen was going to confront him. Then . . . she went missing."

"And you suspected that he killed her over the information?"

"I didn't suspect it. I knew. I confronted him." Ransom got up and paced, the anger and incredulity pouring from him.

Next to Cole, Jo shivered. "Maybe this isn't the best time to talk," Cole said.

"I want to hear everything," Jo said. "I need to know why my mother is dead."

"I confronted him about Helen, and he said it was an accident. He wouldn't want Myrna to have an accident either, which was his way of threatening her. And just like that, I knew that I couldn't win. Troy Martin had friends. His brother was police chief."

"But you could have gone over his head. Directly to NASA."

"I had already tried. You have no idea the bureaucracy and red tape involved when you're talking so many contractors, so many people under pressure to perform or else the government will snatch away the funds—billions of dollars. What was my life worth? Or Myrna's, if even his own wife's life held no value to him? So we made a decision. Myrna and I. Mason had been the one to document everything, and he simply handed it over to me and kept his head down. Myrna and I had to disappear. Just fall off the face of the earth. We knew that Troy would find a way to make each of us accidentally disappear if we remained."

Ransom looked at Jo with tears in his eyes. "So we did. We

each left in a manner that wouldn't leave friends questioning our disappearance, like Helen's. But Mason remained working for Resonant, even after it became Gemini, for a few more years, believing himself safe. Considering he was targeted and murdered, I believe he must have started to doubt his safety, even years later. Maybe he was pressured into tracking Myrna down. Why else would he end up in Michigan? I'm theorizing, of course.

"Regardless, I never saw her again. Still, I secretly kept up with her. I knew that she'd gone to Michigan and that she met and married Dale Cattrel, and I guess pretty quickly, to cover up that she was already pregnant. I didn't know she was pregnant, and maybe she didn't either when we parted ways. Marrying Dale also meant she would have a new name and a new life. She was scared and wanted to protect you. I didn't know about you, Jo. Until that day at the funeral, and then I was afraid that even being there, I had caused trouble. I know now that her death wasn't an accident. She was killed to draw me out. But at first, after I found you, I thought I could keep you safe here in Hidden Bay."

"And the bomb?" Cole asked.

"I got a call from Troy's hitman, warning me just how close he could get to you. Troy wanted me, and he was using you to get to me. I'm so sorry, Jo. I had hoped that I had left the area before anything could happen to you. Two weeks ago, I thought I'd seen Troy driving through town. I wasn't sure if I was imagining it, but I figured that eventually he would find me. That's when I had lunch with Jim Jordan at AT and learned that he had sold me out. Six months ago, he'd brought his grandkids out to Cedar Trails to see the rocky beaches, and his car had trouble. He brought it to the shop and recognized me. I asked him not to share my location with anyone.

But who was I kidding? There was no going back from that. He didn't last six months before giving me up. Jim claimed Troy said he just wanted to reconnect with his 'old friend,' but Jim knew I'd left under the worst kind of circumstances. Troy needed to make sure everyone he considered a loose thread was dead. I was the last one he needed to silence."

"Why didn't you tell me everything? You could have told me."

"No, I couldn't. If I could have somehow persisted and found the right person to listen, though, those *Liberty* astronauts might still be alive today." Ransom paced again. "The truth will come out now. Finally."

"But wait," Jo said. "Didn't you give Troy the space shuttle with a flash drive in it?"

"I gave him a space shuttle with an empty drive. Are you kidding? The power has always been in the solid rocket boosters." Ransom held up the model rocket booster he pulled from his pocket. "I've already uploaded everything, and even now, Senator Goodman, a ranking member of the United States House Committee on Science, Space, and Technology, is reviewing the data. The senator's niece died on the *Liberty*."

"But what about you, Pop?" Jo stood and moved to him. Wrapped her arms around him. "I don't want to lose you. What if you get in trouble for withholding this information?"

"We'll see where the dominoes fall. As far as I'm concerned, I did the right thing at the time—I saved your mother's life. Your life. I don't know how he finally found her, and then Mason. But he's going away for a long time. That's all I care about. That, and for you to live a full life. Get married. Have a family of your own, free of this hidden burden."

A knock came at the door and Remi opened it. Detective Sanders entered, along with Hawk, followed by WSP Detective Hargrove.

"It's time for me to go," Ransom said. "I love you, Jo. I'll be in touch soon."

43

A month later, Jo stood on the beach during low tide and looked up at a calm night sky. Next time she might drag Pop's telescope out here, and she hoped he could join her when he returned from the congressional hearings. In this low-light place on the wilderness coast, she could see the stars so clearly. Even the Milky Way.

A rarity, really, but they were fast approaching the end of the rainy season, and tonight she wanted to walk the beach and look up at the stars.

Space.

Pop had been involved in space travel in the early years. She blinked back the sudden tears. He was busy answering questions back in DC, and this whole situation reminded her of Cole, when he left to answer questions. But the difference was her father was emailing and texting and talking to her daily to let her know how it was going. He was staying in touch. She'd forgiven him for his disappearing act. She thought she might also have forgiven Cole for his disappearing act because he'd come back and given her an explanation.

He'd come back so he could end her reason for hiding.

So, now that she'd hired a company to clean up what remained of Spruce Hollow, Jo had a decision to make. Was she staying here, in the place she'd chosen to hide? Or, with her newfound freedom, did she want to travel or move somewhere else? She didn't have to look over her shoulder anymore.

And maybe she could even return to forensic art and work to put bad guys behind bars. All the decisions that came with finally being truly free. One thing for certain, one thing she knew—no matter where she landed, she wanted Cole by her side.

A flashlight in the distance drew her gaze around.

"Jo?" Cole called out.

"Turn that light off. I'm looking at the stars." He never came onto the beach with her, so his appearance surprised her.

He approached and flicked off the light. "I'm glad I found you. Why'd you leave?"

"You seemed to be having such a good time talking to Brad about some fishing trip to Canada."

He waved his hand. "I'm not going to Canada. I wanted to get to know him. He seems like a nice guy."

"I know what you were doing. You wanted to find out if he was interested in me."

"And he is."

"What?" She swung her face around. "He is not."

"Well, maybe not anymore."

"What did you say? What did you tell him?"

"I didn't have to say anything. He likes you but said he realizes now that I'm into you, and he told me that he could tell you were into *me*. Did you think he was making your favorite dishes just for the fun of it?"

She turned her gaze back to the stars. "Well, yeah, I guess

I hadn't thought of it. But as for you being into me, is that true?"

"You know it is." He wrapped his arm around her waist. She laid her head on his shoulder.

He kissed the top of her head. "It's a beautiful night, isn't it?"

"The best." Jo couldn't remember the last time she'd felt so much at peace. The last several years, fear had always been just one glance over her shoulder.

And now, she only had one minor fear . . . but the smallest details could have the biggest impact.

"What are you going to do now, Cole?" He'd never said anything more than that he loved her. And she believed him. But what did that look like coming from this guy who could blend in and disappear?

Cole turned her to face him, and a rogue wave rushed up and around their ankles, but she barely felt it. When he leaned in, he brushed the hair from her cheek, then captured her lips in a kiss that was anything but hesitant. Jo let him sweep her away until she was floating, weightless and untethered.

Then he slowly ended the kiss much too soon.

"Well?" she asked. "What are you going to do now?"

"Oh, I thought I answered you. I'm going to kiss you and keep kissing you. That's all I have planned. Is that okay with you? What are you going to do now, Jo? Are you going to stay with me, you know, like maybe for a lifetime?"

Her heart jumped. "What do you mean?"

"Let me be clear. Here, under the stars, under the Milky Way, even though I don't have a ring, I'm asking you to marry me. If it's too much too soon, I understand. But for my part, I knew you were the one for me the first time I saw you on the beach. This beach. Why do you think I'm out here? I'm going to learn to love this place as much as you do because I love you. I'd do anything for you."

A shooting star streaked across the sky and then it was gone. A small detail, but it had an impact, kind of like a sign. She didn't need a sign to know she would say yes. "Did you see that?" she asked.

"I only see you, Jo. I'm still waiting on your answer."

Jo stood on her toes and kissed him until he didn't need words to know her answer.

Author's Note

Thank you for reading *Perilous Tides*! I've had so much fun diving deep into this story to bring to life some of the amazing geography of the Olympic Peninsula while creating what I hope you found to be a gripping tale of intrigue. I love showcasing God's creation and building high-stakes stories in unexpected landscapes. I also love to give my readers an unpredictable plot, which is hard to do these days!

As I began writing this story, the whistleblower theme kept rolling around in my mind, and I also knew I wanted to look for a premise related to aerospace. I came across an article about whistleblowers and the *Challenger* orbiter. Bingo. I then read *Challenger: A True Story of Heroism and Disaster on the Edge of Space* by Adam Higginbotham, a 570-page tome about the many facets of the space industry, NASA and its hundreds of contractors, the personal lives of astronauts, and the details behind the engineering of the "most complex flying machine ever built." The author has a way with words that pulled me into this tragic tale, and at some point, I actually cried. I felt like I knew the astronauts so well. If you're old enough, you remember both the *Challenger* and *Columbia* disasters. I lived near Tyler when the *Columbia* disintegrated over the skies of East Texas. My entire steel-framed house shook with multiple sonic booms.

As I read, I was overwhelmed with information that I couldn't possibly include in *Perilous Tides*. Aren't you glad? While reading, I continued writing and created a fictional orbiter and fictional NASA contractors. I wasn't sure that what I intended to occur in my novel was something that had actually occurred with the space shuttle tragedies. I continued to read, hoping that I would find that scenario to lend credibility to my fictional version, though if I never found it, I would have kept my story. It's fiction! But I found what I was looking for.

An engineer who became a whistleblower *feared* for his life. That information helped me to continue to write with confidence because, yeah, this could happen. I hope you'll join me on the next great adventure in the Hidden Bay series!

Read on for
a sneak peek
at the final book in the

Hidden Bay

series

Available February 2026

1

It is not down on any map; true places never are.

Herman Melville, *Moby-Dick*

The sea never gives back what it claims . . ."
Her father's voice echoed through her thoughts, gritty and sharp—like the wind whipping around her and the salt cutting into her cheeks. Cressida Valentine stepped back inside the wheelhouse where Captain Everett "Salty" Malloy stood at the helm of the *Mariner's Gambit*—an older-than-time fishing trawler.

Next to Malloy, she curled her fingers around the binoculars and peered at the dense marine fog chasing the vessel along the Washington coast. Uneasiness pressed down on her as she scanned the mist-veiled horizon. Her father had spent his life chasing secrets buried in waters too deep and too dark to trust.

And here I am, chasing them too.

Out of the white rolling cloud, a speedboat emerged, and

329

it headed straight for the *Mariner's Gambit*, startling her. "Looks like someone's coming toward us," she said.

"Let me see those." Malloy took the binoculars she offered—they were his, after all—and peered through.

Then he swore under his breath. Gave her an apologetic look. "Sorry."

His reaction wasn't a good sign. "Who is it? What's going on?"

Captain Malloy handed the binoculars back, then stepped to the helm. Despite the early morning cold, sweat beaded his temples, his knuckles white on the wheel. A man on a mission to escape?

"Doesn't matter." The tension in his jaw said otherwise.

"What do they want?"

He didn't answer.

Not good enough. Cressida grabbed his arm. "Captain—"

"Not now." He shoved the throttle forward, and the *Mariner's Gambit* groaned as it accelerated, slicing through the swells. "I need to get away from them."

"In this?" She bit her lip, regretting the question. They'd traveled between five and ten knots around the Olympic Peninsula from Port Angeles because fishing trawlers were built for endurance, not speed, Malloy had informed her.

Granted, the old trawler had been updated, boasting modern electronics and "smart" instruments on the dashboard. A necessity, Malloy had told her, since he and his thirty-something son, Dax, were the only ones to crew the sixty-five-foot fishing and charter-excursions vessel.

He didn't respond to her comment that bordered on an insult.

"Again, why is that boat headed straight for us?" She peered through the binoculars again, hoping to see if Malloy had put more distance between them.

"I don't want to find out." He suddenly turned the wheel,

and the boat veered hard to port, into a fifteen-foot swell, throwing her sideways against the wall. She lost sight of the pursuers.

"This can't be happening," she whispered.

But it was.

She wanted to trust Malloy, to believe him, but he wasn't making it easy.

Her mind raced through the possible scenarios and outcomes—the good and the bad. When the trawler suddenly decelerated and the rumble of motors dimmed, Cressida looked out at the fast-moving fog. "We're slowing down?"

"They gave up the chase."

"I'm impressed. I didn't think the trawler had enough speed to escape."

"I only had to beat them to Hidden Bay. They wouldn't have followed me in. But that's not what happened."

The roar of another engine sliced through the chaos. Cressida turned toward the horizon—and froze. A massive Coast Guard cutter loomed in the distance, its white hull cutting through the waves. Relief washed over her, so sudden it left her knees weak.

Malloy exhaled sharply. "The *Kraken*."

"I'm sorry . . . what?" Visions of a mythical creature rising out of the ocean depths, long tentacles flailing, emerged in her mind.

"That's what they call her—the *Kraken*." The ghost of a grin tugged at the corner of Malloy's mouth. "And she's on our side."

Cressida clutched the railing on the wall as the cutter closed in, chasing their pursuers into the eerie fog. Over the last year, she'd traveled the world to research and finish her deceased father's book about shipwrecks, ghost ships, and the maritime folklore surrounding them.

Dad had been on the *Mariner's Gambit* too, Captain Malloy at the helm, giving him a tour of the Washington coast. That's why Cressida had been willing to pay Malloy the ridiculous amount to charter her out of Port Angeles, through the Strait of Juan de Fuca, then down the stunning rocky coast to Hidden Bay. She'd wanted to take the same path Dad had taken before he suddenly cut his research trip short. He'd traveled to DC for an alleged emergency, the details of which he conveniently left out of his journal notes. He hadn't returned to finish his research.

Or his book.

With thoughts of her father's untimely death, her heart edged into a dark place, which she couldn't afford if she was going to finish Dad's manuscript.

"Captain Malloy. I paid you well for this service. I need to know what is really going on. Your pursuers were obviously known by the authorities or else they wouldn't have chased them."

He grunted in reply. A nonanswer. Fine. She got up and took in the scene with his binoculars again, searching for the Coast Guard cutter, but both vessels had disappeared into the fog, which was now rapidly gaining on the *Mariner's Gambit*.

By tomorrow, she'd be in Hidden Bay. Her maritime historian father had already completed most of the research, but Cressida had to go to each place and look for herself because she couldn't write the book he'd wanted to write without personally experiencing the atmosphere of each location where various sunken shipwrecks remained. Of the three million sunken ships, her father had chosen a select few. In his manuscript, he'd focused, too, on ghost ships—those vessels floating aimlessly on the ocean, the crew mysteriously lost.

All the vessels had one thing in common—maritime legend that fascinated her father.

This last vessel was a more recent ghost ship—*Specter's Bounty*. She'd yet to understand the legend because Dad hadn't finished his research, so it made sense for her to travel to Hidden Bay to learn more.

For this charter, she'd requested that Captain Malloy take her to Cape Disappointment at the mouth of the Columbia River—which was around a hundred nautical miles south of Hidden Bay—then return to Hidden Bay, where she would release the charter. Her trip on the *Mariner's Gambit* was almost over. On one hand, she would be relieved to finally be at her last destination. On the other hand, she hadn't gotten much out of this man who had spent time with her father.

The threat of the chase over, she relaxed, though maybe she shouldn't have. "Now that's out of the way, we can get back to the tour."

Another grunt. "I'm cutting the trip short."

"What? Why?" She looked out the window and realized they were approaching the bay, not just traveling past on their way south.

"It's not safe. Told you I didn't want to take more than two days from the start. I agreed to this for your father's sake. I was sorry to learn that he's gone." His tone sounded more ominous than she'd heard from him.

Suddenly, the atmosphere in the wheelhouse had shifted.

"And I had hoped you could tell me more."

"I told you all I could."

What did that mean? That he knew more and was holding back? Or that he'd told her everything? She'd learned that too many questions shut him down.

He continued navigating toward the marina but stopped and dropped anchor out in the bay. "The pier isn't going to work. We'll take the skiff."

"So that's it?" she asked. "You're dropping me off here?"

"This is Hidden Bay. Your destination." He squinted. "I'm not leaving you empty-handed."

"How's that?"

"See that bunch of boats out in the middle of the bay? They call themselves pirates."

He couldn't be serious. "And why would I want to talk to pirates?"

He snorted a laugh. "They're not *real* pirates. That's just what they call themselves. They're liveaboards." Again, he gestured at a group of vessels sprawled out in the middle of the bay, far from the actual marina and dock. "You'll want to talk to Diggins, specifically."

Diggins?

"Just a heads-up in case you were expecting to see fancy yachts instead of derelict boats. This particular group can't afford to live on land, so they live in the water. They were anchored in Puget Sound, but some of them got run off and moved to Hidden Bay, where they're welcome to stay."

"Why are you referring me to this Diggins?"

"You asked about the *Specter's Bounty*."

"And you didn't know anything."

"Didn't say I didn't know anything. I said I hadn't seen it. And if I had, the Coast Guard would have too, and ended the story."

"What *do* you know, then?"

"I know you should talk to Diggins."

"Did you send my father to Diggins?"

"He didn't ask about the *Specter's Bounty*. He didn't ask anything. Mostly let me talk."

"And you don't talk much."

He lifted a shoulder, his face blank. Yeah, he was holding back.

Dad had worked in a museum for a reason. He wasn't an investigative reporter like Cressida before she'd been blacklisted from working as such, thanks to her mother. How had Dad learned so much for his book?

"Can you tell me—was it real or not? Or is it just a ghost story?" Her job was to get as many answers from the locals as possible. She wasn't letting Malloy go without asking.

"I sound like a broken record, but I don't know."

His son, Dax, was sweeping the deck and gave a brief glance up at the wheelhouse. He'd avoided her, and now his father was being short with her. Rude, even. That boat racing toward them had clearly left him unsettled.

Cressida didn't like the idea of taking the skiff—the water looked pretty rough, even in the bay. Regardless, in her cabin, she gathered her things—a duffel, laptop case, and her shoulder bag—then met Malloy and Dax above deck. Her items were lowered into the skiff, and then she descended the ladder and settled in the much smaller vessel. On the deck, Dax crossed his arms and watched her. She looked away, toward the small marina and shoreline.

Settled in the boat, Malloy turned on the motor with a deep frown, looking nothing like the smiling fifty-something man who'd been only too happy to take her money. Once at the pier, he tied off the small boat. "I'll walk you to the dock. This is where I dropped your father," he said.

"Any last words that he said to you?" She had to give it one last try.

His only response was the familiar grunt as he assisted her off the boat and onto the pier and handed off her things. Next to her, he lumbered across the rickety boards, passing between a few other fishing vessels and a couple of older cruisers. The planks clanked as she and Malloy walked side by side up what looked like a recently rebuilt dock. Off to the right, she took in the Bayfront Chandlery, which looked like it also offered groceries, and next to that was a dilapidated warehouse. Weirdly, no town had built up around the marina like one would expect. On the other side of the chandlery, she spotted a partially collapsed dock and a burned-out structure.

The fog had caught up with them and hovered around the older dock, wrapping around the structure destroyed by fire and turning it into an eerie setting worthy of a chilling horror flick. Foreboding goose bumps crept over her skin. This was her last stop on her research trip. She wouldn't be chased away by today's earlier scare or tales of a ghost ship and its missing crew.

At the end of the pier, she stopped and faced Malloy. "How do I contact Diggins when he lives out on the water?"

"Mavis at the chandlery can help you." He leaned in. "I wasn't joking when I said it's not safe."

Before Cressida could process his words or ask him a question that he probably wouldn't answer, he turned and walked away. Still, he called over his shoulder, "Watch your back."

Creepy much? She watched him hurry back to his boat then head out to the bigger trawler anchored in the bay. Good riddance. Adjusting her duffel, laptop case, and sling bag, she glanced at her surroundings.

So this is Hidden Bay.

A sandy and rocky beach for about a hundred yards and then high cliffs that spread a few miles in either direction, carving out a crescent-shaped bay of several miles. She made her way to the Bayfront Chandlery, but Mavis wasn't available. Cressida's cell got no bars, and she wasn't even sure if a rideshare was available here. A young female clerk named Kit assisted Cressida and called for a ride to pick her up here and then take her to the Cedar Trails Lodge, where she wasn't due until tomorrow night. She could sleep in the lobby if she had to. She asked the clerk to store her duffel and computer case so she could walk the beach. However, she kept her shoulder bag containing her wallet with her.

On the beach in the early morning hours, she took in what promised to be an indescribable setting, but with the fog growing thick and suffocating, she couldn't see much—only a few people strolling the beach. While the bay water was relatively calm, beyond the crescent edges, the ocean violently bashed the rocks on the shore.

She didn't want to get too far from the marina, so she perched on a rock to relax and listen to the waves. Maybe she couldn't see everything, but the sounds were calming.

It was too quiet.

Her father's voice echoed once again in her head. *"It's not the storms that sink sailors, it's the calm before them."* A reminder that she shouldn't let her guard down.

Footfalls sounded behind her, approaching too fast and close. She jerked around. "What are you—"

A man gripped her wrist and twisted her arm behind her. He covered her mouth before she could scream. She tried the maneuvers she'd learned, techniques to free herself if she was ever attacked, but against the thick, ropy muscles on this man twice her size and weight, her defensive skills did nothing.

Pain ignited in her head when he grabbed her hair and dragged her out into the ocean, then dunked her. Could no one on the beach see what was happening? Had the fog interfered?

Her heart pounded violently, consuming what little oxygen she'd gulped into her lungs before going into the salty, cold ocean. She tried to punch his vulnerable parts, but his arms were so long, he prevented her from reaching.

Play dead.

Just . . . be dead. She fought until she thought she might actually suck in the seawater. Her lungs burned, then she gave up as if dead.

And floated.

Letting the ocean take her, she drifted along with the waves washing in, then back out, then in again. Salt burned her eyes as she peered underwater, searching . . .

His boots kicked up sand. He was still there. A few more heartbeats and she would die if she didn't breathe.

She had no choice.

She lifted her head to the side, sucked in oxygen, then once again let the ocean carry her. Her body drifted with the current, back and forth, slowly toward the shore, until she washed up onto the beach.

Like a dead body.

Play dead. Let him think she'd drowned. Had this ever worked before? If he wanted her dead, he could have shot her, but why do that when she could just drown and that would be the end of her story? No investigation required.

Limbs numb with cold, pebbles cutting into her palms and arms, she crawled forward on the wet sand. Gut and lungs heaving, Cressida coughed up brackish seawater, then she let herself remain in the sand, unmoving.

Tears leaked from her eyes to mingle with the grit and salt water clinging to her face. Grateful that the ocean had spit her onto the beach, she couldn't fight back the pure terror still racing through her.

Let him believe she was gone. Let the danger be gone.

Acknowledgments

I want to thank all the amazing people who keep me going through the novel-writing process.

The writing life truly is about the friends you make along the way. My writing buddies listen to me vent about the struggles with my plot or a stubborn character, and they listen to me rant about the lack of sleep or my looming deadline. They help me brainstorm out of a corner with no obvious escape. I couldn't do it without you, Susan, Lisa, Shannon, Sharon, Chawna, Michelle, and so many others!

The same is true of my family. To my children—I aspired to become published while you were growing up, and I hope that inspires you to pursue your dreams. To my husband, Dan—you believed in me, encouraging me to attend conferences when we didn't have "two dimes to rub together," if you'll allow me that cliché. I wouldn't be here without you!

A big thanks to my law enforcement expert—Wesley Harris! You're always so quick to give me detailed information about procedural stuff and my characters' actions and reactions. If mistakes are found, these are all on me!

My Revell publishing team—can I just say you guys are

the absolute best! I had the great honor and privilege of having breakfast with you, Rachel McRae, while working on this book. Rachel, you are such a blessing to me and a real gem. I'm so grateful to have you as my editor! Brianne Dekker, you've been an amazing addition to my team! Karen Steele, you always do the best job getting my books out there in the public eye. Art director Laura Klynstra—thanks to you, Revell has the absolute best covers in the publishing world!

To my literary agent, Steve Laube—I'm so grateful you saw something in me fourteen years ago. Sometimes I still can't fathom that the best agent in Christian publishing signed me!

To Jesus—all I am is because of you!

Elizabeth Goddard is the *USA Today* bestselling and Christy Award–winning author of more than sixty novels, including *Cold Light of Day* and *Shadows at Dusk*, as well as the Rocky Mountain Courage and Uncommon Justice series. Her books have sold more than 1.5 million copies. She is a Carol Award and Reader's Choice Award winner and a Daphne du Maurier Award and HOLT Medallion finalist. When she's not writing, she loves spending time with her family, traveling to find inspiration for her next book, and serving with her husband in ministry. Learn more at ElizabethGoddard.com.